Memory Tree

Stephanie—
Best Wishes as
you read bb

Bill Mathis

Bill Mathis

Published by Rogue Phoenix Press, LLP
Copyright © 2021

ISBN: 978-1-62420-597-2

Credits
Cover Design: Designs by Ms G
Cover Art: Arthur Durkee
Editor: Sherry Derr-Wille

Advance Praise for Memory Tree

"For the second consecutive year, an entry of yours finished in the top 3 of the **Chicago Writers Association's** 5th Annual First Chapter Contest. The Board of Directors selected your opening chapter to "Memory Tree" as the Third Prize winner out of a record number of entries."

Bill Mathis understands the passion and humor, but more importantly, the pain and struggle that comes with being involved in an interracial relationship. A timely story as America comes to grips with its ugly past. Louis Butler, attorney.

While Mathis' Memory Tree is set in the past, it holds timely truths for today. Racism is presented in a wholly unique way, as a personal story and journey, as the main character Duane struggles with lessons learned from his father and his own heart telling him there's a different way. Teetering on the edge of death, Duane sorts through all the joys and sorrows of his life as he's tenderly cared for by caretaker Retha, who has a secret of her own. Mathis is a skilled storyteller who knows exactly how to weave us through the unexpected and make the unbelievable believable. Kathie Giorgio, author of *The Home For Wayward Clocks* and *If You Tame Me.*

The Memory Tree is a satisfying tale with an end of life review that offers redemption to a whole host of characters and inspires hope in the reader. Joanne Lenz-Mandt, author of *Remembering My Monk.*

In Memory Tree, author Bill Mathis has brought a new set of characters to life. None of them perfect, but all of them human, though one has transitioned to stardust. Each character looks back trying to make sense of life's puzzle pieces. Like every good story, this book allows us to look a bit deeper, to analyze our own actions and the resulting consequences, our own prejudices, the times we have stood as allies and the times we have looked the other way. There is plenty of regret to go around, but there is also hope in vulnerability, truth and love. Marci Yosef, M.S. in Community Health, also known as Super Mom.

Thank you for allowing me the privilege of reading this story. Memory Tree was deeply moving, meaningful and gripping from the first pages. I think many, many people, especially white Americans, need to read this. The insight into the psyche of non-Southern whites around race is heart-rending, infuriating and humanizing all at the same time. Ron Watson, Ph.D., Associate Professor, Political Science and Health & Society, Beloit College.

THE TREES TALK

The trees talk all night.
They never sleep.
They hug the earth
and never sleep.
The wind which rattles
leaves does not
frighten them.
Their roots hold each
other in such wind,
hold, I tell you.
The trees talk all night
and wait for light.

(Poem by Tom Montag)

Life lasts a long time
As stardust forevermore
Now that's impressive

(HaikuSorta by Bob Wood)

Memory Tree

Split Creek County, Michigan,
Access Road, thirty-five miles east of Lake Michigan

I've been talking to Memory Tree for a long time. Ever since I could talk. Back when I was alive, now through my stardust.

Memory Tree is in my front yard and is old. Really old, and tall. Really, really tall.

We mostly called her Memory because she was kinda part of the family, and she remembers everything.

We always called the tree she. Mommy was glad Memory wasn't called he. She said men couldn't remember things very good.

My name is Eula and you can't see me. My stardust is what's talking to Memory Tree. Yeah, my stardust. That's kinda like my spirit.

Did you know dead people always stay the same age? Like the pictures on Granny's wall. Old people, young people, one, a baby. "They're all dead," she used to tell us.

Anyway, we dead people always stay the same age. We never get older. My twin brother, Jimmy, and I, were nine years and six days old the day we died.

I call it the bad day.

I bet by now Granny has pictures of me and Jimmy on her wall. Mommy, too. She was twenty-nine. I'm not sure about a picture of Dad.

Anyway, Memory knows my stardust is here, all alone in the house.

She remembers Mommy, Dad, Jimmy, and Granny, too.

Memory will never forget us.

I know that for a fact.

Chapter One

My real name is Beula, but I couldn't say the B when I was learning to talk, so Ooola became Eula. Mommy said adding an H to the end of Beula made it sound too old. Besides, I was named after Granny and her name didn't have an H at the end either. She wasn't old yet. At least she wasn't back then.

Some people think stardust is like spirits, which are like ghosts. I'm not like that. Ghosts and spirits can touch things or move things or spook people or animals or birds. I can't. It's like I'm a dandelion, all white and poufy, except I'm a cluster of stardust nobody alive can see. I think where I want to go and somehow, I'm there.

Only I don't want to go other places. Not away from the house. I'm afraid to. I mostly stay at the top of the archway between the kitchen and dining room.

I can hear and see and think. I can't smell, talk out loud, sneeze or touch, but I can remember those things. I don't cry real tears, but I sure remember what they were like, and the pain and fear. In my mind, I'm telling all this to Memory. I always liked writing stories, now it's telling them. I'm just an invisible poof of stardust. Waiting. Telling my life to Memory. And now to you.

It bothers me that there is no—oops, there *are* no—pictures of me or Jimmy hanging in our house now. Or of Mommy. Even Dad. Anywhere. There used to be. Some were of Mommy and us kids. Some were of me and Jimmy with Dad. None were with all four of us together. I don't understand why the pictures are missing. It would be nice to see them every day. Something to look at while I remember, think, and just exist as sawdu…Oops again—I almost said sawdust. Now that would be weird. I mean stardust.

Maybe I was thinking of sawdust because Dad was a wood carver, too. A good one. The wood carvings he made of us are also gone. Why would they be missing, too? Who would sneak in and take them and the pictures? How could I not have seen them do it?

See, I've been waiting a long time in our old farmhouse for Dad to come back. When you're dead, you don't think about time, that's why I can't tell you how long I've been waiting. I won't leave until my stardust meets Dad's or I at least know he remembers us. I don't know where else to look for him, so I'm waiting here.

Things were really scary the bad day. A big angry man attacked Mommy down by the lake. She yelled for us to run and get Dad.

We did.

We screamed for Dad when we got to the house. He hollered to wait on the porch. He was in the shower and had to pull some clothes on and get his gun. He yelled he was hurrying as fast as he could. He sounded upset.

Except we didn't wait for him. Instead, we ran back to the dock. Mommy was gone. Then the crazy man attacked us. We ended up in the lake, next to Mommy.

After Dad didn't rescue us or show up, Jimmy's stardust kept telling mine to go up to the house and wait for Dad's stardust. Mommy agreed. She thought maybe Dad died near the house or on the way to save us. She said I was always a daddy's girl anyway, so I should go. Mommy also said Jimmy's stardust would stay by hers forever and mine could be with Dad's until all four of us can get together. She said Memory Tree would look over me, even inside the house. So, I went. It took a while for my stardust to get through the water.

The only problem was, when my stardust finally got to the house, Dad wasn't here. Not him alive or his stardust. I did see that the barn had burned down. Wouldn't Dad's stardust have found mine if he died in the fire?

How did the barn burn down? It must have burned down after the bad man attacked us. But how? Why wasn't Dad here? If he wasn't dead someplace around the house, where did he go?

Dad was supposed to come rescue Mommy. Me and Jimmy, too.

3

Dads do that. Rescue their family.
Our dad never came.
So, I'm here in the house, waiting for Dad.
Waiting to learn what happened.
Waiting for my forever to start.

Chapter Two

Let me tell you about Memory Tree.

As I said, we called her Memory, like the tree was a person. Dad named her when he was a boy. Said he talked to her, too. He said Memory is an Eastern white pine. That she's over two-hundred years old. I told you she was really old.

Dad said maybe a little Indian kid's foot pushed the seed from a pine cone into the earth and that started her growing. Mom said we should call the Indians Native Americans. She was careful about the names people are called.

Dad told us Memory is one hundred feet tall. He's a forester and he should know. He said she is almost four feet in diameter. There's another measurement, around the tree, but I can't remember what it's called. A hundred feet is very tall. We could see Memory from miles away when we were driving home from town. It's also higher than all the other trees in the national forest next to our place. I suppose it might be even higher than one hundred feet now. Dad did say older trees still grow a little each year, and it's been a long time since the bad day.

Each year, Jimmy and I tried to climb higher in the tree. Just before we turned nine, we made it high enough to look down on the roof of our house. Dad said we were probably thirty feet up. We didn't dare climb higher. Besides, our hands and feet were all covered in pitch and grit.

Me and Jimmy used to crawl in between the lowest branches. We'd listen to the robins, chickadees, and sometimes the mourning doves. Sometimes we talked to Memory out loud, sometimes just in our heads.

It's been a long time since anyone alive talked to Memory. Or climbed in her. Or camped out in sleeping bags on the ground beneath her branches.

Today, people driving by can barely see our old farmhouse. Trees and brush and sumac have grown up to it.

There were no neighbors when Dad, Mommy, Jimmy and I lived here. Back then, hardly anyone knew our family existed.

Memory did.

Chapter Three

January 3, 2019

All of a sudden, it's been busy around here. First, two men plowed out the driveway and shoveled the walk and porch. Next, they got the lights and heat on and the water running.

One of them said, "This is strange. Opening up a home in the winter. Don't we usually open this place in the spring and close it in the fall?"

"Yup. We been doin' this place for twenty-five years. Sad thing is, I don't think anyone has visited here for years."

"So, why we doing it?" The shorter man was working with the pipes under the kitchen sink.

The tall man was lighting the pilot on the kitchen stove. "The owner grew up here and wants to come back and die here, that's why. When you finish the sinks, go bring a good supply of wood from the shed to the porch." The tall man kept talking as he moved to the dining room. He patted the large heater. "The man said he wanted the wood stove to be available, along with the gas heater in the dining room. Ya don't see these kinda heaters anymore. It's vented to the outside, plus the electric fan circulates the warm air. Nope, ain't seen one of these in a long time."

He bent over, opened the small door and lit the pilot light. Straightening up, he said, "This thing will heat the living room and the bedroom, keep the pipes warm at night, too. Good thing, guess there's going to be a nurse staying with him till he kicks off."

Who were they talking about? Did they mean Dad was finally coming home? He did grow up here. Does someone else own our home and I've been waiting in the wrong place? Are they confused? I am.

While those two worked on the plumbing and heat, two more men took the dining room table apart and put it in the living room, against the fireplace that never worked. Next, they brought in a big bed and set it up in the dining room by the heater. Does Dad need a special bed to die in?

All the men left. The next day, a man and woman came and cleaned the whole house. They even stocked the fridge and pantry. I heard the woman say, "Honey, we been cleaning this place for over twenty-five years. You know the guy who owns it?"

"Nope. Everything is handled through West Michigan Property Management in Ludington. The owner of the house has lived in the Upper Peninsula, Houghton, since 1985. Never met him in person. It seems, every year, he still wants the place opened in case he or family come here to get away in the summer." The man stopped talking and sipped his coffee. "Guess, back in the late nineties, several guys came a few times in the fall to bow hunt. Never him or the family. Two weeks ago, Fred, the manager, called, said the old man was dying and wanted to kick off down here. That's all I know."

He poured some coffee for the woman. "While you clean the bathroom, I'm going to fill the wood stove so all someone's gotta do is light it. Every year, Fred told me to make sure wood was cut, dry and ready in the shed. As if the shed ain't been full all these years."

Someone's been opening up the house and closing it down every year. Other than those bow hunters, no one ever came. The first few times, I got excited when people showed up to open the place up. Now I'm used to it. Kinda like part of spring and fall. It was nice to see people. Wow. Twenty-five years sounds like a long time. I told you stardust doesn't keep track of time.

Oh, wait. I do remember that right after I got into the house, several policemen knocked on the door. I heard one say, "I don't think Mr. Gleason has returned. His answering service must a been correct. He's started over up north. Probably doesn't know about the barn and probably doesn't care. This place ain't worth much. Even that hay field is sad looking."

The other one said, "I agree. No sense wasting our time further. If I lived out here, I'd get the hell away, too."

Why would Dad have started over instead of rescuing us? Moved away? That doesn't make sense. He loved us.

Today, I still don't know if they're talking about my dad coming home to die. Will being old make him look different? Will I recognize him? Oh, please, if it is him, let me hear him talk about us so I know he remembers. He's gotta talk about why he didn't come rescue us. Please. Please. Please. If he dies, our stardust can be together and maybe we can find Mommy and Jimmy.

Wait, how long does people stardust last?

January 7, 2019

You won't believe this. A woman came in last night and moved into my folks' bedroom. She's wearing a Detroit Tigers hat, a cowboy shirt, jeans and cowboy boots. She's not fat, kinda skinny. Her skin is dark, but lighter than Granny's, and really smooth, too. I can't tell how old she is, but her hair is all white, short and kinky. She doesn't move like she's old, like Granny's neighbor did.

She checked everything all over, lit the wood stove in the kitchen and pulled something out of her pocket and talked into it, must be like a beeper you can leave messages on. She said, "Okay, Marcy. This is Retha. I'm here to help Duane Gleason die. Everything looks prepared, food, all the medical supplies and equipment. There's twelve inches of snow on the level, at least a week's supply of wood on the porch, and the shed is stuffed with dry wood, oak and pine, all split."

She turned the dial on the heater, waved her hand above it like she was feeling if it was getting warmer. "There's a big gas space-heater in the dining room. It works well, in spite of the drafty windows. I got a supply of Cherry Coke and green tea, so I'm all set. Bye now. I'll keep you updated." She sat down, blew her nose and wiped tears from her eyes.

Duane Gleason? That's my dad's name! I can't wait to see him. My mommy's name was Ellie Bryant. Us twins' last name was the same as hers. My Dad and Mommy weren't married. I don't know why we have Mommy's last name.

9

~ * ~

December 27, 2018, Riverside, Michigan

Retha McGuire entered her two-bedroom apartment tucked under the eaves of an old home on one of the hilly streets in Riverside. She stepped out of her winter boots, hung her expedition coat on the hall tree, turned the tea kettle on, adjusted the thermostat and eased into her recliner.

That was a rough funeral, she thought. Not the hardest she ever attended, but one of them. A seventeen-year old boy finally succumbed to injuries from a gunshot wound to his abdomen. She was with him twenty-four seven the last two weeks of his life. After time in the hospital, he was doing well at home, until infection set in. Again. His family couldn't manage the intense home care and their jobs, so she came in. Slept on their couch, kept him cared for, and dealt with him and the family when the doctors turned the kid over to hospice and her.

After the funeral, the family met with her. "Thank you," the mother said. "My husband and I are each struggling to keep two jobs, plus our two other sons on the straight and narrow. You helped us so much. I don't know how we can repay you."

Her husband added, "I'm still not sure how you helped us find the money for the funeral." He paused, then hugged her. "Most of all, you got us better prepared for our boy's death. As prepared as possible." He wiped his eyes, motioned for the younger brothers to follow him, took his wife's hand and left.

Retha stood to ready her mug. That's what *I do*, she thought. She helped dying people die peacefully, as mentally and emotionally prepared as possible. That's not what the agency brochure said. Not in those words. They used flowery ones, and phrases like, end of life, transitions, as if it were a trip to the botanical gardens with soft waterfalls, birds sweetly chirping, beautiful smells. Similar to death being viewed as floating away on a cloud. Retha didn't use those words. Oh, she adjusted her vocabulary to the clients and the family, but she tended to be very direct. Not obnoxious or in your face. Just calm and honest. More importantly, she got the client and family to talk about their lives. Their past, their pride, their sorrows, often their secrets, especially their fears. Talk about their beginning and their expected ending. She worked with them to understand the grief process, the steps, the ups and downs, how not to rush the process.

Retha took a long view of life. Had to. She loved cosmology, the universe, how it formed over the billions of years, how she knew humans derived from stardust. Neil deGrasse Tyson was one of her favorite persons. Genealogy was also important to her. She managed to integrate those loves into her care for others.

People often looked doubtful or suspicious when she walked through the door with her suitcase and introduced herself as the caregiver sent from the agency. They loved her when she left.

She never got into women's fashions. As a kid and teen, Retha preferred jeans and blue t-shirts or flannels, along with work boots, better yet, cowboy boots. Certainly not dresses. She never wore the big afros when they were popular or, later as she aged, wigs. Her hair, now snowy white, was cut close to her head. She was ten when she informed her mother she would run away if forced to grow her hair out, straighten it, mess with it, and wear dresses. "You learn to cut it and pick it out yourself," Ida, her mother, said. "And your clothes just better be clean."

Her father laughed. "What you going to do when kids laugh at you and rag on you?" She showed him her fist. "Well, in that case, let me show you a few things."

Her aging father, Daniel, the retired educator, local historian, community elder, taught her how to defend herself and emphasized the need for her to always be polite, use humor and not be the aggressor when she faced tormentors.

"You're colored," he said, "White folk don't need an excuse to blame colored people. You can't be seen as the aggressor. Even if you're defending yourself, you will be blamed if you're scrapping with a White person. Just keep that in mind. Don't be afraid, but realize the cards are stacked against you."

During her school years, there were tormentors. Mostly from other colored kids. Tom-boys and masculine-dressed girls weren't always accepted in her community. She knew old folks gossiped about her. Always behind her parents' backs, never to their faces.

The teakettle whistled. She stretched, poured herself a big mug of green tea with honey and returned to the chair.

ELC, End of Life Care, was a small agency that specialized in providing live-in personal care and medical staff for dying people. They networked around the state with hospice organizations, community health centers and social service agencies. Their reputation grew for their willingness to serve the marginalized, the rural, and the fact their staff was willing to live in for weeks, even months.

As she sipped her tea, she let her mind wander over the many years and various clients she helped, how she turned her paychecks back to the agency, her retirement and social security carried her just fine, thank you.

Her cell phone vibrated. It was the ELC number. "How did the funeral go?" Marcy, the staff placement coordinator, asked.

"All things considered, pretty well. I think the fact the kid that shot him wasn't in a gang, admitted he was messing with the gun and it was an accident, helped. I've been to some…" Her voice faded as she recalled some of the inner-city funerals she attended when gangs were involved.

"Yes, I know you have. I think your efforts with the family played a large part in today being such a peaceful experience. Thank you."

Retha didn't know how to respond. She didn't need thanks. She knew Marcy well, they worked together for many years. Retha was glad for her recognition, but didn't need it. "Out with it. You got something else for me, don't you?"

Marcy's chuckle was warm. "Yes, young lady. We have an interesting—"

"Don't you, young lady me. You're just trying to find out my age. Hoping I'll say I'm not young and I'm this many years old. Everyone's always trying to figure out my age. You do know, don't you, there's a note on my personnel file stating that when anyone tries to get my birthdate, I'm to be called with who's asking and why?" She waited a moment. "Go ahead. Answer my question. You know that note is there, don't you?"

Marcy laughed. "Okay, I'm guilty, and truly, I wasn't trying to trick you."

Retha harrumphed. "Guess I'll believe you. My age is unimportant. It's what I can do that counts. Besides, ladies should never be asked their age. Now, start talking. Where you want me to go?"

Marcy tried to sound like the announcer on Wheel of Fortune. "And…Retha…You just won a vacation to the winter wonderland situated in the heart of the national forest…Split Creek, Michigan."

Retha contained her gasp. Her heart raced, tears came to her eyes, her mind spun. Finally, she managed to say, hoping she sounded sarcastic and not shocked, "Wow. Split Creek. A place I've always wanted to visit." She managed a quick sip of her tea, took a big breath to calm herself. "So, tell me about the situation. I have lots of winter clothes. The minivan is running well and the timing for me to be gone is fine. One of my kids needs a place to get his head on straight. Again. It's best he does it alone."

"Oh, Retha, which one of your twenty-some foster kids this time?"

"Jeremy, one of the kids I fostered some years back. Just divorced, lost his job and needs a place to sort things out. He knows I may or may not be here. I'm tired of hearing his love life problems, it will be good for me to get away and him to be alone. Now give me more info. Who, when, where, why?" She lifted the mug to her lips.

"I remember Jeremy and it's been more than some years back. I guess once a mother, always a mother. So, here's the dope. Apparently, an old retired forester wants to return to his childhood home to die. Wants to keep his identity a secret. Doesn't want the info getting out into the community."

Retha sucked in a breath, along with some tea, and began gasping.

"Retha, are you all right?"

Retha managed to swallow, wipe her eyes and blow her nose. "Sorry, I inhaled some tea, that's all. Now go on. I'll try not to drink and think at the same time." She set the mug down and switched the phone to speaker so she could wrap her arms around herself. Focus, she told herself. Focus.

"The man is seventy-four, he's dying of prostate cancer, which has spread. Last week, the doctors told him he has four to six weeks to live. Apparently, this is his childhood home and he wants to die in it." Retha put her head back, making mental notes. "His two daughters are bringing him down from Houghton, Michigan, in the Upper Peninsula. They live on the west coast. Seattle, I think. He refused to move there with them or into a nursing home in the U.P. He'll be arriving Monday, January seventh. Arrangements to have the home ready have been made. I'll mail you the packet."

"Well, I'm available. I'll drive up the day before. It's gotta be seventy-five miles up there." Retha thought a moment. Split Creek. She hadn't visited there since 1985. Why had she reacted to the news that it was an old forester? In that area, there must be more than one. Maybe she could get a chance to visit Fair Haven. Maybe not. There were some memories she might not want to face. Besides, at her age, anyone she knew probably died years ago. "Of course, I'll go. Is the home out in the country? In town? The county seat is also called Split Creek."

Marcy rattled some papers. "You sound like you know more about that area than I do. According to the notes, the whole area is in or surrounded by national forest and lakes. Must be in the county, but it's close to the town of Split Creek. By the way, I already checked, your cell phone should work fine there."

"Do I get there by snowmobile? Horse and buggy? Do they have electricity? Running water? Inside toilet? Am I cooking on a wood stove?" She waited as Marcy burst into laughter. "You laugh, but I can handle all that, I just want to know in advance."

"Oh, Retha, I'm sure you could handle that, but I've been told everything will be working and a week's worth of food will be there when you arrive. There are contacts who will deliver more groceries, plow the drive and shovel, haul up more wood, anything you need. Even sit with the client for an afternoon if you need a break."

"Send me the packet. I'll dig out my map." Retha punched the phone off and sank deep into the recliner. She was glad the home was close to Split Creek. The forester she knew of lived further out, in the woods, exactly seventeen miles from town, on a dead-end road with no neighbors. What were the chances the one she knew of would return to Split Creek to die? Slim to none. She didn't need to check the map to Split Creek. She could drive there in the dark, wearing blinders.

Sunday, January 6, 2019

Retha finished loading her minivan and climbed in. She opened the packet of papers for the exact address to enter into her iPhone. Tears came to her eyes at the name and address. This was the only forester from Split Creek she knew about. She never met him personally, but once planned to. And now, she was supposed to help him die. Why did she avoid opening the packet when it arrived four days ago? She could have cancelled, told Marcy to find someone else. She rarely let her fears go unaddressed. This time, she had.

She climbed back out of the van, went inside and rummaged through her closet for a box she kept hidden for nearly thirty-five years. Returning to the van, she placed it next to her suitcase. She covered the box with the car blanket. Too many memories. All of them connected to Duane Gleason.

She straightened her shoulders, took a swig of her ever-present Cherry Coke, only Coke, always Coke, unless the coffee was black and strong. Oh yes, she liked green tea and Constant Comment Tea, too. Retha backed out onto the street. Apple Maps said it would take one hour and fifty-one minutes on mostly state and county roads, almost straight north. She guessed the last seventeen miles would be slow going on the rural roads. That area always had more snow than Riverside.

Chapter Four

Monday, January 7, 2019

I hear yelling outside. Someone's on the porch.

Retha opens the kitchen door and says, "Welcome." She holds the door wide, but no one comes in.

I see three people. One of them is an old man using a walker. Is that Dad?

One of the women says, "Give us a few more moments. Dad wants to look at that tree."

The old man—Dad?—yells, "Damn straight. That's why I came back here."

I see one of the women shrug, turn and look at Retha.

She smiles.

The two women help the old man squeeze through the door, like they all wanted to get through at the same time.

It's Dad. His hair is all white and stringy and greasy-looking. There's a bald spot. He humps over, looks like he can't walk without the walker. I remember Granny's neighbor using one. His eyes are the reason I can tell he's my dad. Mommy always said they were hazel and that's why she fell in love with him. His voice, it sounds weaker, but still the same. Deep and careful, like he thinks through each word. I know it's him. I'd like to hear him laugh or see him smile. He hasn't done either. He gave Retha, the lady nurse waiting for him, a mean look.

Retha introduces herself to him and the two other women.

Dad looks at her, all strange. "You from Fair Haven?" Mommy would have said he barked his words. She didn't like it when he barked, which wasn't very often.

The two women look at him funny, as if they never heard of Fair

Dad looks confused now, and grumpy. "My inner needs? You sure ask a lot of questions, don't you?"

Retha just smiles at his snippy voice. "Why don't I help you onto the bed and you take a nap while I start dinner. The girls listed brown-gravy swiss steak with mashed potatoes and cream corn as one of your favorite meals. Is that right?"

"It was one of my wife's favorite meals. I'd like macaroni and cheese with polish sausage a whole lot more. Was that on the list?"

"Let me check. It wasn't on the list of your favorite meals the girls listed, but I see the ingredients to make mac and cheese and, look, here's some sausage. Looks processed as hell, but it will work. How about a salad?"

Dad sort of laughs—his first laugh, it was definitely Dad's—and says, "Do I have to eat healthy stuff? Will salad prolong my life or get rid of the cancer?"

I love Retha's laugh, it's like Granny's, even Mommy's, all clear and loud, from inside you, the kind that makes everyone around them laugh, too.

Dad looks like he wants to laugh. Instead, he frowns at her.

Chapter Five

I don't sleep. I just exist. Like, I can hear, see and think, but I can't touch or smell. Through my memories, I feel things, like emotions, but I can't express them. I drift around the house. It doesn't matter if it's cold or hot. I don't get tired, yet I don't feel like going anywhere else or running, which is odd. Mommy told us to run lots, it would help us grow and our brains develop. I should call her Mom. We had our birthdays just before the bad day. She told us nine was old enough to quit calling her Mommy and call her Mom. I don't think she thought we would change in one day, so I still call her Mommy. I'm still just turned nine, maybe if I was closer to ten, I'd be calling her Mom more.

Last night, I watched Dad sleep. We always just called him Dad. Maybe DaDa when we were really little, but never Daddy. Most of the night, he seemed to be asleep. A couple of times, his eyes were open and he just stared at the ceiling. I wonder what he was thinking? Just because I'm stardust doesn't mean I can read minds. I can't. I wish I could.

During the night, I thought lots of things. It's exciting to have Dad home and I want to know so much. I hope he talks about Mommy and us kids and why he never showed up to rescue us.

I thought about lots of other stuff, too. My usual things that go through my mind almost every night and day. Dark or light, it doesn't matter to my mind. I only have nine years and six days to remember, think how many Dad has. Does he remember stuff when he sleeps? I don't think I did when I was alive, just while waking up, going to sleep and during the day.

I love my memories of living here all together. Dad would read to us and take us into the woods when he was home, but it was usually Mom—there, I called her Mom—who took us out, along with the books we got at the library. That's how I learned the names of so many things.

Not the real names, the official ones, Mommy said, but names little kids could say when you're three or four. Sometimes, we still called them those names when we were eight, almost nine, even nine for six days.

"Pink thippies," Jimmy or me would holler. Just like he did that bad day.

"Yes, pink ladies slippers," Mommy would say. We usually called them pink slippers when we could talk better.

We called round-leaved sundew, sunny dews; swamp milkweed, milk shakes; columbine, columbusses; mayapples, baby green apples; Queen Anne's lace, Annie lace; Trillium became trilly; Jack in the Pulpit, jumping jacks.

Our favorite books were by someone named Thornton Burgess. I can see five of them on the bookshelf in the dining room next to where Dad's bed is. We checked out more at the library. Mom said Mr. Burgess died when he was old after he wrote a ton of books. We named animals after his stories with names. A wren was Jenny Wren. "Look, there's a Peter Rabbit," one of us would whisper when we were sneaking through the forest. Mom would say lots of people also called them Peter Cottontail. We were looking for rabbit paths or deer paths and figuring out what kind of poop belonged to what animal. Mom called it scat. Did you know deer scat is smaller than rabbit's poop? It is. Little round pebbles. Goat scat is bigger than a deer's, too. Isn't that neat?

We had a goat. Mortimer. Someone gave him to Dad to eat the grass and weeds around the house so he and Mommy wouldn't have to mow as much. Then he jumped the fence into Mom's garden and Dad took him away. That's all I remember, we were pretty little, maybe four or five.

We ate wild rabbit. Dad would snare them in the fall and winter. He said if you design the snare right, it was the most humane way to kill them and it didn't get buckshot in the meat or let them chew on their legs like they could if they were trapped. We also ate venison. Dad shot two or three deer a year and had the meat processed and put in our freezer. Dad shot the deer that hung around and ate from the alfalfa field. Said the meat tasted better than the ones eating acorns all the time.

Mom ground some of the meat with hamburger so it had fat in it and made hamburgers or spaghetti sauce with it. Sloppy Joes, too. My favorite, especially with chips and pickles. I loved dill pickles. Jimmy liked sweet. We each got to drink the juice out of the jar when the pickles were gone. Jimmy got mad sometimes because he was the only one that liked sweet pickles and it took longer before the jar was empty. Sometimes, Mommy would let him sip some juice before he ate up all his pickles.

Did I tell you we spent gobs of time outside? We did. Dad was gone a lot, three or four days a week, sometimes for weeks if his work was far away. He pulled his old Airstream camper and stayed in it. Mom said if she hadn't met Dad and had us twins, she wanted to study wildlife and nature at college, then go stay in the woods. She always said living with Dad was better because she could live in the woods, love Dad, plus have us kids. Mom also said Dad taught her stuff he learned at college. He studied about forests, said it took him six years to get a four-year degree. I didn't understand that, but he always laughed.

Once, we were playing with some kids by where Granny lives. They asked where we lived most of the time. We told them about living next to the forest. One boy said, "Ain't you got no neighbors to play with?"

Jimmy said, "No, Mom and Dad do so much stuff with us, we don't get lonely."

I said, "But it's fun to play with kids when we come to Granny's, which is about every week. Besides, living in the woods means we see and learn lots of things. We like it."

The boy looked surprised. So, we told him all about woods stuff. Stuff he could learn not too far from Fair Haven, if he was interested.

I just looked out the window. It's almost all frosted over. I remember standing on the couch or a chair in winter, to peek through the top of the window, above the frost, to check on Memory.

In the summer, if Mommy was busy, she'd tell us to go visit Memory. Somedays, we just sat in its shade. Other times, we crawled in between the lowest branches and laid down. If we kept our feet toward the trunk and looked through the tips of the branches, we could see the clouds and sky between the needles. It was cool. If we kept our heads close to the tree, we couldn't see as much sky, but the limbs hooked to the trunk going in circles were cool, too. Did you know trees grow a new ring of branches each year? At the top. Not at the bottom.

A few times, Jimmy and me were naughty or upset. Mommy would ask us everything she could to see what bothered us. If we couldn't tell her, she'd say, "Okay, I can't figure you two out. Go tell your problems to Memory, maybe she can help you. Just come back in the house in a better mood."

I don't remember what we told Memory, but it usually helped.

How did Memory get her name? Mom told us to ask Dad. He pulled one of his old college books down and had us sit on either side of him. Like he always did when he read to us or wanted to show us things. He showed us a picture of a tree stump, magnified. He explained magnified to us, but we already kinda knew because we had little magnifying glasses from Christmas. Anyway, he showed us a black ring about halfway in. He told us to count the rings out to the black one. It was twenty-three.

"Each ring represents one year of growth, like how we mark the stairway door frame on your birthday. When this tree was twenty-three years old, there was a forest fire. It must not have been a bad one because the tree lived and you can count the rings after." There were thirty more and he told us that meant the tree was fifty-three years old when it was cut for lumber. "So, that's part of the reason trees have memories. You can tell other things, too. Like, how close and far apart each ring is, tells us how much moisture it got that year."

Jimmy wanted to know how our tree got its name. "Because when I was little, my dad showed me a stump and explained the same things. He said he believed trees remembered more than what we thought, but he couldn't explain it to me. So, I decided to call my favorite tree Memory Tree."

I asked him if he ever had to go talk to it when he was naughty or upset. He said he was never naughty. Mommy heard him and yelled for him to go talk to the tree for not telling the truth. They both laughed. He said he went there a lot, how he didn't have other kids to play with at home, so he liked talking to Memory, especially when he was lonely.

Right now, Memory looks like a dark frosty shadow. I wonder if she remembers everything I've been telling her all these years since the bad day. How many new layers of branches does she have now? She knows I'm talking to her through my stardust. Does it matter if I'm not sitting under her? I hope not. I don't want to go outside and get blown away.

Chapter Six

Tuesday, January 8, 2019

Duane startled awake. Where was he? This dark was different than his subdivision home in Houghton. He stared at the ceiling, trying to remember. The warmth from the heater close by and whiff of burning oak and pine from the kitchen, sent him back years to when he was growing up. He remembered making the girls wait on the porch yesterday so he could look at Memory Tree.

I'm home. At last, in my own home. He sighed, *that's right, I'm home to die.*

He sniffed the air again, sensed the draft from the windows, could smell the outside winter air filled with oak and pines, sumac and snow. The cold. The silence of the forest. He glanced at the clock on the buffet. Three a.m. Too early for the chickadees and blue jays or the crows to start making noise. A branch lightly scratched at the metal roof. He remembered when their yard went from the house, past Memory Tree, to the road. How once his parents died, and he was in and out of college or away working, he let the undergrowth move closer.

After he left the area, the sumac, weeds, grasses, and vines grew close to the house. Now, it was barely visible from the road. Access Road, it was called. Even his mail said Access Road. No number, just Gleason, in hand-printed letters barely visible on a mailbox, mounted on a pipe, cemented into a rusty milk can.

Access Road ran straight north to the Pierre River, where a small turn-around awaited with a narrow ramp into the river to launch canoes. An outhouse, infrequently serviced, along with several parking spaces, were hidden among the trees. He recalled being excited when he was young, and cars with canoes on top went by. Especially watching the lumbering Chevy Suburbans with summer campers hanging out the windows, singing camp songs, a canoe trailer tagging behind in a cloud of dust. The kids always waved at him. He waved back, unless Ralph was with him or his dad was around. Occasionally, Dad would take him to the access where the two would wind their way along the foot trails to several clearings. Spaces where they could fly fish. He never got too good, but it was fun being with Dad.

His dad was almost fifty when he married and Duane was born. Dad was a lumberjack in his younger years. Rough, tough and outspoken, especially when he drank. That's what Duane's mother told him when Dad wasn't around. "He was a good man," she said several times. "Except when he was drinking."

"When did he quit drinking?" Duane was about eleven when he asked her. He never saw his father take a drink of anything other than lemonade or hot tea.

"When he asked me to marry him. I'll tell you the story sometime. Just know, if you want to be a good husband and father, you have to control yourself. Don't ever think you can drink a lot and raise a proper family."

Duane felt the urge to pee. Damn old age and men's prostates. My walker's right next to this fancy bed. Wonder if I can make it across the kitchen to the bathroom without bothering that woman? She tied a bell to the bed. I hate tinkling a bell just to go tinkle. He found the bed control and after several jerks found the right button to sit the back up.

Retha was by his side in an instant. "Time for a middle of the night pee? Remember, I showed you the urinal hanging by your right hand."

"I'm trying to keep going in the toilet as long as I can," he muttered, swinging his legs over the bed.

"Best lower the bed. You raised it higher, trying to make it sit up." She took the controller and lowered the bed.

He slid the walker over, stood, and shakily pushed it through the kitchen toward the bathroom, past the woodstove and the humming fridge. It was bought new in 1975, along with the range and the big chest freezer in the basement.

He tried to ignore Retha walking beside him, her hand holding his elbow. "I don't want to be a nosy woman, but I don't want you falling in there by yourself. Can you sit down to pee? Some men hate that."

"I sit. I'm not proud and I sure as hell ain't steady enough to stand and wait. My pissing like a racehorse days are long over."

He liked her laughter, but didn't join in. Who was this skinny Black broad? Was she truly a nurse, or just some aide they hired cheap to sit by him till he croaked?

Once back in his bed, he surprised himself when he said, "You must be a light sleeper. Sorry to wake you up."

"I've learned to be and don't apologize. I don't need as much sleep as most people. I'll tell you more about myself and I want to hear about you. Talking is healthy in your last days. Better than keeping things in or carrying stuff to your grave." She adjusted his covers, patted his shoulder and went to the bedroom situated off the living room.

What did she mean? He came home to die, to sense the woods he grew up in, to remember his childhood. Keep things in? I didn't come home to share things. Never. Especially with her. Still, he liked her pats.

He drifted off to sleep, only to jerk wide awake. The nightmare came back. Only it wasn't horrifying dreams. It was scary reality. May 29, 1985. Racing through the woods toward the pier. Hearing the twins screams suddenly stop. Firing the pistol. Starting over, living with guilt and fears.

He calmed himself, wiped the sweat from his face, took deep breaths and gradually slipped back into sleep.

He awoke to the smells of bacon and coffee, the sounds of wood going into the woodstove and FM classical music playing on the aged kitchen radio.

"You want to eat in your pajamas or get dressed before your breakfast?" Retha stood next to his bed.

He wondered how old she was. She couldn't be his age. She was far too energetic. Why did she dress so masculine? Western shirt, blue jeans and cowboy boots, the kind made for street wear, not busting broncs or roping cattle. "I need to hit the john, then I'll get dressed." She helped him through the kitchen. He noticed the portable TV that sat on the fridge forever was gone. "What happened to the TV? I like to catch the morning shows."

"I put the TV upstairs. Looks like the antenna wire into the house is shot and I'm not about to climb that rusty old tower to install a new one. Besides, everything's gone to cable, or out here in the boonies, satellite, and that's expensive. Especially when you must sign up for six months or a year." She patted his back as he entered the bathroom. "Bet you can sit on the john to shave and brush your teeth, too. I'll be right back with your toilet kit."

He peed, maneuvered himself closer to the sink, used his electric razor, and brushed his teeth. Retha helped him back to the bed, had him sit on the edge and assisted him with getting dressed. He was tired when he shuffled into the kitchen and sat at the table. She found a radio station with local news, set a cup of hot black joe in front of him and began frying eggs and making toast.

The food revived him and he decided to remain at the table. His curiosity got the best of him. How long could he sit here and not talk? Especially to someone who seemed so nice, even if she was Black. He startled. Those words sounded like his old man. "So, this is what you do? Go around to care for old folks who are dying." He tried not to sound sarcastic.

"Yes, but they're not always old. My last client was a seventeen-year-old shot accidently in the stomach by a friend. A very sad case..." She stopped talking as he put his head in his hands.

"That must have been horrible," he muttered, more to himself than her. He didn't want to hear about kids dying. He straightened and took a sip of his coffee. He needed to change the subject. He glanced up to find her studying him carefully.

Thankfully, she changed the subject. "I was an OBGYN nurse for years in Riverside. Delivered lots of babies. I never married, but I did foster a bunch of kids, sometimes through the State, sometimes on my own. Later, I heard about this agency, so I've been doing this for over fifteen years."

"How old are you? Seems like you've packed in a lot."

"Didn't your mother tell you it was impolite to ask a lady her age? That black don't crack? I never tell anyone my age, so don't go trying to trick it out of me."

He couldn't tell if she was joking until she started laughing. Somehow, he knew she was both, serious and joking. He watched her wash up the dishes and start browning ground beef. He noticed the red beans soaking, the chili powder, and the onions on the counter. He loved chili. That part, the girls got right. Of course, he usually made the chili, his wife's was terrible.

Retha refilled their coffee and sat down. "I've had quite a life, but I bet you have as well. Tell me about your girls. I was very impressed with both of them. Are they twins?"

Chapter Seven

Oh, goody. I can't wait to hear about Dad's daughters. Hey, they must be my half-sisters. Isn't that the way it works? We have the same dad, but different mothers. Their mom must have been all white, like Dad.

Retha seems so cool. I think she wants to get Dad talking. I think he's trying not to. Maybe he can't help himself. I don't know how talking will help him die better, but I bet I learn a lot. All these years, and other than seeing the people who opened and closed the place, and cleaned it every year, there's been no one. Boring. Dull. Just waiting. Oh, wait, twice, some men came bow hunting in the fall. Now, Dad's here. Retha, too.

~ * ~

Duane thought for several minutes. Where did he start? It couldn't be in his late twenties, no way, but she hadn't asked about that time period. He didn't want to share too much, but his girls were special. "The girls are Irish twins. Ashley was born in early September, 1991.We wanted our second about fifteen months later, but things happened sooner. Jessica was born six weeks early in mid-August 1992. They both ended up in the same grade."

Retha nodded for him to continue.

This was the easy part, he thought. "We lived in Houghton, in the U.P. My wife taught high school English. I pretty much did what I've always done—been a forestry consultant. The U.P. is a good place for that kind of work, even though I was gone a lot."

"Did you live in the woods or in town?"

"Unfortunately, in town. That's why I wanted to come back here to die. I love the woods. Been working in them my whole life. The wife said town was better to raise kids in. Course, she wouldn't consider moving out of town when the girls went off to college." He noticed Retha looking at him, a questioning expression. He didn't want to go there. He frowned.

"Does the wife have a name?" Retha's eyes twinkled. She turned, drained and rinsed the beans, added them to the cast iron pot, plus canned tomatoes, chopped celery, some pepper, salt, a few shakes of chili powder, and turned the flame down to simmer. Putting the lid on, she turned and waited.

He couldn't help his smile. "Did you put more chili powder in when you browned the meat and onions? As long as you don't drain it, the flavor is better. I used to add black beans, too." He watched her check through the cupboards, pull a can down, open it, drain it and pour the black beans into the pot.

"Now that we're on the same wavelength with the chili, does she?"

"Oh yeah, she does." He waved his hand as if a pesky fly was near. "It's Pamela. Not Pam. Never Pam. Pamela." He looked away, then back.

Retha nodded, a small smile on her lips. "Where did your girls go to college? What do they do?"

He drained his coffee mug and slid it across the table for a refill. "Just half. They went to the University of Oregon. Ashley got a degree in public relations and Jessica in computer science. Both have good jobs with the high-tech companies. They rented a four-bedroom house outside of Seattle and commute by rapid transit. Their boyfriends rent from them. I told them on the ride down that I guessed their boyfriends sleep with them which means they could still rent out the other two rooms."

Retha laughed. "Were they shocked their old man figured that out?"

"Nah, they just laughed and said it was a great idea. Housing is so expensive out there." He fidgeted on his chair. "I need to drain this coffee and empty my bowels. I think I can still handle all that by myself, but I'm not looking forward to when I can't."

"Duane, we'll figure it out as we go. I think there's more important things to worry about." She helped him to his feet and guided him toward the john. "There's a bath-seat in the tub. Think you can step in and I'll give you a sit-down shower?"

"Nope, I'm getting tired and ready for a short nap. Maybe you can give me a sponge-bath later."

Besides, he didn't want to share anymore. It was like this woman could see right through him. That seemed scary, and somehow, all right.

Helping him onto the bed, Retha asked, "I'm thinking the chili would be good for supper, maybe with some shredded sharp cheddar and chopped onions. How about a grilled cheese for lunch? I've got some bacon left over, plus a tomato, if you like."

"Is there a can of tomato soup out there? I figure grilled cheese and tomato soup always go together."

"There is. Long as you don't mind having two tomato dishes in a row." She pulled the covers up and adjusted the bed. "I'll turn the heat up a bit. The wind's picking up and this old place is pretty drafty."

Chapter Eight

So, Dad's wife's name was Pamela, and he has two girls, almost twins, I never heard of Irish twins before, whose names are Ashley and Jessica, and they're very smart and went to college and live in a big house and have boyfriends that live with them, but aren't married, and have good jobs. Whew. That's a long sentence to think about. Mommy would have said it was a run-on sentence if I wrote it on paper. We were home-schooled. Mom listed us with the state as third graders, but she said we were doing fifth grade work.

Me and Jimmy are twins, too. We're full twins. Irish twins must be kids born close together. Hey, do Black people call kids born close to each other Irish twins? I wish Granny was around to ask her how that works.

Mom and Dad weren't married. They just lived together. Mommy said she didn't need some priest or preacher telling her she was legally hitched in God's eyes. She loved Dad and wasn't leaving, no matter how peculiar he was sometimes. Dad said he couldn't get rid of her anyway so he'd stay around, too. They always laughed, then kissed, which was yucky and cool at the same time.

I watch Retha stir the chili. Wish I could smell it and taste it. All of us loved Dad's chili. Except he put hot peppers, jalapenos, in his own dish. I touched one once and licked my finger and yelled cause it burned my lips. He just laughed. Said it was an acquired taste. Whatever that meant, I didn't want to find out.

Retha pulls a flat thing out of her bag and sits at the kitchen table. It's like a thin Etch-A-Sketch with a TV screen on it. She starts tapping and typing on it like Dad used to on his typewriter. I can see words and pictures come up, but I can't read or tell what they are. She sighs several times. Next, she plugs a cord into it and the outlet. How does that work if we don't have TV? Her phone, too. I could tell now it's a phone, not some kind of beeper. It's not connected to the one on the kitchen wall. Several of the people who cleaned and turned the heat on had them. Once, one of them forgot theirs and came running back in, saying he left his cell. I don't know who he was talking to, but he seemed glad to find it.

Dad's still sleeping. Actually, it's napping. He's snoring, too. Just like he always did. Only this time, it's a different sound. Harder, deeper, slower. Is that part of dying? Could he die now, before I can hear him talk about us? Tell why he didn't make it down to the lake?

~ * ~

Retha plugged her iPad in to charge, poured herself some coffee and sat back down at the table. Marcy was correct, there was good cell coverage out here. Thankfully, she had a hotspot on her phone to provide WIFI for the iPad.

She found Pamela Hopkins Gleason online, still living in Houghton, but at an address different than Duane's. She found no divorce records, but did find their marriage information and the girls' birth records. Pamela retired as the high school principal three years ago, at age sixty-four.

How long did she and Duane live apart? Why?

While on the iPad, she used Google Earth to view the house and Pamela's apartment. The house was a comfortable ranch on a cul-de-sac, probably built in the early eighties. What looked like an Airstream trailer sat next to the garage. The apartment address was in a rehabbed historic building downtown.

She wondered what happened. Why didn't Pamela assist with driving Duane down here? Why did the girls never mention their mother? They held medical power of attorney and durable power of attorney. None of the papers mentioned Pamela's name.

She picked up her phone and dialed. "Ashley, this is Retha. I just wanted to give you a quick update on your father. Don't worry, no big changes yet."

"Thank you, Retha. That's so thoughtful of you. Is he talking much to you? Jessica and I were worried he might not want to communicate."

"Somewhat. I sense some hesitancy. He's eating well, still going to the bathroom by himself. He told me all about you girls after breakfast. He's mighty proud of you two." She paused. "Why wouldn't he communicate with me?"

Ashley's pause was longer. "Sometimes…I hope this doesn't offend you. I'm sorry to say it, but sometimes he has problems with race."

"I already sensed that. Now, do you have a problem with my race? A Black woman caring for your father?"

Ashley snickered. "Oh my, Retha, heck no. We don't. My boyfriend is African American and Jessica's is Pakistani. We all met in college and have been together seven years."

Retha's voice softened. "I think that's wonderful. Now, what do you think your father's problem is?"

"We're not sure. Our mother thinks his father was very racist and some of it rubbed off on him. Our mother was very open. Surprising for someone raised in the U.P." Ashley was silent a moment. "Once, when we were kids, I remember her giving Dad the evil eye for saying something derogatory about Black people. Mom knew next to nothing about Dad's life before they met. Other than he loved forestry work and being out in the woods alone."

"I noticed your mother's name wasn't mentioned while you were here. I had to point blank ask your dad what his wife's name was. He said Pamela, but wanted to go take a nap. I don't mean to pry, but what is their relationship?"

Retha heard Ashley take a big breath. "It's distant. Very distant. He was a good father, but gone a lot. I think when we became more independent in our senior year of high school, my parents each realized they had no other common interests. Mom hated the forests. She loved town, education, knowing nearly everyone because she taught them or knew their parents, being social. She became even busier when she became principal. The superintendent was older and Mom pretty much ran the district till he retired. She was passed over to fill his position. They said, because they wanted someone younger. She stuck it out a few more years and retired."

Retha could hear her sipping something.

"I'm sorry to talk so long. The bottom line is, they separated shortly after we started college. Once Dad's health went down, Mom agreed we should be in charge of his care and life. She wanted nothing to do with it. We'll inherit whatever is left. Mom has excellent retirement income and benefits."

"Why do you think they married in the first place?"

"That's a good question. We think because they were both older. Mom did not want to marry another educator. Her biological clock was ticking. Dad was interesting, not rough, but definitely not smooth around the edges. She said, when they met, he was extremely interested in having kids. He represented biology and ecology, lived it. I think she saw him more as a botanist than a forester. Neither realized how little they had in common till us girls were getting ready to leave. We had no intention to return to Houghton, not even summers during college."

"Was there any violence, abuse?"

"None. It was just two people who desperately wanted children and failed to realize that was the only bond they had. Sad. Once we were gone from their daily lives, I think it was like the Grand Canyon between them. Dad spent more time in the woods and Mom immersed herself further into the community. It was rather gloomy. Listen, Retha, if you discover why Dad's jumpy around minorities, could you tell me? It hasn't been a big issue, just an attitude that sometimes crops up."

Retha cleared her throat, unsure how to reply. Was it her job to inform them about this, too?

Before she could speak, Ashley said, "I'm sorry. That request wasn't fair to you. It's just…It's just that there's so much we don't know about him…"

"Thank you, Ashley. That's a question I haven't had to answer before, but I will try, child. I will." She took a breath. "Thank you for sharing so much. I'm an old pro at helping people die. My job is to get him talking, yelling, if he has the energy, anything to help him clear his mind out so he's at peace with himself. Whatever informed some of his feelings and attitudes happened well before your time, so don't feel guilty."

Ashley's voice became plaintive, soft. "Retha, do you believe in heaven and hell?"

"That's a good question. I usually address that with my clients, and plan to with your father. I'm always dead honest if asked about my own beliefs. I think humanity evolved from stardust and we return to dust. I like what Neil DeGrasse Tyson says. I hope I haven't offended you, young lady."

There were sniffles. "You haven't. We believe much the same way, it's just there's sometimes a guilt thing from our mother's Lutheran upbringing. I'm so glad you're taking care of him. I want to learn everything about him that's possible." Ashley paused. "Can I ask one more thing? What are you fixing him for lunch? That's crazy, but you sound so homey, I was just wondering."

"Grilled cheese with bacon and tomato, and tomato soup. Child, supper is chili."

"Oh my God. If your chili is half as good as Dad's was, it will be fantastic. I am so jealous. Wait till I tell Jessica."

Retha joined in with her laughter. "It's going to be good. He told me to add black beans to it. Now get back to work. I'll call you tomorrow. Tell Jessica I'm thinking of both of you."

"I'm telling her we're talking with you together. I'll connect her in."

"Ashley, one more thing, quick-like. Does your dad have any hobbies?"

"No problem. He loved to carve things. Wood. Nature things, sometimes faces. Jessica and I each have several he carved of us. They're very good, his nature work is wonderful. Take care till tomorrow."

Retha got up and peeked into the dining room. Duane was still sleeping. *That's good. Dying people sleep and nap a lot. Hopefully, it helps him get the energy he needs to talk with me. Of course, I've figured out sometimes he naps just to avoid talking. All normal behavior for an older man in this situation, especially one that doesn't want to face the past.*

She walked across the kitchen and opened the door leading to the basement. The basement was damp, with stone walls and heavy, rough-sawn, beams. A large chest-freezer stood near the bottom of the stairs; its lid propped open. She noticed a string to a light and pulled it. In the light, she saw another light-string over a workbench along the wall. She pulled it and sucked in a quick breath as bright florescent light filled the area.

A long shelf held hand-carved wooden pieces. Above it, tools, files, and small knives were neatly arranged on the wall. Some of the carvings appeared finished, some barely started. All were covered in years, decades even, of dust. She blew the dust off several and gasped again. The work was exquisite, detailed, the faces lifelike. So were the leaves, the animals, the trees.

Some pieces were carved from oak, others walnut, pine, maple, even balsa wood. Pieces of wood were stacked under the bench. She noticed a box that said soap and pulled the lid off. Inside were bars of soap, still individually wrapped. She looked toward the end of the bench and saw carvings in soap. Bending over, she grabbed four bars, turned out the lights and went up the stairs. She left the knives hanging on the wall.

At lunch, Duane ate quietly, as if his mind was elsewhere. He sopped his half-sandwich into his soup, but waved her off when she offered him the other half. "Thank you, that hit the spot," he said as she cleared the table.

She set the bars of soap in front of him. "I spoke with Ashley while you were napping. She said you used to carve. I found these downstairs and thought you might like to do something with your hands."

He stared at the bars. "How dare you go down there and snoop around?" His face reddened; his eyes squinted. "You nosy Black bitch. I came home to die, not answer questions and not to have someone digging around my house." He tried to stand, but couldn't get his balance and sat down again. "God damn you."

"All true. I'm nosy, ask lots of questions and I'm Black." She glared at him and waited till he looked her in the eyes, "And guess what? I do not appreciate being called a Black bitch, and if you want me to stay it better never happen again."

Duane's eyes watered. He lowered his gaze to the table. His mouth opened and closed several times, but no words came out.

Retha sat back down and slid a grapefruit spoon and a paring knife over. She gave him a sassy expression. "I'm stubborn about some things like that and ain't about ta change. Now, why don't you do something productive and start carving. Make your daughters or something from the woods. Ashley said you were really good. Prove it." She shoved her chair back, stood, and started washing the dishes.

She didn't turn to watch him till he muttered, "Never used a grapefruit spoon. It's not too bad on soap." He glanced at her, then focused as his hands slowly worked the knife and spoon over the soap.

Chapter Nine

Wow. Dad didn't talk nice to Retha. Those were bad words. Why is he talking that way? He never said Black bitch to Mommy or Granny. That's not like the Dad I knew. Why is he acting so crabby?

Another wow. Retha said we came from stardust and return to dust. Here I am, stardust, watching and listening to her. Isn't that cool? Oh, I wish I could talk with her. I'm so glad other people know about stardust. That has to mean Dad will turn to stardust when he dies.

I like seeing Dad carve. He used to carve at home, especially when he was waiting for another job to start. He went downstairs to use his electric tools and hand knives on different kinds of wood. Sometimes, he used soap first, and would bring it upstairs to show us what he planned to make. We used to have all his pieces upstairs. Mommy told him unless he started dusting them, he could keep three upstairs and the rest had to stay downstairs. He put the ones of me and Jimmy and Mommy on the buffet. She told him, "There's too many important things to do in life besides dust. Now, D," that's what she called him sometimes, "I've cleaned enough houses and dusted enough pretty things to last a lifetime. It's more important that these kids learn about nature, math and science, than dusting." Then she would kiss him and tell him she did love his art and why didn't he think about selling some, that way he could hire someone to dust.

I can't wait to see what he's carving now. I just hope he gets in a better mood toward Retha. She's just trying to help him.

~ * ~

As he cut excess soap from around the corners, Duane thought, wow. I gotta watch my mouth. And attitudes. Where did that come from?

40

I was sounding like my old man. Still, I hope she didn't go through all my carvings down there. How would I explain some of them?

He loved carving. Missed it. He quit six months ago when he got his diagnosis. He took a few more short forestry jobs, parked his Airstream and did nothing. Didn't drink, barely ate, avoided answering the phone when Ashley and Jessica called, rarely left the house. The girls flew in to check on him. That's when he opened up and said he wanted to die down here. He didn't tell them he considered this to be his real home, that it wasn't just an old family summer home. He never spoke about his life before them.

Carving always took him to a different place. The good times with his father. His boyhood. Especially the woods, the birds, plants, flowers, streams, trees, lakes, even the woods after a selective logging. Yes, the forest looked terrible, the ruts, the trampled brush, but he knew how the forest rebounded. The brush sprang back, new growth had a chance, dead wood and branches could break down faster and feed the soil.

He wished he felt stronger. He'd love to go downstairs and see his work still on the shelves. Carved in the years before he left so suddenly. That day, he didn't take any of the carvings with him, nor his tools. He sighed as the thought hit him, maybe he didn't want to see all the carvings. He didn't want to think about what feelings they might bring up. He pushed back his chair. "I need to use the john, then might take a short nap. Sorry about the mess I'm making on the table."

"Better the table than the floor." Retha helped him stand and assisted him to the bathroom. Afterward, she helped him onto his bed and covered him.

"Don't look at that piece on the table. It's not done yet. I'll finish it when I get up."

"No problem." Her voice was cheery.

Why was she so content? He envisioned a nurse, if she was a real nurse, who dealt with dying people to be…To be what? All sad, down in the mouth. Spiritual? Religious? Talking about Jesus, heaven and hell, confessing your sins. New agey, whatever that meant. Lighting incense or having solemn music playing. How had the girls found this agency?

Why had they chosen it? Why was Retha the one caring for him? There must be other nurses closer than Riverside. Why was she so dedicated to helping people die? Why did she have to be a Black?

All he wanted to do was slip quietly away, with his secret grief, his guilt, his regrets, his unspoken questions. No way some Jesus like magic guy in the sky could help with that, nor some old Black nurse, if she was truly a nurse. She had to be close to his age. He dozed off for a short time.

He woke, thinking about his inner complaints with Retha being Black. Why was that upsetting him? Now? At seventy-four? He listened to Retha stirring the chili, tasting it and using the electric mixer. What else was she making? He twisted around on the bed, hoping she didn't realize he was awake.

He was nine when he saw his father become enraged over a Black kid coming on their property. When he was home, his dad frequently bitched about Black people, especially after he saw some in town, or some tried to get work in the lumber camps or sawmills. Sometimes it related to what was mentioned on the radio news, later the TV. He only complained out of earshot of Duane's mother.

It was summer. Duane sat in the front porch swing, drinking cold lemonade after weeding the garden and picking some beans. He noticed an old Chevy Suburban towing a canoe trailer stop in a cloud of dust just past their driveway, headed south, away from the river. "Flat tire," someone shouted. "We gotta patch it, there's no spare."

A few minutes later, a lanky Black kid, probably around sixteen, and a White lady with long blonde hair came up the driveway. Duane raced to meet them. He didn't want his father to see them. "Have you got any patches? We've got a hand pump and jack," the woman asked. She was wearing blue jeans cut off at the knee, a swim suit and a wide hat.

"Umm, yes. Go back by your car and I'll bring some to you," Duane almost whispered.

As they turned to go, his father roared from the garden. "Get that darky off my property." He marched toward them, waving a hoe.

Duane's mother stepped from the kitchen side porch and ran to her husband. She put her hand up. "Take one more step and I'm gone. I still have my travel money." Duane watched his father glare at her, then slowly turn and head to the house.

His mother smiled at the camp people. "I'm sorry about him. He's a good man, but has some terrible remembrances. Now, what do you need?" She took them to the shed and Duane found the inner tube patches, glue and another jack. "Good idea, son, two jacks will be more secure." She turned to the leader. "Make sure those kids sit on the bank above the ditch or around that big pine while that tire is being fixed. It's safer if they're not close to the car. How many of you are in the group?"

"There's ten of us. Three staff and seven campers." The two headed down the driveway with the equipment.

"Son, come in the house and count out two dozen cookies while I throw some powdered lemonade together." They carried the snacks down to find seven Black boys who looked to be twelve to fourteen years old, lined up on the bank. Duane almost dropped the bag of cookies. He saw Black people before, especially in the summer when events were hopping at Fair Haven, but never this many Black kids at the same time out in this part of the national forest. His mother poured each person a plastic glass of lemonade as Duane handed out the cookies. "Duane, you wait here and bring back the jack. Tell them to keep the patches. By the looks of their tires, they may need more."

He stared up at her, shocked that he was to remain here without her. She ignored his look, waved at the staff members sweating over the tire and went back to the house.

"You can sit by us." One of the boys patted the dirt next to him. "C'mon. We won't bite." Several other boys snickered as one muttered, "Poor little White boy afraid of us city kids."

Duane sat down, staring at the dirt. The boy next to him tapped his arm. "They call me Shrimp. You really live out here all year round? Ain't you scared of all the dark?"

"I like it. You from Riverside? That's a big town." Duane grew braver and looked at the kid next to him. "I'm Duane."

"Nah, man. We're from Chicago. We're at the Y camp and us

seven passed our deep-water test, so they took us on a canoe trip. It was scary at first, but fun when we got to tip the canoes."

One of the kids hooted. "Not fun if all your clothes and the tent was still in the canoe."

"That's why you were supposed to unload it first. You tipped goofing off when you were s'pose to be paddling. How's your drawers, man? Still wet?" The boys whooped more.

"You go to school around here?" Shrimp looked at him, as if still surprised anyone would live out here.

"Yeah, about five miles away. A bus takes us. There's four classrooms plus the kindergarten room."

"Four classrooms. Hey, this kid has to go five miles by bus to a school that only has four classrooms. Go on, you serious?"

Duane's memories stopped when he felt a hand on his arm. Retha stood beside him. "You're not sleeping, are you? Why don't I sit you up and you tell me about what you're thinking?" She started adjusting the bed.

"I—I need to pee," he snapped, struggling to move his legs.

"You're going to use the urinal. By the way you were tossing around, not sleeping, I can tell you got something on your mind, and you don't need to waste your energy trying to walk." She swung his legs around and helped him scoot to the edge of the bed till his feet were on the floor. "Now, pull the front down and pee while I hold onto the urinal. C'mon, you're too old to be embarrassed over someone seeing your junk."

Duane couldn't help his snicker at her saying junk. He finished.

She took the urinal to the bathroom and returned, hanging it below the bed. She helped him get situated. "So, what was running through your mind?"

He shook his head, looked toward the window, at the shadows of the few leaves on the sumac crowding the house, the snow on the trees across the road, Memory Tree, shadows barely visible through the frost on the window. Taking a big breath, he muttered, "Seeing as you won't leave 'till I talk, I was thinking about my dad."

"You're right. I'm just doing my job. Now, what about your father? Was he mean to you or your mother?"

Duane waited, trying not to look at her. "He hated Black people. I was remembering when he got mad because a camp group coming back from a canoe trip had to work on their tire by our driveway." He glanced at her and slowly told her about the day he'd been thinking of.

"So, what happened, tell me about the rest of the day." Retha pulled a rocking chair next to his bed, along with a knitting bag. "You talk, I'll knit, and I'll try not to ask too many questions. Deal?" She waited till he nodded.

What choice did he have? He didn't think he was going to die today, probably not for several weeks. Why was he so mixed, hot and cold, about race? His daughter's boyfriends were both dark-skinned. Sometimes, that bugged him. Other times, it didn't matter. Why was he so inconsistent? He'd been that way all along. That was part of his guilt.

"I told them a little bit about my school. The boys started getting restless. It was taking a long time to patch the tube. The tall teen was a junior counselor, so he said he'd take us for a little hike down the road, and the guys could pee out some of the lemonade they guzzled." Duane leaned his head back, closed his eyes as if seeing that day all over again.

"I told them I knew some trails near the road, so I showed them tracks and scat and tiny trails where rabbits ran or fox snuck around. I told them to be quiet and listen to the birds, then told them which sounds were which birds. I showed them sassafras, and they told me they made tea from the roots on their canoe trip." Duane opened his eyes to see Retha, head down, knitting away.

"Were you thinking of them as Black, or just boys who didn't know as much about the woods as you did?"

"That's a good question. Maybe a little of both. When we got back, one of them pulled an old volleyball out of the Suburban. Another drew one big square, divided into four quarters, in the middle of the sand road, and they started to play four-square. I never saw it before. I loved it. I think that's when I totally forgot they were Black. We were yelling and hollering and having so much fun..."

"What happened? You quit talking."

He shifted himself on the bed, shaking his head. "My dad had to leave for a job. He had a pickup with a camper on the back he stayed in. He drove down the driveway, stopped and stared at me. Glared at me, pointed his finger at me and wiggled it, like telling me no. I took off, running back toward the house. The boys were confused and hollered for me to come back, that I was up next."

"Why did you run? What were you feeling?"

"Fear. I knew Dad hated colored people, that's what he sometimes called them, though usually he used the 'n' word." He lowered his eyes till he heard Retha whisper to go on. "I was afraid of what Dad would say when he came back in several days. He never hit me or even spanked me. He was a rough man who bragged about all the fights he used to get into and what he'd do to people who crossed his way. Sometimes he beat up the coloreds who joined the crews, or tried to. I—I don't know. It's like I just did something he didn't like and it scared the hell out of me."

"What did you do in the house?"

"I never made it to the steps. Mom came out and told me to get back down to my friends. 'Friends never quit in the middle of a game. Your father's problems with colored people don't have to be yours. There's good ones and bad ones, just like us White people.' So, I went back down and soon was playing again. One of the boys asked who that old mad man was. I told them it was my father, that he worked in sawmills or cutting trees. He was gone a lot and he lived in his camper." Duane stretched and watched Retha knit. "They finally got the tire fixed and back on, loaded up, and left. I carried our jack back and put it away. Mom just smiled when I came in the house, said I was filthy from playing in the dirt road and to go take a bath."

"What happened when your father returned home?"

"Dad never talked about Black people in front of Mom. The day after he came home, he and I were in the garden. 'Son, your mom thinks different from me, but she's not been around the colored people like I have. Trust me, stay away from them, never become friends. Have as little to do with them as possible. They'd just as soon stab you or steal from you as they would breathe. Never let your guard down.' A few minutes later, he said, 'I hope you took a bath after playing all crazy with them.' I nodded and said I did. Even then, I didn't think Mom had me take a bath because I was close to Black kids. It was because I was filthy with sand and dirt from head to toe. Usually, you play foursquare on cement or blacktop, not in the middle of a sandy road."

"Did you ever see any of those kids or staff again?"

"Yeah, the staff heard me say Dad lived in his camper when he was gone. Every week, they brought kids for canoe trips. They'd drive real slow, and if Dad's camper was gone, they'd honk and holler. One time, the woman came to the door and asked Mom if she had any female things. I kinda knew what she meant. Mom gave her some. She had me run down to the freezer and bring a bag of frozen cookies up for her." He laughed. "Over the next few summers, I saw Shrimp, the kid who friended me. A few years later, he popped in, said he was a counselor leading the trips. Said he refused to lead the trips without a good spare. He was in some college in Chicago." Duane sank back in the bed, tired.

"You want some coffee or tea? Maybe a cookie? Think any are left downstairs in the freezer?"

He laughed while Retha bustled off and returned with green tea and store-bought cookies.

He sipped his tea and chewed a cookie. Not looking at her, he swallowed. "I even went on canoe trips with them. Not that many people around here actually canoe. We fish on the lakes or fly-fish. Canoeing's for the tourists and summer folk."

Retha almost dropped her tea. "You what? Good Lord. What happened?"

"That blonde lady was married to the trip director. They did all the out-of-camp trips every summer. I think they were school teachers during the year. Anyway, she got our home phone number and called Mom one morning. Told her a camper got sick and couldn't go. Did I want to? Mom checked the calendar, saw that Dad was gone for five more days and told her yes. She hung up and told me I'm going on a canoe trip for three days. They'd be by in two hours."

"Oh Lordy. What did you do?"

"I was scared and excited. I was thirteen. I had a blast. I learned a lot about how they lived in Chicago. Several just moved into new apartments they called Lathrop or Cabrini Green. They said they were nice and new. A couple lived in really bad areas, all squeezed in, but their folks were trying to get into better places. Two lived in what sounded like nice homes, back yards, gardens, garages. The staff wouldn't let them tease each other about the differences in their homes."

"What else did you learn? What did they learn from you?"

Duane snickered. "Well, I learned a lot more about sex than I had from my parents." Retha laughed. "I think I was able to teach them about the woods, flowers, trees, wildlife. I told them stories Dad told me about his lumberjack days, riding the logs, living in the camps, fighting." He sipped his tea and looked at Retha. "They wanted to know why he hated coloreds so bad. I think you were going to ask about that, right?"

Retha collected his cup. "Well, if you already know what I'm going to be asking, better just start answering."

"I was twelve when Mom told me why she thought Dad hated Black people so much. Apparently, he and his friends used to go over to Fair Haven to take in the music and performers, in the summers. Lots of Whites did. The place was really swinging in the 1920's. Fair Haven was like the only Black resort in the state or the Midwest. White people loved the music they brought in."

"That's my understanding, too."

Duane thought her voice sounded purposefully vague, as if she knew more about Fair Haven than she wanted to admit. "Anyway, one summer, he took a girl. They were dancing and having a good time. Dad thought one of the colored guys was paying too much attention to her and tried to pick a fight with him. Dad's friends and several Black guys got him and his girl out to his car and told them to leave."

"You mentioned your father bragged about his fighting. Did he still fight after he married and you were born?"

"He was big, tough and rough. He drank a lot and fought a lot. Sometimes, in the bars. Other times, in the boxing rings they set up to kill time."

"What else did your mother tell you about him?" Retha handed him another cookie and waited till he ate it. "I'm planning to make some real ones today or tomorrow. Hope you like oatmeal raisin."

He chewed and swallowed. "I love them. Must have been on the list of foods I like." He smiled. "Mom told me that the following week, he was at Fair Haven without a girlfriend, just some other guys. He was drinking heavy and started hitting on one of the Black girls. He was warned to leave her alone, but guess he became insistent. Anyway, he started a fight and got the crap beat out of him by the Black guys. Really did him in. Teeth out, black eyes, sore kidneys, even his crotch. His White friends waited till the Black people were done, before driving him home. They said he deserved it. Mom figured from then on he hated Black people, plus anyone White who was okay with Black folk."

Retha adjusted the heater, went to the kitchen and threw some more wood in the stove. "That wind's whipping up." She tucked another blanket around him. "I hate to sound mean, but your father didn't seem like much of a catch. Any idea why your mother married him?"

"I agree. He was older than her and was slowing down when they met. He wooed her for three years. She kept telling him he had to quit drinking and fighting. He must have complied, though he probably drank when he was away from us. The fifth time he asked her to marry him, she reached in her purse before answering and pulled out two fifty-dollar bills. 'This is my travel money,' she told him. 'If you ever come home drunk, get in another fight that I hear about, or threaten anyone else, White or Black, I will leave you immediately and with any kids, if we have them.'"

Retha broke into laughter. "Oh my God. My kind of woman. This must've been during World War II. Whoopee. Good for her."

Duane couldn't help laughing with her.

They both stopped laughing, as if each knew there was more to talk about.

"Did you ever do anything more with the Black campers? Did you have Black friends in high school?"

Duane sighed and looked past Retha toward the wallpaper he

remembered helping his mother hang. "I did go on several more canoe trips over the next summers. Mom took me to Fair Haven to listen to music and hear some of the entertainers in the late fifties and early sixties. Dad was always out of town. We never told him. In terms of race, I was pulled between them. Dad telling me how terrible Blacks were, telling horrible jokes about them, threatening me if he ever saw me with a Black person." He thought a minute, staring at the wallpaper pattern. "Then there was Mom, not talking, but always showing me people were people. It was like walking a tightrope between them. I wanted to please both. Mom even made friends with several women in Fair Haven. I remember one was called Granny—" He jerked, quit talking. He'd said too much.

Retha stood, patted his hand. "So, now I have an idea of how being pulled between your mother and father could affect your views on race. Maybe make you ambivalent, but that was a long time ago. How else has it affected your life?"

Duane shrunk into the bed and looked toward the frosted window. "I need to take a nap." He closed his eyes. *Granny. He had no intention of mentioning her name, was glad Retha was from Riverside and didn't know of her. There was Ralph, too. If he talked about Ralph or Granny, he had to talk about May 29, 1985. He couldn't speak of that day without speaking of the ten years prior to that. Couldn't tell her he was in a mixed-race relationship.*

He didn't think Retha noticed when he didn't answer about Black friends in high school. During school hours, he nodded in recognition, spoke with them if necessary, for an assignment or on a sports team. Outside of school, he ignored them, never tried to stop his White friends when they were harassing them or making racist jokes. Sometimes it felt like his mother was sitting on his shoulder, whispering not to be afraid, to stand up for what is right. Harassment and racial jokes weren't right. He was such a chicken shit. His guilt grew throughout high school. Before his mother became too sick to attend sporting events his senior year, she often sat by Granny in the stands or bleachers. He never forgot the comments White friends made to him about his mother sitting with a colored person, sometimes surrounded by other Black people. All cheering the same team. Duane always ignored both his mom and Granny, never spoke to either in public when they were together, never Granny— even if no one else was around them. He never forgot the hurt in both of their eyes. Back then, he couldn't understand why she was called Granny. She certainly wasn't much older than his mother.

Chapter Ten

Wednesday, January 9, 2019

Last night, Dad talked about Granny. Well, he said her name, then stopped like he didn't want to talk about her. Why doesn't he want to talk about Granny? She loved him. He loved her. He always said she was like a second mother to him after he and Mom met. Both him and Granny remembered they met each other when he was young, like twelve or maybe in high school.

I loved going to Granny's house. Every Sunday, we went over after she got home from church. We didn't go to church. Mommy said she got more of God in the woods and being with us kids than she could in a church. Granny just smiled and told her, "Just as long as you believe there's a God." Then she'd talk about something else.

On the way home one day, Jimmy asked Mom if she believed in a God.

"I don't like you to keep secrets," she said, "please don't tell Granny. I don't think there's a God, but I'm not positive. However, if there is, he or she isn't like the one in the Bible, nor any other religion. Mostly, I think religion is made up by men trying to control people, especially women and minorities." She turned and grinned at us. "When you're adults and independent, I want you to visit churches, synagogues, Muslim places. You decide what you want to believe about a god. Just make sure you read their Bible or the Koran by yourself, alone, and ask good questions."

She liked us asking questions. A lot of times, she told us to think about the question and all the answers that were possible, then pick the one most likely. "I won't think for you," she'd say.

I wonder if Dad is thinking about Granny, he doesn't seem fully asleep now. He came almost every Sunday to Granny's house, too, when he was home. He drove separate, always said he'd meet us there. On nice summer Sundays, he would take us swimming in the lake Granny lived by. A few other dads did too, but Dad was the only White dad there. We'd learned to swim, but not real good yet. We couldn't swim in the lake by our house. It's a bay off a bigger lake, but it was so weedy and there was so much brush around the edges, we couldn't wade in and swim or play.

One time, I guess when we were little, Dad took us to swim at the public landing on Big Grassy, four miles from our house. Us kids were hot and hollering we wanted to go swimming and cool off. Dad finally said we didn't have enough time to drive over to Granny's, but he'd run us over to the public landing and dunk us in. He said, "No one will probably be swimming there anyway, just some boaters going in and out." So, we went over there. Several other families were swimming there. They were all White. Me and Jimmy didn't notice or care. They were kids having fun. Something happened that Jimmy and I don't remember. All I know is, some other dad talked to Dad and all at once he picked us up and put us back in the truck. He said something about never coming back.

Once in a while, after we got bigger, I heard Granny and Mom talking about it. Mom said Dad wouldn't take us back there to swim because people yelled at him for bringing us. He said he wouldn't have us kids exposed to racists. Granny always shook her head when they talked about it. She said, "He just don't realize he should ignore the naysayers, and how he could be hisself around everybody, especially his family. There's nothing to be ashamed of in a mixed family."

Then Mommy said, "I know. I hoped that when he took the kids over there, maybe it would mean he was changing, getting more relaxed about being out in public with us." Her face got sad. She said, "It may have made things worse."

Back then, I wasn't sure what she meant.

Jimmy and me loved going to Granny's to play, eat and talk. When Dad was gone, Mommy would take us to Granny's during the week, sometimes we got to sleep over.

We liked Sundays when it got dark. Dad would take us home from

Granny's in his truck while Mom stayed later or overnight to help Granny clean houses the next day. Sometimes, Dad would drive into the forest on a trail, turn the lights off, roll down the windows and tell us to just listen. It was so cool. We could hear all kinds of noises, the owls starting to hoot, one flew right by the truck and we could feel the wind from his wings. It depended on the season what we could hear, even mice or moles and the squirrels moving through the leaves and grasses.

I loved summers when Dad was home. At night, we'd sit on the porch steps and whistle the Whip-Poor-Will sounds, or the Bob-White. Dad was so good, the birds would answer and come closer and closer. It was usually too dark to see them, but a few times, we could see them near the driveway or almost to Memory Tree. Jimmy got better at whistling than me, so I'd listen. I could tell by their answers when they first moved closer, even about where they were, the hay field, the garden, near the old barn, maybe across the road in the sumac or the ditch.

We had a record with all the bird sounds. Mommy or Dad would play it and we'd go outside to listen to the real ones. We helped Mommy make a bird chart and every time we saw a different kind, we marked it down. The spring we turned eight, we saw around one-hundred fifty different types of birds. It was so cool. We used colored pencils to draw them. After, Dad or Mommy got out the bird books and we compared them. Jimmy is a good artist, better than me, but I'm better at writing stories.

Jimmy and me were going to make a book someday. I'd write the story and he would draw the pictures. We made little books for Granny all the time, but someday, ours was going to be a real book about kids who lived near the woods. The daddy would be White and the mommy, not dark like Granny, but not White like Dad. His hair would be light brown and his eyes green-brown, hazel, Mom said. He would be tall, over six feet.

The mommy would be tall for a girl, five-nine. She would have green eyes with sparkles, except when she was mad and fire came out of them. Jimmy hadn't figured out how to draw them with fire, so we decided the book wouldn't have her mad in it. The mommy would be curvy, that's what Dad said. Only sometimes, he said mommy had great boobs and a sweet ass. We knew we couldn't say those words in a book. Besides, when he said those words, she always said, "I'm a lot more than those two things. I'm smart, and you dang well know it." She'd try to look mean at him till they both laughed.

He always said, "I know. I know."

In our book, the mommy's hair would be loose, afro curly and reddish. Not carrot top red, but definitely reddish. She would have freckles. Lots of them. I have some, but Jimmy has a lot. He has brown eyes and darker skin than me and darker hair with a red tint. My hair is brown, kind of curly-wavy, but can get frizzy, and I have blue-green eyes. Sometimes White people look surprised when we tell them we're twins. Black people don't seem to care or be shocked.

Daddy showed us pictures of his parents, they're still hanging on the wall in the living room. Mommy said her mother died in a bad fire in Detroit when she was little, so Granny raised her. Mommy's mom, my grandma, was named Naomi. Once, Jimmy asked Mom if she had pictures of her parents. They would have been our grandparents. At Granny's house, Mommy showed us one of her mom Naomi, hanging on the hallway wall. She was beautiful, too. A lot like Mommy. Just like Mommy and Jimmy and me, my Grandmother Naomi never got any older either. I wonder if she has stardust somewhere?

Mom said she didn't have any pictures of her father. She never met him or knew nothing about him. One time, Granny said, her voice real low, he must have been a redhaired White man or light-skinned Black mixed with a redheaded Irishman. They both changed the subject. Big people do that sometimes. Change the subject when they don't want to answer you. Jimmy and me figured that out when we were eight.

I don't think much talking is going to happen today. Dad's sleeping again. I think Retha is, too. Her head is back and she's not knitting. Sometimes, I wished stardust people could read minds. I wonder what she's thinking, or maybe she's dreaming. That would be cool to see people's dreams. Mostly, I just need to hear Dad talk about us and Mommy, and his stardust be with mine so we can go find Mommy's and Jimmy's.

Chapter Eleven

Glad I'm good at catnapping, Retha thought, as she lowered her knitting needles, leaned her head back and closed her eyes. We're making progress. His anger has to come out before he can figure out why he's angry. I think he's starting. Still, I won't stand for being called a Black Bitch. That may be part of the territory, but I think he got the message. If he says it *again*, I'll inform him that within four hours I can have someone haul his skinny ass to the nursing home in town. I don't want to do that. We both got stuff to get through.

When Duane mentioned Granny, I almost dropped my needles. It was all I could do to focus on his words and not think about Granny. There is so much pain and love tied up in that name. That tiny little woman was known throughout the area as Granny, even when she wasn't old enough to be a granny. She was the unofficial mayor, the hub, the sparkplug of Fair Haven. Well, what was left of Fair Haven. After Naomi died in the apartment fire, Granny must have made sure Ellie called her Granny. I'm sure Granny didn't want Ellie calling her mom.

Retha let her mind drift to Fair Haven, the African American community east of Split Creek. The place started before World War I, as a place where financially secure Black people could get away to vacation, hunt, fish and recreate without facing discrimination. The old folks said several White families bought the land and sold it to them, so colored folks could have the same rights to relax as White folk did. The place grew. Trains brought guests from Chicago and Detroit, even Riverside. Lots were sold, cottages built. Entertainment spots constructed, a roller-skating rink, night clubs. Big name entertainers came, Cab Calloway, B.B. King, even Aretha Franklin, late in the town's heyday. Twenty to thirty thousand people visited in the summer, with thousands owning properties.

People settled year-around to serve the community. That's what Granny said her folks did. They came up one summer from Detroit to wash dishes, clean resort rooms and cabins and keep the grounds up. The second summer, they rented a little cabin, saved their money and managed to survive the winter without freezing to death or starving. They bought the little cabin, two blocks from the main lake and beach. They gradually fixed it up and did anything necessary to keep food on the table. Granny's dad eventually got a job at the post office that was built and they added on to their cabin. Growing up and all her life, Granny cleaned cabins and rooms, cooked, bartended, and waitressed. She inherited her parents' home, along with their leadership amongst the working class of the small year-around community.

Retha shifted in the chair, her butt was getting tired of sitting. I can't be thinking like Wikipedia, she thought. She picked up her knitting. Recalling all she knew about Fair Haven was fun, but dangerous. She didn't want to go there. Not yet. She knew she would have to sometime. She changed her mind. Guess I'll play encyclopedia awhile longer, it's safer to do at this time, in spite of my sore butt.

She recalled how one of the greatest moments in the nations' life was the signing of the federal 1964 Civil Rights Act outlawing discrimination in services and accommodations nation-wide. With increasing opportunities and competition, the demand for places like Fair Haven all but disappeared. Was the leadership of their unique community so entrenched, they couldn't figure out ways to adapt? All Granny knew, she used to say, was, "We shrunk down to almost nothing. People who owned cottages still came, but not as much. They got old and died and their kids didn't want the place up here in the middle of nowhere. The resorts closed, the restaurants and bars, the church barely hung on for years. Our little grocery store closed. The place became almost a ghost town." She'd sigh. "After 1964, all us Black folk could start going to other places for fun. Folks soon discovered there was lots of other places besides Fair Haven."

Oh, Granny, Granny. Thinking about you is too close for comfort, but I am going to get Duane talking about you, and Ellie. She glanced at him, noticed his hands opening and clenching.

He muttered, "Shut yer mouth. Jist shut yer mouth…"

Who was he muttering about?

Next, he spat out, "Ralph!"

She knew who Ralph was.

Chapter Twelve

Ralph? Dad just said Ralph in his sleep. Wake up, Dad. Please wake up and talk. Who was Ralph? Talk, Dad, talk about the bad day and why you never came.

~ * ~

"Wake up. You're talking in your sleep and throwing yourself all over the bed."

Duane opened his eyes and almost yelled for this Black lady to leave him the hell alone. He got his bearings. It was midafternoon, must be Wednesday. Had he slept most of the day? He shook his head to clear it and tried to rearrange the bedding. He couldn't rearrange his mind. Ralph. His father. Granny.

"Guess you won't leave me alone till I talk. Right?" He tried to smile, hoped his voice wasn't too grouchy.

"You're catching on, young man. Catching on. Sometimes talking brings up painful stuff, but you gotta get it out." She straightened out the bedding and adjusted his bed till he was sitting. "Now, who was Ralph?"

He grimaced. "A boyhood friend." He looked around for something, anything, to give him time to think.

Retha hustled into the kitchen and returned with a small bowl. "Chocolate-covered peanuts. Are these your favorite or your wife's?" She winked at him.

"Mine." He bit carefully into one, chewed, swallowed and looked at her. "Ralph Sims was a neighbor's kid, four years younger than me, moved in when I was eleven. He just showed up one day…" He grabbed two more peanuts and slowly ate them. "He—he was pretty needy. No dad, mother on welfare, she bartended at the dives. They moved down the road, little over a mile, into an old trailer house, barely habitable."

"How did you meet?"

"Mom, Dad and I were in the garden and we heard someone say, 'Can I help?' Sort of scared us as we never heard him approach. Dad looked him over and said, 'You the Sims kid? What's your name?' 'It's Ralph, I'm seven, but I can beat up most twelve-year old boys.' He was big for seven, stocky, big head and shoulders." Duane paused again. "My dad just laughed. Mom looked at Dad like he was crazy, like she was surprised he knew who the kid was. She said we didn't fight around our house and invited him to start picking beans, if he knew how. He did. When we finished in the garden, Dad asked Mom what was for lunch. He winked at her. Of course, she'd have fed the kid anyway. Ralph started hanging around, especially when Dad was home."

"Did you play with him? You said you were boyhood friends."

"Yeah. He became sort of a younger brother, but his main attraction at first was Dad. He couldn't get enough of him. Being four years older meant we were on different wave lengths in some ways. I taught him the woods, how to play four-square, fish, track animals, play checkers. He loved the woods. Sometimes Dad took both of us." Duane shifted his body. He was beginning to ache more.

"Ralph wasn't much for reading, though Mom and I both tried to work with him. He was in and out of the house and our lives for a while. Mom got tired of his language and told him he could only show up when Dad was home. The kid was devastated when Dad died, he was fourteen."

"Were you devastated when your father died?"

"Not like Ralph was. By then, I came to see Dad in a different light." Duane thought a moment. "I was sad, but in some ways his death meant I could focus on Mom being so sick, plus planning for my future."

"I can understand that." Retha popped a peanut into her mouth, chewed as she looked at him. "What else about Ralph?"

Duane shrugged and looked toward the frosted window. "Guess that's pretty much it."

Retha glared at him till he looked at her. She reached for two more peanuts, her eyes flashing. "Duane, I flat out do not believe 'that's it' about a guy who still gives you nightmares at age seventy-four." She sat back in her rocker and motioned for him to continue.

Duane sucked in a deep breath. As deep as he could, given his condition. "Dammit. Who said I have to play this stupid talk game with you? What gives you the right to force me to talk? Will it speed up my death? Will I get to hell faster? Christ, I came here to die peacefully, not play some talking-to-a-fake-shrink game. Leave me alone." He turned away from her, muttering. Angrily, he turned back. "Goddammit, now I gotta pee. Can you help me?"

"Of course, we'll use the urinal." She helped him swing to the edge of the bed and pee, tucked him back in and left the room. In the kitchen, it sounded like she started cooking something.

Chapter Thirteen

Dad sure is crabby. Why won't he talk more about that Ralph boy? I'd like to hear what happened to him. Especially when he was all upset after Dad's dad dying, my grandfather I never knew, except from pictures on the wall in the living room.

Will it be good for Dad to talk more about Ralph? I wish he would talk about us. I think Retha's right. Dad needs to talk.

~ * ~

Retha emptied and rinsed the urinal, washed her hands and went to the kitchen. No sense riling him up more. Why is he being so stubborn about sharing his past life? The one before the big girls. The man is wound up tighter than a watch spring, with guilt over something. What was it? She knew part of the story, but needed to hear it from him. He needed to tell it. She needed to tell her part in his story, too.

She checked the time. Three hours' time difference between Michigan and Oregon. She'd wait to call Ashley and Jessica. Maybe they could do FaceTime or Skype with him and the girls. That might be good for him.

She turned the oven to two-seventy-five and began browning a roast and prepping the potatoes, celery, carrots and onions. She put it all together and slid the Dutch-oven into the stove. She warmed up the leftover tomato soup, poured it into a mug and took it into him. "Here's some tomato soup and crackers. Want to eat it in bed or have me help you to a chair?"

He mumbled, "Bed's all right, for now," and added a soft thank you. He finished the soup and handed her the mug. "I'm sorry I exploded. Don't know why I did…"

"I know why." She waited till he looked at her. "Most people have regrets, guilt, things they've kept stuffed, hidden, whatever, all down inside. I've found, and research shows, that getting that out of you is good for you. Why die with regrets buried? It's obvious you have some. I think you need to get them out while you can. I'm not being nosy, just want you to die with a clear mind."

He nodded. "I'm trying to understand that. It's hard. I didn't think that's what I wanted when I decided to come here to die. I figured I'd just die with them." He scratched the stubble on his chin, stretched, then pointed at her. "How about you, you got regrets? Secrets? I keep feeling like you know more about me and this area than you're letting on. Like you're holding back, too."

"You're pretty perceptive. I guarantee you I will share my story. Our lives do overlap, even if we never met each other." She patted his shoulder. "Tell you what. Let's take the rest of the day off from storytelling. Tomorrow's supposed to be a sunny day. Think if I get some help you might feel well enough to take a drive? It's been years since I been to this area, maybe a ride will be good for both of us."

Duane looked surprised. "I'd love to get out and see the area again, but there's no way I could even walk down those steps now, let alone get in and out of a car. Most are set so low. What do you drive?"

"I drive a minivan. I can even take wheelchairs in it. I have some contacts for local folk who could help with your transportation. I'll make some calls. The snow people plowed and cleared right up to the steps so, with some help, we should be fine. How about it?"

He smiled. "Yup, this will probably be my last time outside until they scatter my ashes. What's the worst that can happen? We end up in a ditch, freezing to death." He tried to laugh.

She shook her head. "I love gallows humor until it includes me. Now, what games do you like to play? Checkers, cribbage, cards, Monopoly? Just not chess. Maybe you just want to carve soap?"

"Let's play some cribbage. After that, I want to carve a bit."

She scooted his legs over, rolled the hospital lap table over him and climbed onto the bed facing him, her legs under the table next to his.

"Bet you're surprised a white-haired woman can be so agile, ain't ya?"

"No comment, any answer I give will get me in trouble."

"Smart man. Smart man, you're learning fast."

They played several hands of cribbage before he began carving. Retha texted Ashley about a time to Skype or FaceTime. Both girls said they could be home by five-thirty their time, which was eight-thirty Retha's time, shortly before Duane would go to sleep.

At eight-thirty, Duane was in bed, apparently finishing his soap carving. Retha purposely avoided looking at it, though she knew it was a person's face. Her iPad buzzed. She carried it in, laid it on the lap table, slipped a fresh bar of soap under it to raise the camera toward Duane, and pressed the button. Ashley's and Jessica's faces filled the screen, their squeals echoed through the room.

"Oh my God," he said, "I didn't know we could do this out here. How wonderful. What a surprise."

They chatted away. He updated them on what Retha was fixing him to eat. They told him about their jobs and their new puppy. Finally, Duane asked, "So, how are Ahmed and Mark doing?" The girls were quiet. "You're making them pay rent, right? Did you rent out your empty rooms?" He waited before adding, "It's okay. I'm trying to be funny. I sincerely want to know. I'm sorry I've been so up and down about them. It sounds like you both have excellent relationships. That's all that counts." He teared up and looked away.

"Thanks, Dad," Ashley whispered. "Hang on, the guys are in the kitchen, making dinner. You want to say hi?"

He nodded.

The men joined the girls and all chatted a few minutes. Jessica sent the guys back to the kitchen because she smelled something burning. "Dad, have you been carving? Can you show us?"

Retha caught his look of surprise and quick glance at her. What was that about? She watched as he slowly brought the carving up from the table.

"Dad, hold it closer to your face, turn it toward us."

Retha took a deep breath as the girls exclaimed, "Oh, Dad, that looks just like her. Retha, Retha, get in the picture and hold the carving next to your face. I wish it could be in wood. Don't ever wash with it, Retha."

Retha teared up and shook her head at Duane. "Dang you. Why'd you do that? How can I be mean to you now?"

He grinned as he put the carving into her hand. "I didn't start out to carve you. It just happened. Sometimes carving takes on a life of its own." He shrugged and waved goodbye to the girls. "Thank you, that was a nice surprise. I hope we can do it again."

Retha set the soap carving on the buffet. She winked at him as she removed the iPad. "You're welcome. We will Facetime with the girls again. Now, let me help you pee, then I gotta go wash my hands."

He laughed. "I'll take that as a thank you from an agile white-haired lady."

Retha settled him for the night, damped the woodstove, adjusted the heater and crawled into her bed. I think that was a breakthrough. Maybe for both of us. I hope tomorrow helps open him up more, I'm guessing it will me as well. She thought a few more moments. The rough stuff is yet to come. It won't be easy from here on.

For either of us.

Chapter Fourteen

Thursday, January 10, 2019

Dad slept like a baby all night. He just had to pee once. I wish I could go in the van with them. I probably could, but I don't know how to time it to go out the door with them. Would I be blown away? That would be horrible. How did I get into the house that day after the bad day? I don't remember. Did I float through the walls? A window? Do I have more supernatural powers than I think I do? I don't think I have any. I'm just stardust. Nine years and six-day old stardust waiting for Dad's stardust to appear or at least to learn why he never rescued us. I think I'll be meeting his stardust. Still, I'd like to hear him talk about us before he dies. Is that strange? I think this whole thing is strange.

Dad and Mommy said they didn't believe in heaven or hell, that our people-spirit wasn't religious. It was just stardust. People remembered things about us, good and bad. That's how we lived on, in people's memories. I still don't get it. Maybe dead people are the only ones who understand stardust. Is it just Mommies and Daddies stardust that communicates with their kids' stardust? Why doesn't mine talk with Mommy's and Jimmy's? It only did for a short time. I hung around, hoping to talk more, but it didn't happen. So, I obeyed them and somehow came to the house. I was too upset and scared to remember how I did it.

What will happen when Retha dies? She doesn't have any real kids, just foster ones. Does her stardust meet up with her parents? Will her foster kids' stardust meet up with their real parents? Is stardust only for kids? All I know is I'm stardust who can see, hear and think. I'm not sure about going through walls or getting blown off the porch. I'm sticking here, inside.

Oops, someone's knocking at the door. Retha let a man in. He says he's here to help transport Dad and did she need anything else. Retha tells him to go start her van and bring more wood in from the shed while she gets Dad ready. She asks if he could do some grocery shopping while she drives Dad around in town. "We won't be gone long. Can't keep this young man out."

The man laughs and says, "I don't think we should be gone too long, no matter how young he is. There's a front moving in this afternoon and it's bringing some snow, maybe a blizzard."

They rush around and leave. I'm glad I stayed home. I don't know how stardust kids do in blizzards.

~ * ~

Arturo—call me Art—wheeled Duane onto the porch and picked him up like an infant. Art carried him down the steps and tucked him into the front seat.

Duane couldn't take his eyes off Memory Tree. He missed her so much. It was becoming easier to talk with Retha. Maybe it would be even easier if he thought about talking with her as if he was talking to Memory.

He heard Art place the wheelchair in the back of the van before asking Retha, "Want me to drive? I'm used to this area in winter."

Duane smiled as she puffed up and snorted. "Get in the second seat, young man. The day I can't drive in a Michigan winter is the day I quit breathing. Now buckle in." She buckled in and drove smoothly down the drive and over the icy hardpacked roads into Split Creek. She gave Art some cash, along with a list, and dropped him off at the grocery store. "I'll be back in half an hour. Don't make me wait. These are just a few things so I can do some baking. The store already has a large order I called in to deliver on Saturday."

She drove them slowly around town. Both remarked at the changes, the newer high school and junior high, the elementary school. It appeared every child in the county was now bused into town. Duane noted how none of the stores or restaurants were the same. Retha agreed. She drove them by the nursing home where Art and his wife worked. Different shifts so someone was home when the kids were out of school. Today was Art's day off. He seemed appreciative of the opportunity to make extra money.

"When we get home, pay Art well," Duane said.

"I already planned to. Besides, it's not my money." She winked at him.

Both noted the number of run-down homes. He thought there were more trailer homes than years ago. It appeared the poverty level was high, opportunity for jobs was low.

Retha headed east out of town and turned into Fair Haven. There was little left. More trailer-homes, a few, very few, of the nice homes that once surrounded the lake still looked good, if they were in view at all. A combination gas station and convenience store was the sole retail operation in town. Several small restaurants were closed for the season. The post office was shuttered. The church looked rarely used, except the parking lot between it and the cemetery was partially plowed. Retha pulled in, parked, and flipped the heater to high. They sat there, the tension building. Why did she stop here?

"Granny's buried over there. Count four rows back and six headstones to the left of the tree. Everybody chipped in to make hers a nice one."

Duane wiped his nose. *Try not to cry, try to keep in my grief. I let Granny down.*

"They're buried next to her. Flat headstones."

Duane gasped and choked. He tried to unbuckle his seatbelt. Their graves. She could only mean Ellie's and the twins' graves. How does she know about them? Who is this woman? The twins, Ellie, their graves only seventy-five feet away. Next to Granny's. He managed to unbuckle his belt and reached for the door handle, but couldn't figure out where it was. The door locks clunked.

"Duane, you can't get out. I'm sorry. Even I'd have trouble walking through the deep snow when we can't see the paths or most of the headstones."

He sagged back into his seat, defeated. Who buried them? Why was Granny's grave next to theirs? When? When did this happen? How does she know?

Retha handed him some water, patted his shoulder, wiped her eyes. "I told you our lives overlap. We have a lot in common. We each need to talk." She leaned over and buckled his seatbelt.

He saw tears streaming down her cheeks. Who was she? How did she know about Ellie and the twins? He was too stunned to ask. That day ran through his mind like a herd of galloping mustangs.

Retha sniffled a few times, didn't speak, as she put the car in gear, drove back to town and picked up Art. No one talked on the way home. The wind picked up, whirling around, the big flakes making the atmosphere inside the van even grayer.

Art settled Duane in the house, said he had to use the john. After washing his hands, he hollered, "Hey, I caught a whiff of gas by the basement door. I'm going to check it out."

They heard him poking around in the basement. Duane didn't smell gas.

"Maybe the water heater kicked on and gave off a whiff," Retha said, her voice still strained.

Art came back upstairs and ran some water in the bathroom. He went back downstairs for a few minutes and trotted back. "There's no leaks in the basement. I checked every joint with soapy water. Only place it's coming from is the hole for the tube leading from the outside to the inside. I'm thinking the outside valve may give off a whiff now and then. Call the company and they'll send someone out. I stuffed the hole with rags. You're good." He laughed. "That copper tubing down there is one hell of a Rube Goldberg job. I'm guessing the only shut-off valve is outside. Anyway, I'll throw some more wood on the porch. I gotta get back so I can pick my wife up from work."

Duane managed to say, "Yeah, my father ran that copper just before I was born. I always intended to re-do the runs."

He watched Retha pay Art, who looked happy with the amount. Retha asked Art to quickly move the recliner from the living room into the dining room. Art shifted Duane's bed, and the rocker, dragged the recliner out, shook their hands again, and left. Duane was surprised when he heard Art open the kitchen door and haul the wood in from the porch.

"Retha, put some towels down. There's no sense you coming out on the porch and dealing with snow-covered wood. This will be easier if it's all inside. Let me know next week and I'll run back out and haul in more."

Retha thanked him again. Duane thought she slipped him another ten. She hurried into the dining room and pulled the covers tighter around him. "With the wind rising and temperature dropping, I'm going to close the pocket doors into the living room and sleep out here in the recliner. Lord knows I've slept in enough of them. This'll keep the heat closer." Her voice sounded strained, not light and cheerful.

Retha warmed up some leftover chili and served it over cornbread. Neither spoke, they just ate. She took to sitting on the edge of the bed to eat when he remained in bed for a meal. Right now, he was too wiped out to try sitting at the table. He felt numb, yet comfortable. He shoved the sight of the graves to the back of his mind. It was too much to absorb all at once. He wanted to ask her all kinds of questions, yet didn't feel ready. Though he was at ease with her, he reminded himself he had a lot to get through if he wanted a clear mind and soul before he died, and he did. He didn't have the energy right now to begin talking or asking her questions.

He knew his prostate cancer metastasized into his bones and organs. The meds currently kept the pain mostly at bay, but he knew more pain meant more meds which would make him dopey. Duane knew his departure was approaching, that he wasn't looking at several weeks like he thought. Maybe one week, if that. He understood the end could come quickly with someone in his condition. Still, he wanted to know how their lives overlapped. How she knew about Ellie and the twins. Who Retha really was? Exhausted, he leaned back and dozed off as she covered him with another blanket.

He came to when he felt her undressing him.

"Here," she said, "I'm putting you in an adult diaper and a pair of sweats. Drink a little of this Ensure. After today, you need a good night's rest. So do I."

He reached for her hand and squeezed it. "Thank you." He took several sips of the Ensure and let his head fall back against the pillow. *I can't make it to the bathroom on my own anymore, I'm in a diaper, I can't make it to the kitchen to eat. Damn, how life changes when you get old. Except, I'm not only old, I'm going to die. Soon. At least that's not a bad excuse for being upset about losing control of my life. I can't change anything. Worrying won't help. My life is what it is.* He took a big breath and let it out slowly before he slipped into a deep sleep, his mind quiet.

When he awoke the next morning, Retha removed his diaper and put another one on him. He didn't object. Wasn't this what happened when you got old and were dying? While she was in the kitchen, he thought about yesterday. Somehow, he felt calmer. At least he knew Ellie and the twins were buried. Someone found them and made sure they were taken care of. He winced as the acid taste of guilt rose in his gullet. Someone took care of them, even if it wasn't him. Big chicken shit. He looked up to find Retha watching him. She held tea and a piece of toast.

"I put peanut butter and jam on it." She sat on the edge of the bed to feed him.

He ate several bites and sipped the tea. He motioned the toast away. "I can't eat much. Leave the tea and I'll sip on it." He patted her arm. She squeezed his back and took the toast to the kitchen, returning with a shoebox.

She moved the table over him, placed the box on it, then climbed onto the bed, facing him, her legs under the table. "Okay if we're close for this?"

"That's fine. I think we're comfortable enough now to share a bed." He tried to smile. It was true, he did feel comfortable with her, yet he sensed both had a ton of history to unload. Yes, he wanted her close for that. Under the table, he patted her leg through the bedding.

Her eyes serious, she looked at him with concern. "Opening this box is going to be rough on both of us. Take a big breath."

~ * ~

72

Dad must have plum wore himself out yesterday, riding around in the van. Granny always said plum wore yourself out, I like the way it sounds. Plum wore out. It's not about plums, either. Her neighbor had a plum tree, but the birds usually got them before we could. Oh, I remember. It's plum with a b on the end. Dad showed us a plumb line, and how if the weight was swinging, you couldn't tell if something was straight or not. "It's out of plumb," he said. "Plumb crazy, that's where the expression comes from." I just remembered that.

After that nice man Art left, Retha and Dad ate some cookies before he fell asleep. Hard. He barely woke up when she changed him. She even put diaper pants on him cuz he was too asleep. I know he's breathing, so he's not dead. She slept in the recliner Art pulled out for her. Guess it's really getting cold. Now they don't have to heat the living and bedroom. There's a board over the vent that goes through the ceiling from the dining room to my old bedroom, so no heat's going up there.

Mommy moved us upstairs, after we got potty-trained. She said she wanted a dining room back. She made one room our play area and we slept in the other, the one with the vent. She said we were getting old enough to sleep in separate rooms, but hadn't moved Jimmy's bed over yet. On real cold nights, we slept in sleeping bags in the dining room next to the heater. Sometimes when Dad was gone, Mom slept out there with us, like a little party.

Oh, he's awake. Retha puts another diaper on him, feeds him some toast and tea. She puts a box on the table and climbs up on the bed. He seems okay with her being on the bed. I bet he's liking her a whole lot better than he did at first.

What the heck is in that box?

Chapter Fifteen

May 19, 1975

Duane, age twenty-nine, ran through his mental checklist. Clean clothes packed in the old Airstream. The hubs greased on the battered aluminum land-ship that looked like a beached whale. Fresh water tank filled. Black and gray tanks emptied into the septic system. Inside the house, his bathroom was clean, bed made with fresh sheets, dishes drying in the rack—he rarely put them away. His clothes were folded and in dresser drawers, the furniture quick-dusted, floors swept or vacuumed and the fridge checked for anything that might go bad. Only thing left was to pick up some fresh food for the Airstream.

It was eight-thirty in the morning. He didn't have to leave until one p.m. Hating to wait till the last minute, or have to park in town with a trailer, he decided to run into town in his International Scout to shop. The love of his life. He bought it brand new in 1971, a year after he finally graduated from college and established his forestry consulting business. Yellow, with a removable hard top, V-8, stick-shift, air, and a custom radio with speakers, it was a beauty he kept locked in the shed when he was away.

He eased from the driveway and noticed a vehicle off to the side of the road where Grassy Lakes Road curved west and Access Road split off north, about a quarter mile from his driveway. The hood up grabbed his attention. Wonder what I can do to help? He rarely passed anyone in distress on the road. He knew what it was like to break down and was always thankful for help from strangers.

As he drew closer, the second thing that grabbed his attention was the long light-brown legs of someone in blue-jean cutoffs, leaning under the raised hood of a rusted Ford Falcon. He couldn't tell what the original

74

color of the car was because he was so entranced by those long legs and sweet butt.

He pulled to a stop and climbed out of the Scout as the young woman straightened up and turned toward him. She had long arms, was wearing a man's red-checked flannel shirt over a blue t-shirt with the tails of her shirt pulled and tied around her waist. Her face was full of light freckles, her eyebrows slightly reddish. He couldn't stop staring at her eyes—green, flashing with anger. She wore a blue knit winter stocking hat pulled low over her ears, forehead and back of her head. A wisp of reddish black curl poked out near her left ear.

"Bad decision," she said, looking at him. "Bad, just bad. I thought it might just be the air filter, but I managed to bang a lot of crap out of it and it still wouldn't start. Looks like a mouse nest was in it. Now I think it's the fuel filter. Plugged." She wiped a greasy hand across her brow, leaving streaks. "This thing's been sitting all winter. It started off okay. About halfway here, it began sputtering. I cussed it along, but it died anyway. Maybe I should have been praying for it, that's what my granny would have done. It's her car."

"Can I take a look?" It was hard to take his eyes off of her to concentrate on the car. Not that he ever looked much. Too busy with his forestry business. Besides, what woman would want to live with a forester in an old farmhouse next to the national forest and who was gone all the time?

"Be my guest." Her eyes changed from sparks to sparkles.

He grabbed a small tool kit from the Scout and began poking around the air filter and carburetor. He slid halfway under the car and pulled the fuel filter. It was jammed full. "Bet you didn't put any gas winterizer in, did you?" He crawled out and dusted the grit and rust off his pants. "Your carburetor is gummed up, too." He loosened a spark plug, shook his head. "This old girl needs some work, nothing major, just a good tune-up."

She looked at her watch. "Can you do it in five minutes? I'm almost late for a job." She flashed him a grin.

"Where do you work? What do you do?"

She pulled off her stocking cap and ran her finger through reddish-black, loose-curly Afro looking hair. "I clean houses. Things got so slow over where I live, I've started a business, cleaning summer cabins for White people."

He was stunned. Still by her looks, but also by her frankness, and that she wasn't White. "You—you mean you're Black?"

She threw her head back and laughed. "Yeah, if I cover my hair, I fool most White people. That's why I'm wearing my hat to work over here. I don't want those nice White people from Riverside, Detroit and Chicago to think we've invaded. Do you blame me?"

Visions of his father flew through his mind. "No. No, I don't." He scratched his head. "Just what was your plan, Miss…"

"It's not Miss and sure as hell not a Mrs. I'm Ellie Bryant, and since you're still staring at me, I'm nineteen, almost twenty. I live in Fair Haven with my granny who raised me." She reached out her hand and shook his. "She had medical tests in Ludington, so she took my car and I took hers. We contacted the property manager who opens these summer places up, gave him a good price to clean them. He's got four or five lined up for me." She sighed and twisted several curls. "I brought my sleeping bag, planned to squat a night or two over here, 'cuz I wasn't too sure about this old Falcon. Now, I don't know what to do."

"I can run you over. It's only a couple of miles." He thought of his plans for the day and pointed toward his house. "I'm Duane Gleason. I live in that house. I'm a forestry consultant. You got anyone who can come pick you up if I drop you off?"

She thought several moments. "Granny's going in for several days of tests, so she can't. There ain't a whole lot of other people hanging around Fair Haven anymore, but I can probably round up someone if I can get to a phone."

It dawned on Duane the summer cabins might not have phones, or they may not be turned on yet. He glanced at his watch. Maybe, just maybe, he could get this Falcon running. "Tell you what, load your cleaning gear and that sleeping bag into my car. We'll run back to my house. You can take the Scout to work. I'll take my work truck into town

76

to pick up some supplies. I'll pick up some parts, come back and see if I can get this thing running."

"Are you kidding me? That sure would help."

"Yes, it's no big deal. Listen, if I can get it running, I'll drive it over and switch. If I can't…Well, I guess you can drive the Scout to your home. Do me a favor, just swing by the house and leave a note with your address and number so I can call you to bring it back."

"That's very nice," she said as she hauled her supplies and sleeping bag and placed them in the rear of the Scout. "Won't you be home later today? Are you going away?"

"Oh, yeah, I forgot to say that part. I have to leave right after lunch with my truck and camper for a job on the other side of the state. I'll be back Saturday. I leave again the following Tuesday." He smiled. "So, in case I don't get the Falcon running today, I can work on it over the weekend. Deal?" He stuck out his hand.

"Not so fast, buddy. I got like five buck's cash. How am I going to pay for these parts before I even get paid for these cleaning jobs?"

He grinned and shook his head. "Well—"

"Don't you well me. You were going to say you were sure we could work something out, weren't you?" Her eyes spat daggers. "I'm not innocent, but I sure as hell don't trade myself for goddamn car parts. Give me back my stuff and I'll walk to those cabins." She yanked the tailgate open.

"Ellie, dammit. Wait a second. In the first place, I wasn't going to say that. In the second, I was going to say I have plenty of money. For Christ's sake, I own my business and do fine." Now his eyes were burning, and she looked surprised. "In the third, I was going to tell you to pay me when you could afford to and over time if needed. I never hound people for money they owe me, unless I think they're trying to stiff me." He climbed into the Scout. "Now, are you walking or borrowing my car? It's up to you."

She slammed the tailgate and climbed into the passenger seat. "Guess I'm borrowing." She looked around the vehicle. "This thing is gorgeous. Anyone else ever drive it?"

"You'll be the first. Make sure there's not a fingerprint on it when I see it next." Both laughed. He drove back to his house. She used the bathroom. On the way out of the house, he handed her a note. "This is my home phone. This number is my answering service. They give me my messages. I call in at least once a day. And…" He tapped the beeper on his belt. "This number is for my beeper. Coverage north of M-46 isn't as good as the southern half of the state, but it's getting better." He followed her onto the porch. "By the way, if you don't feel safe squatting in those cabins, my back door is never locked. You can stay here, if you want." He watched her back stiffen. "I'll be gone, no strings attached. That's just in case I can't get your car running today."

She turned, looked at him silently, gazing into his eyes, her eyes soft, sparkling, not flashing arrows. She stuck her hand out. "I think you're a good guy. Thank you."

What did I just do? Duane wondered as he watched her drive his precious Scout down the drive. He jumped into his truck. Now, he had even more to do. He stopped at the Falcon and checked the carb again. It needed more than a cleaning, it needed to be rebuilt. No way could he get that done today. He drove into town, bought the car parts and groceries. On the way back, he managed to tow the Falcon and park it next to the shed where he kept his tools. He replaced the plugs, wires and condenser, the fuel filter, and pulled the carburetor, then took a shower. He left a note on the back door of his house, stating he would finish her car over the weekend, hitched his trailer to the truck and pulled out.

~ * ~

Driving toward town, he sighed. Now he just had to put up with Ralph Sims till Saturday. No way was he mentioning Ellie to him. The man always seemed jealous when Duane dated anyone, which wasn't often. He was glad Ralph rejoined the Army and was leaving next week. The man needed the structure to control his aggression and attitudes.

He pulled the truck and trailer to the side and beeped his horn in front of a rundown house set close to the street. Ralph had been home from the army for a month and Duane was ready for him to leave again. Ralph worked for him before he went into the army and when he was home on leave.

Still, he wondered why he felt like he was Ralph's caretaker. *I don't know why he sticks to me like a fly on flypaper when he's home. He's been that way ever since Dad died, eleven years ago. Sometimes I think he needs a father.*

Sometimes I think he wants to be in love with me. It's just weird.

Two men in love? Yes, the gays were starting to make themselves known, especially in the big cities. That was all about butt sex, wasn't it?

Yuck.

He startled as Ralph yanked the door open and climbed in. "You asleep? You didn't even move when I opened the trailer door and put my clothes in."

Duane watched as Ralph turned and waved at his mother standing partway in the open door. She appeared to be still in her nightgown, a cigarette dangling from her lips, a can of beer in her hand.

Duane pulled away and carefully drove through downtown Split Creek. The tourist season was starting, mostly senior citizens before Memorial Day. A fair number of people were wandering the stores or going in and out of the main grocery store.

"Goddammit." Ralph pounded the dash. "Look at them people going into Frank's Restaurant. Why can't they stay with their own kind out in Fair Haven where they belong?" He acted like he wanted to jump out of the truck and go after them.

Two blocks later, while stopped at a red light, he yelled out the window, "Go back to Mexico." A Hispanic looking couple was crossing the street. Duane swung his hand, cuffing Ralph's shoulder. "Do you want to get out here? Right now? I'm not listening to your shit about colored people and Mexicans."

"Ooh. What's'a matter? You in one of your kume-bye-ah moods again? Gotta love all them people that don't belong with us Whites?"

Duane flicked his signal on and slowed down to turn onto a side street.

"Wait. Wait. You serious? You're gonna take me home?"

"It's up to you. Can you keep your race shit to yourself or not? It's also a long walk from north of Higgins Lake."

"Oh, all right. You know me, I don't mean anything by it. 'Sides, your old man talked this way all the time. Even worse. Why you so shocked about it?"

"I'm not shocked, I don't like it, not in these times. Things have changed, plus Dad never said that in front of my mother and you know it. He talked that way to you because you ate it up. You should have grown out of that crap. How can you get by in the Army with those attitudes?"

Ralph seemed to shrink back in his seat. "Army's different. I'll be good. What am I doin' on this trip?"

"You're marking. We got a section, plus some, to go through. Mostly oak, some walnut and maple. Just the bigger stuff."

"How we gonna get that done in five days? You know I'm leavin' Monday."

"I know. I'm leaving the trailer and going back by myself till it's finished."

Ralph leaned against the door and stared out the window before dozing off.

That week, Duane kept Ralph out in the woods, measuring and marking the trees. They used a compass, along with a grid on a map, and checked in with each other several times a day. Duane occasionally double-checked Ralph's work, mostly so Ralph realized he was being supervised. He was a good assistant in the woods. He was just so damned obnoxious out of them. Evenings, in the trailer, after Duane worked on his records, they played checkers, cribbage, and cards. Occasionally, Duane carved in soap or pine, He also brought the food so there was little liquor to throw Ralph off base.

There were times Duane wondered if Ralph wasn't related to him. He was just like Duane's father in so many ways. If they were related, his mother must have never suspected. He remembered her travel money story.

On Wednesday, Duane checked in with his answering service.

Roberta, who handled her answering service from her home, using aging equipment, chuckled as she read a message. "From Ellie, 'Cabins not safe, thank you. Got more jobs. Update you later.' Now, that's the strangest message I've ever taken for you. Do you want to leave a response?"

That must mean she's staying at my house, he thought. "Nah. I got it. It's just a friend."

"She's just a friend. That's what all men say." Roberta laughed. Her voice purred. "Sure you don't want to leave a message for her?"

"Roberta, did you hear about the new answering service company that just started up in town? Full-time, trained staff, twenty-four seven, work in shifts, latest equipment, bonded for privacy."

"Oh, Duuwane. Don't go getting touchy. I've been teasing you since you started with me five years ago. You know I'm discreet. There's only two dogs and three cats that live with me. Besides, I got so excited a girl left you a message that wasn't about cutting trees, well, I just couldn't contain myself."

On Friday, when he called in, Roberta could barely contain her cackling. "From Ellie. 'More cabins, been busy. Bring bacon, eggs, bread, cheese and milk. Granny's tests were fine.'" Duane heard her snort. "Ain't saying a word, Mr. Gleason. Sir, would you like to leave a professional return message for your caller?"

"No, thank you. I'll check in with you when I get home tomorrow."

"Okay, I'll be right here awaiting your call. And, Mr. Gleason, sir, don't forget the bacon, eggs, bread, cheese and milk. Sounds like omelets to me."

Duane hung up before she could hear him laughing.

He thought about Ellie all the way back to the woods. Part of him couldn't wait to see her again. She was intriguing. Oh hell, she was beautiful and spirited. Part of him was aware of his father's voice, as if he was looking over his shoulder, yelling in his ear.

He returned to the trailer where Ralph was waiting. My father's twin, he thought.

Saturday, he dropped Ralph off about noon. Ralph acted like he was going away to war and might never return. He served in Vietnam, but that was over. The U.S. lost. He told Duane it was a safe time to be in the Army. He re-enlisted for six years.

Today, it was almost like Ralph wanted to cling to him. "I'm going to really miss you, buddy. I've loved these last thirty days hangin' with ya."

"I'll miss you, too. You've been good company and help." Duane kept thinking of Ellie. Was she at his house? What did she mean, to bring home food? Did she eat his up? Was she going to cook for him?

Ralph slid his bulk across the seat and wrapped his meaty arms around Duane. "Well, take care." He briefly touched his lips to Duane's cheek and clambered out.

"Jesus, Ralph. A kiss on the cheek? I'm twenty-nine, you're twenty-five. You're only going back into the army with no wars going on. Not off to Vietnam like you did in Nineteen Sixty-nine." He wiped his cheek off and put the truck in gear.

Ralph waved at him like a little kid.

There was no sign of his Scout when Duane pulled into the driveway and parked alongside the shed. The house smelled fresh and of cleaning supplies. He unloaded his cooler and put away the groceries.

Why did the house seem so bright? He realized the windows had been cleaned, inside and out, the heavy drapes removed and just the sheers left hanging. They looked clean, too. The linoleum in the kitchen and bathroom shone with fresh wax. The sinks, tub and toilet gleamed.

There was no note. *She must still be cleaning cottages or took the Scout to her granny's house. I'll check for messages later this afternoon.*

He went to the shed and started working on the carburetor.

Thirty minutes later, he heard the well pump kick on and stepped outside. A hose ran from the outdoor spigot toward the barn and snaked around to the shady side. Who hooked up the hose? He followed it around the corner to find Ellie drinking out of the nozzle, his Scout washed and gleaming with new wax.

"Just making sure there's no fingerprints," she called, shutting the nozzle off.

"Looks like there's none in the house either. You didn't have to clean my house when that's all you've been doing for five days."

"Granny always says to leave a place better than you find it." She tossed him the keys to the Scout. "Don't move this till the sand around it dries. I won't be responsible for any dust or mud-marks." She pointed at his greasy hands. "Is that from my carb?" She didn't wait for a reply. "While you finish that up, I'll go in and throw together an omelet. I'll leave after we eat. Granny needs me at home."

Duane finished installing the carb, turned the motor on, listened, and readjusted the plugs and carb. The car ran fairly well, not great, but it wouldn't conk out driving down the road for a good while.

He washed up at the outside sink and went inside, nervous, yet fascinated.

Ellie chatted away, telling him of her adventures cleaning houses. How the property manager that hired her loved her work. "He liked my body, too. Kept telling me, following me around the first day like I was in heat. He started to touch me and I pulled my knife out. It's a switch blade. I told him I was there to work, not for his pleasure, and if he ever tried to touch me, his wife would find him emasculated." Her eyes narrowed. "You do know what that word means, don't you?"

"I most certainly do. Is it safe for me to keep eating?"

Her face flushed. "I'm sorry. I just refuse to be patronized as a Black woman."

"Did you still have a job?"

She laughed. "To answer your question, he became very respectful. Still, I didn't take my cap off till after he paid me and told me he wanted me back Tuesday and every week to clean up after the people leave."

"What happened when you pulled your cap off?"

"Nothing. He stared at me, said he liked my guts, but just wear my cap when I was working around there. A lot of these folk wouldn't care, he said, but some would. I told him I could live with that. It was sad, but I could live with it." Her expression changed, not to anger, but to sadness. She stared out the window a moment.

Duane collected the dirty dishes and began washing them. The drain rack was empty.

"Oh yeah, I put things away. The right way." She stood, patted his shoulder. "I saw the receipt for the parts on the counter. There's the cash, plus five for the groceries. I'm leaving now. Thanks for all your help." From the porch, she called back through the screen door, "My numbers on the back of the receipt."

Chapter Sixteen

Duane finished the dishes and put them away, the right way. He wandered around the house, still surprised at the light, the fresh smells, heck, she'd even rinsed the screens. He went upstairs to the two bedrooms to find them dusted and swept. In the basement, he checked his workbench, his carvings, but didn't think anything was touched. At last, he went into his bedroom off the living room. It was spotless. The bed looked exactly as he left it.

Walking back through the living room, his eye caught something pink tucked between the cushion and arm of the couch. It was a pair of pink footie-socks. Behind the couch was a sleeping bag. He sat down, fingering the socks, imagining her slipping them off, along with other clothing. He jumped up. He needed to keep his mind occupied.

Sunday, he washed the truck. He didn't bother waxing it. It was four-wheel drive, heavy duty and meant for driving narrow forest roads and two-tracks. He finished several proposals and dropped them in the mailbox, knowing they wouldn't go out until Tuesday. Monday was Memorial Day. He started some vegetable soup for his supper, simmered it for several minutes and decided some fresh panfish sounded good to go along with the soup. He flipped the burner off.

The lake was a twenty-to-twenty-five-minute walk, across the road, down a hill, through the woods. Not strenuous, but not easy due to the shrubs and roots, along with the twists and turns. Plus, the last twenty yards went through the lowlands and swamp. Over the years, he helped his parents put planks down for when the water level was high. They led to three ten-foot floating sections made with scrap lumber attached to metal barrels. A rough ramp went from the boardwalk up to the dock.

Every spring, he cut back the brush to keep a small clearing open just before the dock. He also trimmed the brush back along the dock, starting with the second section, in order to provide space to get the boat out.

He kept a small john boat tied to the second dock, the oars left in it, soggy seat pads that might or might not float rested on the seats, bamboo poles stuck over the front. The boat was not locked. The area was so desolate, either from the road or the rest of the lake, that there was no need to worry about someone stealing the little boat.

He grabbed the spade from behind a tree, scanned the cleared area and dug in. As always, he found big fat worms to throw into the coffee can. He shoved off and rowed to the middle of the bay.

The bay was surrounded by woods and brush except for a fifty-foot entrance into the main lake, Big Grassy. Other fishermen rarely ventured into the bay. Which meant there were lots of pan fish and bass waiting for Duane. Sometimes he brought his rod and reel for bass. Except the lake was so weedy and the brush around the bay so dense, it usually wasn't worth the effort. Especially when the panfish all but jumped on your hook. From the middle of the bay, he had to look closely to find his dock. That was how thick the brush was around it.

He caught two dozen fish in forty minutes—sunfish, crappies and bluegill. Way more than he needed, but enough that he could freeze some and take them to eat in the camper. Once home, he filleted the fish behind the barn.

What was there to do now? He double-checked the soup, then the fish fillets resting in the fridge, and did what he almost always did when he was bored. He grabbed his camera and headed for the woods.

He was never bored in the woods. Everything was constantly changing. Wild flowers emerging, showing off, before fading as other types came in. A pileated woodpecker shredding a pine tree for grubs, the crows cawing to announce his arrival, the different sounds of the breeze amongst the mostly pine and oak trees. He knew these woods like the back of his hand, as his dad always said. He composed and snapped several pictures of Pink Lady Slippers to later have printed and add to his collection of favorites.

Relaxed and hungry, he came home, warmed the soup up, fried up several of the fillets and ate. Someday, I'll learn how to make fish soup, like I've heard about. His mother's cookbooks were still on the first shelf in one of the cupboards. He never touched them.

It was eight o'clock and a long way from darkness in Western Michigan. He noticed the receipt for the auto parts and cash on top of it. Pocketing the money, he turned the paper over. It read Ellie Bryant and her phone number. A sunflower was drawn next to her name. Without thinking, he picked up the phone and dialed the number. He went mute when, after the third ring, someone picked up on the other end of the line.

"Bryant House Cleaning, this is Ellie…Hello. Hello. Is anyone there?"

"It's me. Umm, you left your sleeping bag behind the couch." He waited. "I—I just thought you should know." He wanted to hang up. How stupid was this, calling her without even thinking about what he was going to say?

Ellie laughed. "Does Umm have a name? I might have more than one sleeping bag."

"Your pink socks, too. They were tucked in the end of the couch."

"How do I know you have the correct number? I don't usually talk with strange men who call me and tell me I've left my pink socks and sleeping bag."

"Your number, it was the one you wrote on the back of the receipt for the car parts. You know, for the Falcon. Oh, I'm sorry. I'm Duane." He couldn't help laughing along with her.

"Ohh, you're the guy where I forgot my sleeping bag. I remember you."

They started talking and didn't stop for forty-five minutes. She wanted to know about his day, his walk in the woods, the things he saw, the fish he caught, how he fixed them, did he use cornmeal instead of flour, what did he put in his soup? She kept coming back to the woods, the flowers, the plants, the birds.

"Your woods are so much different to ours," she said. "Yours are in the national forest. It's like another world over by you."

"You live near the forest, too. How are they different?"

"It's just ours are so much closer to civilization. There's more people been through ours. Yours, it seems like you could just start wandering and go all the way to the Mackinac Bridge and not see anyone. By us, you keep running into roads." She paused. "I realize that sounds silly. We're part of the same national forest."

"Well, you're right in one respect. The western part of the county has more rivers running through it, so there's been less development in terms of roads and private settlements."

Both went quiet for several moments. Finally, she asked, her voice pensive, "What are your plans for tomorrow? Anything special?"

"No. I'll probably review some paperwork, do a little laundry and spend several hours in the woods. I think there's some Yellow Lady Slippers hanging on, and I want to find them before they die."

He heard her sigh before she said, "I'd love to see them. I'm jealous. Well, I gotta go help Granny make some potato salad. Thanks for calling." She hung up.

What was that all about? Why was his heart fluttering? She was so easy to talk to. He went downstairs and picked up a carving he was working on. A flower.

Monday morning, he fixed eggs and sausage, ran a small load of laundry, grabbed his camera, and strode into the woods. He found the Yellow Lady Slippers, they were several days past peek, but still gorgeous. He kept an overflowing album of photos he shot in the woods, mostly flowers and plants. They were good references for his carving.

He wandered around till his stomach told him it was time to go home. Sitting down to eat a sandwich, he was startled when a car drove in. He stepped onto the side porch. It was a black Rambler station wagon. A tiny African American woman with white hair jumped out of the passenger side as Ellie climbed out of the driver's seat.

"This is Granny. She knows you." Both came up the porch steps.

"I know you, Duane Gleason. Your mama was Bernice. She used to bring you to the concerts in Fair Haven till you got too big and embarrassed about bein' with Black folk and your mother." She stuck her hand out and grabbed his and shook it twice. "You even met Ellie back then. 'Course, she didn't look like she does now. She musta been in first grade and you in high school."

Duane stepped back. "I do remember her." Visions of a young girl whipping around, red curls bouncing, those same eyes and freckles rushed through his mind. Granny was either bartending, waitressing drinks, or both, while Ellie trotted around, greeting everyone, carrying the soft drinks, wiping tables and returning the glasses. He glanced at her and smiled. She looked down.

"Yup," Granny chortled. "I'm guessin' you remember me too, but those last few times, you didn't want to admit it. You always looked embarrassed to see me and your mama sitting together at the ball games or huggin' when we ran into each other in town." She poked his arm. "I was at your mom's funeral, too. Lots of folk were. Ellie, here, came with. There was so many people crowded into that tiny funeral home, we had to sit in the annex."

Ellie looked flabbergasted. "That was his mother? I remember going to a funeral with all white people, but didn't know it was Duane's mom."

Granny poked his arm again. "Bet you wonder why we're here, don'tcha?"

He nodded and grinned like she was going to tell him anyway.

"First, when Ellie started describing this place, I was ninety percent sure it was Bernice's place, it being so isolated and all, and that I knowed you. Second, I've never seen Yellow Lady Slippers, just the pink ones. Thirdly, Ellie told me you got extra fish to eat up. I brought some of my killer potato salad, baked beans and leftover ribs I grilled yesterday. Figured all that would go good with some fried fish, especially if you use cornmeal."

Ellie shook her head, blushing. "This was all Granny's idea."

"You didn't protest much, didja? Go get the food and put it in his fridge." She poked him again. "I wore hiking boots, even brought bug dope and a hat. Let's get movin'."

He led them into the forest, getting more animated as he explained the flowers, plants, trees, insects, birds and faint animal trails. After

Granny and Ellie dropped to their knees to better view and exclaim over the Yellow Lady Slippers, he led them down by the dock.

Granny pointed toward the water. "With all this brush and weeds, I can see now why Bernice always said you couldn't swim in the bay area of this lake."

Back in the house, Granny supervised him frying the fish like he was counting gold. Ellie set the table.

"Does everyone call you Granny?" Duane asked as he adjusted the burner under the fry pan. "That's the only name I remember Mom calling you, too."

"My real name is Beula. My husband started calling me Grand Lady when we married. Little kids in the neighborhood started to call me Grandy. Don't ask me why, but Grandy became Granny shortly after I birthed this one's mama." She pointed at Ellie. She was quiet, staring out the window. "This one's mama died in a fire when she was fifteen months. I was already her granny. Still am." Granny blew her nose, wiped her eyes, turned and grabbed the turner from Duane. She lifted the edge of one of the fish simmering in the cast iron fry pan. "You done good, boy."

Duane plated the fish and motioned for Ellie and Granny to sit down. He sat down and looked around. Wow, he thought, this is different. People at my table. We feel like a family. He lifted a forkful of potato salad to his mouth, chewed and swallowed. "Hey, now that's got some kick to it."

"There's a touch of cayenne pepper in it," Granny said. "Old people like spicy food." She bit into the fish. "Boy, you sure know how to fix this good. Ol' Bernice taught you the right way." She watched him as he turned his face away, pulled his handkerchief out and blew his nose.

"She did teach me right. I wished I remembered more of what she told me when it came to cooking. She never measured much or followed a recipe." He took a bite of the cold ribs. They were delicious, too. He glanced at Ellie.

She smiled back. "You were pretty lucky, getting to grow up in the woods like this. Still, how did you learn so much about everything?"

Duane explained how his father took him into the woods, how that exposure developed his love of nature at a young age. "I learned a lot in college, as well. It was a good program. We had wonderful professors who got us out in the woods, showed us things first-hand, rather than just from books." He couldn't help smiling at her. "I don't know, guess this type of work and living in the woods always seemed to be who I was meant to be."

"Jist what do you do out in the woods?" Granny helped herself to several more pieces of fish.

Duane took a quick bite of the baked beans before answering. "I'm a consultant. An individual or organization who owns woods or a forest contracts with me for several reasons. Frequently, it's to go through their property and assess the trees for lumber. We call it a selective harvesting or cutting." He stuffed another fork of beans, chewed and swallowed. "I mark the trees that have lumber potential, put out bid requests to logging companies, hire the best one, coordinate and supervise the cutting to make sure the loggers only take what was marked and in the most efficient manner, so as not to destroy to much of the undergrowth and potential for future growth."

Ellie giggled. "That's almost word for word from your little pamphlet you send out. Isn't it?"

He laughed. "Yes, I guess it is." He grinned at her. "Just how do you know what my flyers say?"

Her face turned pink. She threw her head back and laughed. "I picked up the stack of them on your desk to dust. Besides, I'm plain nosy."

Granny snorted and shook her head. "Girl, sometimes I don't know about you." She looked at Duane. "So, what else does a woods consultant do?"

Ellie jumped up, went to Duane's desk and picked up one of the flyers. "I know what he does." She read from it, "As a forestry consultant, I use my education and knowledge of science, ecology, chemicals, contractors, lumber markets and forest management to help landowners achieve their goals and objectives for their property. That may mean selective lumber sales, improving the health of the trees and growth, identifying and removing invasive plants and shrubs that are robbing the soil of nutrients for healthy environments or devising a plan to expand forest operations." She placed the flyer neatly on the stack and sat back down at the table. "Granny, you got all that?"

Granny shook her fork at Ellie. "Well, if I don't, I can always ask you to explain it again." She gave Duane an admiring look. "You done your mama good. She's right proud of you."

After eating, they relaxed on the front porch chairs, sipping iced tea Granny made sometime during her supervision of the frying of the fish. Ellie talked about some of the cabins she cleaned. How they were more like expensive homes than simple cabins. Granny spoke about all the changes in the last ten years with Fair Haven. How she was glad she always paid into social security so she had some, plus some of her husband's social security and a small pension from the post office. He also left her enough in savings to keep the taxes up on the house and its repairs. "Not enough for anything else," she said. "But that's okay. I'm doin' just fine."

A beat-up pickup, muffler dragging, roared up the driveway. Duane jumped to his feet. It was Ralph. He felt the color leave his face. He glanced at Granny and Ellie. Should he ask them to hurry inside, hide in the bedroom? He didn't want Ralph to see them. Maybe he could head Ralph off at his truck.

"What's wrong?" Granny asked.

"Umm, nothing. Just wait right here. Please." He hoped he didn't sound rude.

Both gave him a perplexed look as he rushed around the corner from the front porch to the side one.

He waved for Ralph to wait by his truck. They met at the end of the sidewalk.

Ralph looked bleary-eyed and smelled of beer. "I just needed to say goodbye one more time. I'm hungry. You got somethin' to eat?" His words slurred as he stumbled closer to Duane. Ralph froze when he saw Granny and Ellie standing where the front porch joined the side one. "What the hell are those people doing here?" He pushed past Duane and started up the walk.

Duane whispered, "Ralph, wait. Just leave." He wanted to run and hide.

"Them kind don't belong here. Tell 'em to go back where they came from and stay there." He turned on Duane. "Why the hell are ni—"

"Don't say it." Ellie's voice was a growl. She stepped down from the porch as she flicked out her switch-blade. "Get your ass in your truck and never come back here."

Ralph puffed up. "This ain't your place."

"It ain't your place either. Now go." She stepped toward him and sliced the air with her knife.

Ralph wilted, backed up, spun around, and stumbled past Duane. "I just wanted to say goodbye." Almost to the truck, he turned back. He puffed up, then spat on the ground toward Duane. "You're a real pussy, gotta have bodyguards. Black-assed, female guards. Your dad would be ashamed of you."

"Never come back here, Ralph." Duane's voice was soft. Weak. Now what did he do? Why was he so weak? Why did it feel like that horrible time in the barn with his father? That time, he had no control. He shook his head to clear those images, sat down on the edge of the porch and put his face in his hands. What did he say now? He had such a good time. Lunch felt like a family. Something he hadn't experienced in over ten years. Granny? She was like a mother and she knew his mom so well. Ellie? Well, he was falling for her.

Granny squatted beside him. She tapped him. Almost a pat. "Boy, you don't need friends like that. Ellie's gettin' the dishes and we're headin' back home. I've enjoyed myself and then some. Yellow Lady Slippers, watchin' you fry fish the right way, learnin' all them plants and trees." She stood, patted his head. "Why, other than Ralph, this has been a wonderful day. Don't let him ruin it for you. C'mon, Ellie, we gotta get some rest, we both got cleanin' jobs tomorrow."

He watched them march to the Rambler and drive off. Ellie never looked at him. What did she think of him? What did he think of her? The way she pulled that blade and snarled at Ralph was like nothing he encountered before, and he'd been around a few fights. Loggers weren't the most sophisticated guys to work with. He felt sick. His father's words kept echoing, 'Don't ever be friends with colored. Don't ever be friends with colored. Don't ever...'

He went inside and did up the dishes, this time leaving them in the rack. There was no right way to put things, dishes, or his life with a Black woman, even if she was light-skinned.

He spent most of the night trying to quiet his brain, only to be awakened by the blaring of his alarm at six-thirty. He stumbled to the bathroom, took a shower, wrapped a towel around himself, and walked back through the living room to dress in his bedroom.

"What the heck."

Ellie sat on the couch, holding the pink socks in her hands. "I'm sorry to bother you. I need to talk a few minutes. Besides, I thought I'd pick up my socks. I forgot them." She smiled, completely at ease. "Go get dressed. I'll make some coffee and set out some cold cereal and those sweet rolls."

He stared at her, felt like his feet were nailed to the floor.

She flapped her hands toward the bedroom door, like she was shooing a fly away.

As he sat down to the table, she slid an orange juice across and watched him pour milk over his raisin bran. "Yesterday kind of messed me up. I didn't know if I jumped in too soon with Ralph. Maybe I should have let you handle him. I didn't really give you a chance."

Duane set the carton down. "I—I froze. I feel embarrassed. I should have done more to stop him."

She put her hand up. "Don't beat yourself up too much. It's just that being Black, I've put up with White people's attitudes all my life. I've learned that I'm responsible for my own well-being. No one else is." She bit into a sweet roll and watched him as she chewed. "I will never wait for someone else to step in to protect me or to get me something I want. Most White people in this area are okay, some aren't. Ralph is known in the Black community, that's all I'll say about him."

Duane sipped his coffee. "I'm not sure what to say, other than he will never work for me again or come here." He attacked his cereal.

Both ate silently.

After several minutes, she reached across the table and touched his wrist. "I love it out here. I've got at least three days of cleaning jobs around the lakes, maybe four. Would you care if I slept here again? I'll be gone before you get home. It's Friday this week, right?"

He loved her eyes. At that point, he wanted to tell her she never had to leave. Did that make sense? He grinned at her. "*Mi casa, su casa.* That means—"

"I know what that means." She swatted at him. "I took Spanish. Several of my friends are Mexican."

He laughed hard.

"Why are you laughing at me?"

"I was just thinking how glad I was you were swinging at me and not poking me. I think I have bruises from Granny poking me all day yesterday."

She laughed, too. "That means she likes you. If she ever grabs your ear and pulls you someplace, you know you're in trouble." Ellie jumped up and put the milk and juice away. Pulling the dishes out of the rack, she said, "Dang it. If I'm going to spend another week here, the dishes have to go in the right places and not stay in the drainer."

They both left the house together. Ellie stopped him, lightly touched his arm. "Thank you. You're a good man." She looked around. "It feels so isolated out here. Do you think Ralph will come back?"

"No, he was supposed to leave for the army today. As you saw, in the bathroom, over the door, is my deer rifle. It's loaded. There's more ammo in the bottom kitchen drawer. Keep the back door locked at night or when you're here alone. There's a key inside the shed, over the small door." He watched her look around at the woods to the north and west of his house, the barn and hay field to the east and scrub woods to the south. "Are you afraid of the remoteness out here?"

"No, I love it. How close are the neighbors?"

"Not close. Five miles south is an older couple that rarely get out. As you probably noticed, driving out from town, the last home is at least ten miles from here."

"Does anyone ever drop by?"

"Rarely, the mailman is about it. The only traffic by the house is in the summer when canoeists and fisherman go by. They're mostly tourists. Locals can fish easier places than the river." He looked at her. Loved those eyes looking directly back at him. "You sure that doesn't bother you?"

She looked away. "No. Not at all. I can't tell why I love it out here. I just do. It feels so comfortable for me." She turned back. Her eyes glistened.

They looked at each other until he thought they might embrace. Finally, she poked his arm. "See ya."

He poked hers back.

That must mean we like each other, he thought as he climbed in the truck. If so, he'd take all the bruises he could get.

Chapter Seventeen

That evening, Duane couldn't wait to get out of the woods. At eight-thirty, he drove to the nearest gas station and parked next to the pay phone.

Ellie answered on the first ring. "Oh, good, it's you."

"Who else would it be? Oh, I suppose it could be Granny."

"Yes, it could. I still have some fears about Ralph. I'm sure he knows your number. Anyway, I'm glad it's you. I have a question for you. Are you allergic to dogs?" She giggled.

"No. Why? Did one wander in?"

"No, even better. When I got to work this morning, the manager asked me if I liked dogs. I said yes. Well, to make a long story short, a family left their dog and didn't realize it until they were halfway back to Detroit." She sighed. "I guess both parents drove up separately and, when they left, each thought the other had the dog with them. Their kids figured it out when they stopped at a rest area."

"So, you're now a dog caretaker and a house cleaner?" Duane laughed.

"That's what the manager asked. His wife hates dogs. He said the people will pay three dollars a day if someone will take good care of it till they come back up. He said I can stay at their house, it's a beautiful place. One of those A-frames, only a big one."

"So, you're staying over there till they come up Friday? Why are you at my house?"

"Umm, I'm not that comfortable there. It's like living in a glass house, so I brought the dog back here. Besides, it's not till just Friday, they won't be back up for almost two weeks. He's a beautiful dog. A black poodle, the big kind, called a Standard. He's very well behaved. I'll take him to Granny's over the weekend."

Duane added more coins. "What's the dog's name?"

"Murphy. He has a fancy pedigreed name, too. Listen, it's expensive shoving coins in the phone. Give me your number and I'll call you right back. That way, it only costs you standard long-distance rates on your home line."

Duane gave her the number. They continued talking till the mechanical-sounding operator cut in for more coins. He waited until she called back. He told her about marking the trees, using the grid in a selective logging operation. She wanted to know about the flowers he noticed. He heard the dog bark.

"I've got to take Murphy out. Can you call me tomorrow night from wherever you're at? Call collect. I'll write down the number the operator gives and call you back. Unless you like carrying a ton of coins and don't want to be racking up long distance charges on your home line."

He tapped the phone three times.

"What was that?"

"I was poking you. Good night."

He heard three taps back. "Pokes. Good night." Her voice was soft.

Wednesday night, they talked for an hour and twenty minutes. She told him she had work on Friday, was staying over Thursday night, then taking Murphy to Granny's for the weekend.

Thursday, he didn't call her. He was able to finish his work by six, hitch up the trailer and leave. It would be fun to surprise her. The kitchen and dining room lights were off when he drove up Access Road at nine o'clock. He shut his truck lights off just before the driveway and crept slowly through the early summer dusk to the barn. He forgot about the dog. By the time he sneaked up to the back door, the dog was barking.

"I got a gun and know how to use it." Ellie's voice was strong. He was sure her eyes were throwing swords at him.

"Don't shoot. Don't shoot. Ellie, it's me, Duane. I'm sorry, I was trying to surprise you."

A flashlight glared in his eyes. She unlocked the screen door and flew into his arms. "Don't ever do that again. Especially when I'm still

98

afraid Ralph is around."

He held her tightly as Murphy sniffed him. "That was pretty stupid of me. I'm sorry. For some reason, I wanted to get back home and decided to drive in this evening."

She pulled back, wiped her eyes and poked him. "Just what might that reason be? To meet Murphy?" She took his hand and led him to the couch, sitting close to him.

He poked her.

She poked him back

"How long does this poking stage last in our relationship?" he asked. "I'm starting to get bruises on top of bruises. If poking means we like each other, can we try kissing? There might be less bruising."

She swung onto to his lap, straddling him. "You're a good guy. How about trying now?" After several tentative pecks, they were soon lip-locked and moaning in desire. Murphy nudged them, whined, and finally barked.

Duane groaned. "Is he trained to do this?"

Arms around each other's waists, they walked the dog down to the road and back near the alfalfa field. "Wow, look at the stars." Ellie squeezed Duane's waist.

"I love being in the woods, but at night, I also love to come out here to watch the sky." He pointed out the constellations, the bear driver, Libra, Ursa Minor, the Little Dipper and Polaris, the North Star. He led her over to a log against the garden fence. They sat and continued to gaze at the bright night sky as Murphy sniffed around on his long leash. Duane kissed her on the cheek. "I'd love to take you into my bed. Are you ready for that? Or do you want to wait?"

"Can I have some time to think about that?" Before he could reply, she jumped up and pulled him into a hot embrace. "I thought about it long enough. Let's go. I've wanted to get you naked since you asked me if I was walking or taking the Scout." She tugged him toward the house. "That, plus the first time I saw your eyes. I'm on the pill, but you might want to wear a condom to slow you down. I don't like to be left hanging."

The alarm went off at six-thirty Friday morning. Duane rolled over to find Ellie gazing into his eyes. "I love your eyes. I set the alarm last night. Had to. I have to start one of the summer homes at seven, the owners are coming in around two. Can you keep Murphy?"

"Of course, but when did you find the time to set the alarm clock? We were pretty busy till we wore ourselves out and fell asleep."

"Speak for yourself, old man. I was good to keep going. I set the alarm on one of my pee breaks. I read a woman should pee each time after she screws to avoid infections." She kissed him and trotted off to the bathroom. "We need a microwave," she called back. "Then we can nuke the leftover coffee."

Duane took that as a hint and went into the kitchen. He poured yesterday's coffee into a pan and turned the burner on. He took Murphy out and was coming up the drive when Ellie flew out of the house, screwing the lid on a metal thermos. She kissed him, told him she'd be back by two, jumped in her car and tore off down the road in a plume of dust.

He never thought about having a microwave before. They seemed to be the new fad for kitchens. After some breakfast, he put Murphy in the Scout and drove into the Sears appliance store. He came home with a microwave—the thing seemed huge for such a limited dish space—and the receipts for a new kitchen range, refrigerator and deep freezer to be delivered Saturday morning at ten. The old appliances were purchased when his folks married. It was time to upgrade.

It was also time he spent some of his money on something besides film and his cost of living. What good was it doing building up a big balance in his savings account? He kept a five-thousand-dollar balance in his checking account and at least fifteen grand in his passbook savings. Twice a year, he met with the investment banker at his bank to invest everything above that into long-term growth stocks and bonds. At their last meeting, his banker told him he would be able to retire comfortably in ten years. That seemed unimaginable.

Ellie rolled in at one-thirty. They met on the sidewalk. "It wasn't a good morning," she said. "I forgot my stocking cap. The neighbors stay all summer and came over and asked what I was doing." Her eyes were angry. "I told them, nicely. They said they didn't believe me. I looked like a Black person, they never saw one before around the lake, and they were calling the police." She slid into his arms and let him hold her tight. "I told them, fine. Thank God the house I was cleaning had a touch-tone phone. I went in and paged the property manager. He was in the area and came over and explained who I was. Even told them I'd cleaned their place before Memorial Day, when they moved up."

"Did they calm down?" Somehow, Duane wasn't surprised. He knew exactly how it felt when one realized a Black person was in a place they rarely were. How threatening it felt to White people's security.

"Yes. I put on my best manners, didn't get sassy, almost did my step-and-fetch-it routine. Yes, ma'am. No, sir. Flashed my bright white teeth at them." She smacked her fist into her hand. "The worst was when the manager yelled at me for not wearing my cap. I found my cap on the floor of my car. I pulled it so low I could barely see out of it." She took several steps, turned and stared up at Memory Tree.

Duane watched her walk into the front yard. He followed, but at a distance. The impact of her being criticized, having to defend herself because she was Black, struck him. He watched Ellie pause almost at the same place where his family used to have a bench. He stepped closer, but not too close, about ten feet away. "That tree is called Memory Tree. We used to have a bench about where you're standing. I used to tell her my problems and dreams." He walked back to the sidewalk, turned to watch her kneel and pull Murphy into a long hug.

A few minutes later, she strode back to him, kissed him, and said, "Thank you. I'm hungry."

When they stepped inside the house, she squealed and almost knocked him over. "Why did you do this? A microwave? I was joking."

"Well, I heard they're good for people in a hurry and you're always in one. So, I didn't want to slow you down."

Her face registered surprise. She stared at the floor, as if she was thinking of something. "I was planning on going home to Granny's for the weekend. Could I stay here several nights next week while you're gone? Is that still okay?"

"Yes, but it's even better when you stay over when I'm here." He tried to laugh, make it a joke, but turned away to wipe his eyes.

She turned his face toward hers and wiped his cheeks. "We have time to be together right now. Later, I'll go home. Is it alright if I come back in the morning to spend the day?"

"Can you be here around eleven?" Who knew what the White delivery men might think if they encountered Ellie in his home? Best not find out...

Saturday morning, Duane watched from the porch as dust boiled up from a delivery truck coming down the road. It was followed by a smaller cloud of dust. Both vehicles pulled into his driveway. The truck parked at the end of the sidewalk. Ellie parked her Rambler across the driveway under the oak tree. As the two delivery men hopped out and opened the rear door of the truck, Ellie climbed out of her car. Duane was thankful she leaned back in and pulled on her stocking cap. Why did her car contain clothes on hangers, and several boxes? His body tingled at the thought.

Ellie marched up to him. "What's going on? I followed this truck the whole way since town."

He pointed to the boxes containing the new appliances. "I figured if it was time for a microwave, I might as well get all new appliances. My parents put the ones I have in over thirty years ago, right before I was born."

"You're thirty?"

"Almost. Does it matter?"

"Nope." She poked him. Lightly.

While the men hauled the boxed range on to the porch, Duane stepped towards Ellie's car and pointed at the hanging clothes and boxes. "What's all this?" Why was his heart beating so hard?

"I figured if you liked me staying over when you're here, well, I needed more clothes. Besides, you have more closet space than I do." She looked across the road, blushing, avoiding his eyes.

He led her to the far side of the delivery truck, out of sight of the men, and kissed her. "What did Granny say?"

"She said I found a good man. Don't wait around." She giggled. "Actually, she said if I found a man who can fry fish that good, keep him on the hook." She kissed his cheek. "She also said this place was perfect for me. She knows how I don't like living around a lot of people."

"Fair Haven isn't that big. How many? Maybe two hundred still live there year around."

"That's about one hundred and ninety-eight too many for me."

Chapter Eighteen

Six weeks later, in July, Duane was on a creeper under Ellie's car, changing the oil and lubing the joints.

She sat on a stump, handing him tools as he needed them. "You know I can do this myself, don't you?"

"Yes, but I wanted to check it over. Do you want to finish? I'll gladly get a beer and sit in the shade to watch you. Of course, you'd still have to take the clothes off the line."

She laughed, then leaned down till he could see her face. "Have you ever wanted children?"

Duane jerked, bumping his head. "Ouch. What brought that up? I thought you were on the pill." He tightened the drain plug and slid out. He sat up, wiping his hands, staring at her.

She leaned in and kissed him on the nose. "We'd make great kids. Your sperm's not going to get any stronger, so why wait?"

"Are you saying I'm getting old? What brought this on?"

"I've always wanted kids. Two, close together. I thought about going to college to study the environment, nature, but could never focus and didn't want to be far away from Granny." She thought a moment. "Besides, you're already teaching me about forests and eco-systems. I found your textbooks from college and I've been studying them, too. Here, I can live in the forest, Granny is close, you're the right man, we don't need to be married, our kids will be beautiful, I can teach them a lot, practical stuff and books stuff, so can you." She shrugged and stood. "Another thing, I don't mind you being gone. I don't need a man twenty-four hours a day. I love being by myself in the woods, just like you. So will our kids. You look shocked. Think about it." She moved to the clotheslines and began taking down the laundry.

Duane did think about it as he poured in the oil, checked the battery levels and the radiator. He thought about it as he aired the tires, washed the inside of the windows. It made no sense cleaning the outside when living on a dirt road, unless they were muddy. He thought about kids as he washed her car anyway.

He never expected to be thinking about children. Vaguely, he thought he might meet a woman someday, fall in love, get married. He never thought about what type of person she'd be, other than someone who could adjust to his being away, which made the prospect of marriage even more doubtful.

He definitely never considered that the color of her skin would be anything other than White. Nor the woman's age, younger or older than him. He barely noticed the ten years between him and Ellie. Oh, he could recognize some emotions, or uncertainty at being nineteen, almost twenty, but overall, Ellie was pretty damn mature. Definitely independent, not a clinging vine looking for someone to carry her. He liked that.

He wondered why Ellie mentioned they didn't need to be married to have kids and be a family. Was she worried about marriage to a White man? Was it that younger people in the seventies seemed to be living together before or in place of marriage? Did she think marriage would hinder her independence? Be too stereotypical? The wife at home serving the husband. Did she feel free sex was fine with kids? Obviously, or she wouldn't have brought it up.

Duane realized he felt surprised. Actually, honored, that Ellie wanted to have children and raise them with him. She wasn't waiting around for him to figure things out and propose. Maybe she recognized something in him that might take him a long time to figure out. Like kids. Like marriage or a relationship. Maybe that's why she took the lead. He did love her and wanted to spend the rest of his life with her.

He stretched, twisted a kink out of his back. Would he be experiencing these same thoughts if Ellie was White? Would he even have doubts about marrying a White girl? He shuddered at the pain of that thought. Dammit. I'm not going there. It's the seventies. I'm independent, too. We don't need to be married to be in love and have a family.

He paused, staring at the water running over the car, the suds washing off the cement apron into the sand. How would he father? Would he be like his dad? The good things his father did with him, teaching him the forest, how to hunt, fish, being responsible, not taking risks with your money, living on less than you made, those parts were good parenting. However, there were the other parts. Why did it feel like his father still sat on his shoulder, shouting racial epithets in his ear? Something dawned on him. He usually only heard his dad's harsh voice when he was in public, when he saw minorities, when he was with Ralph. I also am part of my mother and absorbed her parenting style, too. If I can take the good from both...

He shut off the water, coiled the hose and hung it in the shed, put his tools away. He used degreaser to scrub his hands, wiped them off on a rag, headed toward the house, then turned back and began waxing the car.

His mind wandered off to taking kids on hikes in the woods, fishing, teaching them science and nature, watching the stars from the alfalfa field, taking canoe trips down the river. He thought about Ellie as a mother, about Granny.

He remembered Ellie, young, the two or three times he saw her at Fair Haven, attending music sessions with his mother. Wednesday nights were often jam sessions, practice for the musicians. There was no cover charge, just buy something to eat or drink. Ellie whipping around, laughing, being teased and teasing back, her innocence at five or six, those green eyes sparkling. The last time he went, age sixteen, him being so uncomfortable, so torn, knowing his father would blow a gasket if he found out where he and his mother were. Yet the music was so good, the atmosphere so warm and supportive. Were Black people staring at them? Dared he speak to anyone other than Granny?

One time, they were the only Whites in the place. Other times, several more were present for the jam sessions. On concert nights, he figured twenty percent of the audience might be White. Why did it matter? Granny never cared and Ellie didn't seem to know the difference. Not at that age. She did now. Is that why she liked the woods so much? She could just be herself? Not have to wear her stocking cap when going to areas where Black people rarely went. He knew she usually didn't wear it in Split Creek, even though he sensed some people would stare at her.

What would their kids look like? Probably well-tanned, tall and slender with dark hair. What did it matter? What about going out in public with them? With them and Ellie? He shuddered as his fears edged in again. Dammit. Just goddamn it. He sprayed some water into his hand and swiped his face to clear his head. It didn't clear, so he stuffed those thoughts. Deep. I'm not thinking along those lines. Things will work out.

He always liked seeing babies, no matter their color. Wanted to hold them, feed them, play with them when their backs grew stronger, or they started to crawl, run around. Changing diapers didn't seem like a big deal, just a smelly one. He was an only child. He realized he missed out on growing up with other children, missed the good, the bad, or instead of good or bad, was it just the reality of growing up with brothers and sisters? Of course, there was Ralph. He turned and spat at the name. Why did he have such ambivalent feelings toward him? He was glad Ralph was in the Army for at least six years, maybe more. Didn't want to go there.

He put the wax and cloths away and jogged toward the house.

Babies, kids. His life had so many changes in the last two months and was so full, why not keep the ball rolling?

Babies, kids. He couldn't wait to hold one.

Chapter Nineteen

Duane came home from a job in mid-August. Ellie fed him some gumbo, something he never had before he met her and Granny. Her eyes sparkled. With what mischief now? "Let's go into town and get an ice cream cone, then come home and roll in the hay. I think I'm ripe."

He raised his eyebrows like she was nuts. "Ripe? What are you talking about?"

She watched him try to process the information. He still didn't get it. "Remember? I went off the pill. I had a period. I counted the days. If I'm right, I should be ovulating over the next few days." She laughed at his expression. "You do know what ovulating means, right?"

"That fast? You could get pregnant so soon? Hey, what's the ice cream got to do with things?"

"Granny says it helps, especially the first time." Her laughter pealed out. "C'mon, you can keep control till we get back." On the drive in, she told him the doctor at the clinic told her she might need to go through several cycles before she got pregnant.

Duane listened to Ellie chat on the way into town. The closer he got to town, the harder it was to focus on her words. The only place to get an ice cream cone was at the Dairy Queen. He didn't want to pull in there. It was warm, late afternoon, right after many people got off work. The place would be busy.

He turned his blinker on and slowed to pull into the grocery. "I'll run in and get us some ice cream and cones we can take back home."

Ellie stared at him. "No way. It has to be DQ. Something special to celebrate. Common old frozen grocery store ice cream ain't going to do it. Keep going." Her eyebrows raised in surprise.

Duane switched off the blinker and veered back into his lane. Without saying a word, he drove to the DQ, and just like he worried, there was a good-sized crowd of people. Some sat at the picnic tables, others waited in line, some sat on the parking curbs and everyone seemed to be eating and laughing. They were all White. He recognized many of them from when he'd gone to school. Especially John Anderson, who stood at the end of the line with his wife Sue, and their three kids.

He froze, but managed to park in the back corner. He quickly opened his door. "Why don't just I go? What flavor do you want? Let's eat them in the car."

Ellie looked with concern at him. "Why didn't you just park over there? On the side. It was closer." She pulled him back into the Scout and stared into his face.

His face flushed as he realized she saw his fear.

She shook her head sadly. "I'll go. I don't have my cap anyway. Never wear it in town. Now, white or chocolate?"

"Chocolate," he muttered, feeling his face grow even warmer, not looking at her. This was his problem, not hers. The guilt went deeper.

"I want a twist. Imagine that." She waved his money away, slammed the door and marched to the end of the line.

From the side mirror, he watched her stand behind John. He watched John glance back, notice Ellie, and move in front of his wife and kids so that Sue now stood in front of Ellie.

Sue turned and began chatting with Ellie. It looked like she introduced her kids as they each shook Ellie's hand. Several other women joined the long line with their kids. He watched as Ellie all at once broke from the line and ran across the street into Woolworths. She returned, carrying a small sack. She got back in line and resumed chatting with Sue and her kids. John seemed to be engaged in conversation with another classmate Duane recognized. John never looked back at his wife, kids or Ellie.

John Anderson was one of the kids Duane went through high school with. They were never close friends, John being a town kid and Duane a country boy, but in the small high school they did a lot of things together. Especially sports.

John was also the one who confronted Duane in his sophomore

year because Duane was helping a dark-skinned girl with math. Esther wasn't from Fair Haven. She was the adopted daughter of the Methodist minister in town. Rumor had it the pastor and his wife adopted her and several other children of various hues when they were on some far-off mission field. They moved to Split Creek just before school started that year.

Esther was smart and outgoing. After the second day of geometry class, she asked Duane a question. He explained the answer. During study hall, she sat down at his table and asked him several more questions about geometry He explained them and walked with her to their history class.

He found her easy to talk with. As easy to be with as Shrimp had been from camp. It was obvious she lived in various places and met many different people. He wondered if they could develop a friendship. He wasn't thinking of a relationship. Just that here was someone who lived with and met other people from a larger world than his. People different than around Split Creek.

For two periods that day, he wondered about Shrimp. About Granny. About his fears of what his father would say if he knew Duane was friendly with another colored person. Somehow, for that short time, he glimpsed an opportunity of a different world. A world without his father's belt, a world where he wasn't afraid to be seen with Granny in public, or embarrassed when his mother and Granny hugged in public or sat together at ball games.

After classes ended, he found himself walking and talking with Esther as they exited the school building. She turned toward the sidewalk to walk home, he turned toward the buses.

John Anderson fell in step with him, even though John didn't ride the bus. "Duane, you're looking awfully friendly with that chocolate bunny."

Duane replied, "I was…I was just explaining geometry to her."

John pulled Duane around in front of him. "Right. Tell her to ask the teacher her questions. It's bad enough Fair Haven closed their school and them cotton pickers gotta come here, but we don't have to like it or them." He poked Duane in the chest. "It's embarrassing enough to see your mother sitting with the colored at ball games. Your dad's got the right attitude." John walked away.

After that, Duane avoided Esther as much as possible. Answering her questions in short syllables, telling her he didn't know and to ask the teacher. The girl and her younger siblings soon became ostracized in the school and community. The family left the church before Christmas of that year. Duane never heard where they went. He did hear that Esther was born in India.

He roused as Ellie showed up with two large cones, a chocolate and a twist. She handed them through the window to him. "Hold both for a second." She pulled a blue knit stocking cap out of the bag and put it on. "Now get out, we'll sit on the curb. This hat stays in the Scout. I bought another for your truck. Relax. We're going to eat our cones right here like White people do." She poked him, hard, her eyes flashing, not sparkling.

A Ford station wagon drove by. John Anderson glanced quickly at Duane and Ellie. He looked confused, then scowled as he looked away to concentrate on the people walking in front of him to their cars. Sue was looking ahead and didn't see Ellie, but the kids saw her and waved enthusiastically. Ellie waved back.

Duane and Ellie continued to eat their cones without talking. On the ride home, each stayed silent until they pulled into driveway and he parked. He wondered what she was thinking. He knew what he'd been thinking. Guilt. Fear. His father's voice shouting in his ear. John's look at him as he saw him sitting next to Ellie. Poor Esther being ostracized, the words whispered behind his back about his mother sitting with Granny. Had John's words reinforced Duane's father's words? Why did he hear those words rather than his mother's actions? Was it the beating with the belt? How did he overcome these thoughts and fears?

Ellie put her hand on his arm as he turned the engine off, kept it there till he looked at her. "I've been thinking…" Her voice trailed off as she stared into his eyes.

Her pause worried him. Was this the end of their relationship? He could understand, well, sort of. He did have a problem, but no idea how to address it or to change himself.

"I don't fully understand you. Hopefully, you can think your fears through." She slid over and pulled his arm around her. "I think your problem has to be your problem. I can't solve it for you. I'm strong and I'll always love you." She kissed him on the cheek. "I still want you and your babies. Hey, I think the ice cream made me hornier." She leaned across him, yanked his door open and pushed him out. "Oh yeah, Granny never said anything about ice cream. We don't have to do it next time we want to get pregnant. Let's go."

At that moment, sex and making a baby seemed more important than figuring out his fears.

Chapter Twenty

May 23, 1976

Duane pounded several stakes in the ground, tied the strings, walked the strings to the other end of the garden, pounded in the matching stakes and tied the cords off. He hoed a groove to plant vegetables in.

He never thought he'd be a gardener, always figured he did enough of it growing up to last him a lifetime. Of course, he now found himself doing a lot of things he never thought he'd do. The biggest one was expecting twins. They were due in a week, and the doctor told Ellie he was happy she carried them this long and thought they would arrive around June first or later. Maybe she hadn't got pregnant when she thought.

The dining room became a nursery-in-waiting after she directed him to disassemble the table and store it upstairs. Ellie found two used bassinets at a yard sale and painted them a soft green. She made mobiles of twigs and pine needle clusters and hung them over the tiny beds. "We won't know what sex they are till they're born," she said. "This shade of green goes better with the woods, anyway."

Duane finished the trenches, carefully fed the seeds—carrots, peas and onions—into the earth, poked the packets over the stakes and covered the seeds. He began more rows, lettuce and beans. Ellie was cleaning houses today. He was not happy about it. They had one of their few arguments that morning.

"You're as big as a barn and you're going to go scrub and clean. Does the doctor know how active you still are?"

"Don't worry about it. My body will tell me when to stop. Yes, I told the doctor I was cutting back on housecleaning, but it's a busy time and I didn't want to stop yet. Know what he said?"

Duane shook his head and rolled his eyes, which produced more sparks from hers.

"He said do what I felt like. If I was running a roto-tiller last week and it didn't shake the kids loose, they must be as stubborn as me and would come when they damn well pleased." She shook her fist at him and laughed.

That morning, she led him out to the nicely tilled garden and showed him where she thought things should be planted and why. "I read expecting husbands get antsy and need to stay busy. Sometime today, run into Woolworth's and pick up marigolds. You can plant them around the edge of the garden. I'll show you tomorrow where to do the melons, squash and potatoes." She kissed him and barreled off.

Duane finished planting the vegetables. He glanced at his watch and decided to run into town and get the marigolds and seed potatoes before he fixed lunch. In town, he picked up a local newspaper.

Back home, he planted the marigolds and decided to go ahead with the potatoes. After all, wasn't he supposed to be the antsy father keeping busy?

Around two, he made a sandwich and sat down with the paper. A headline on page two grabbed his attention. **Local Man Sentenced Five - Ten Years for Assaulting Area Woman**. A picture of Ralph was in the article. Duane knew Ralph had been discharged for dishonorable reasons from the Army, but thought he left the area after getting into trouble. The authorities must have caught up with him. He was glad Ralph was going behind bars. Ellie could relax even more, once she knew he was sentenced.

Nearly two months before, in early April, Ellie decided to keep chickens for eggs. She read up on it, talked Duane into helping her put some chicken-wire fence and roosts in a corner of the old barn, with a door to the outside and a small fenced yard.

She bought a dozen hens and one rooster. A week after their arrival, she asked Duane to kill the rooster. "I have enough trouble sleeping through the night with twins fighting in me without being woke up by that noise."

The rooster did make a good southern-stewed dish. Granny told her how to fix it.

Days later, Ellie was in the barn, collecting eggs and chatting with the chickens—she claimed it helped to be friendly to them—when she heard a vehicle. She stepped to the barn window and watched a battered pickup come slowly up the drive and park. The driver got out and walked up to the house.

It was Ralph Sims.

She stayed in the barn as he beat on the door, yelled he knew someone was around, that he'd be back, and then left. She told Duane she was scared to death, but managed to lumber up to the house, get the deer rifle, some shells and go back to the barn.

Twenty minutes later, Ralph drove back in. This time, he checked the shed where Ellie's car was. She heard him mutter, "That bitch must be living here now."

She watched him go up to the house, try the kitchen door and step inside. He hollered hello, turned and came back out. "He was empty-handed. He didn't spend any time in the house, so I know he didn't come to rob us," she later told the police.

He stood on the porch and yelled, "You little Black whore, you've got no right to live here. Watch yourself because I'm coming back to get rid of you once and for all."

Ellie told Duane that, as Ralph came down the porch steps, she stepped from the barn and fired a shot over the house, racked the lever and yelled, "That was a warning. Now leave."

He ran to his truck, yelling, "You bitch, I'll kill you someday."

Ellie went inside and called the police. Next, she called the answering service. By now, she and Roberta joked around like friends. "This is Duane's friend. Tell him Ralph stopped by."

When Duane called home that evening, Ellie told him the story and how she filed a complaint with the police. He was ready to drive home immediately, but she told him she was going to Granny's till he came back for the weekend.

Duane chewed his sandwich as he reviewed the news article. Later that same night, Ralph tried to pick up an African American woman in a bar. When she wasn't interested, he assaulted her. The bartender called the police and they arrested Ralph. The article didn't mention Ellie's name, only that another woman filed a complaint the same day about him threatening her. Duane cut the article out and left it on the table. He was sure it would help Ellie.

Her words over the phone when she was telling him that day still haunted him. "Don't worry, I spoke with the police over the phone. Told them they didn't need to come out here, but I wanted them to take me seriously. They agreed because I gave them Ralph's name and type of vehicle. Even the license plate. Besides, I didn't want to embarrass you by them coming out here."

Duane bought her a small twenty-two caliber pistol. On one of her yard sale expeditions, she picked up a cuckoo clock. The clock apparatus didn't work, but it looked beautiful, hanging on the kitchen wall. At her suggestion, he removed the inner works and adapted a side panel into a door to hide her pistol and shells.

Duane washed the plate and silverware he used, dried them and put them away, the right way.

The phone rang. It was Roberta, his answering service. "Always carry your pager, Daddy. Your friend's been trying to reach you for four hours. A boy and a girl. She's over at Redding at that satellite E.R."

"What? She wasn't due till the first. She was fine this morning—"

"Son, you got a lot to learn. Now get your ass over to Redding and meet your babies."

He ran into the bedroom for his pager. How stupid to forget it when your girlfriend is expecting babies any day. He checked the calls. At least five since nine-thirty that morning. Who knows how many times she tried the home phone?

What the hell happened? Why Redding?

She was supposed to deliver in Split Creek.

He sped off, driving twenty-five miles northwest to the satellite E.R. and hospital operated by the Ludington Hospital.

Ellie smiled at him as he entered the room. "Meet Jimmy and Beula. They just nursed for the first time."

A nurse walked in and paused as Ellie introduced Duane as the father. The nurse looked surprised, but smiled and asked, "So, Daddy, do you want to hold the babies? Yes. Alright then, sit down on the bed, scoot back, and I'll place the babies into your arms."

Duane gladly complied, snuggling the babies close to him.

"Hey, you look pretty relaxed, holding them. Have you held babies before?"

He looked at Ellie, tears in both their eyes. "No, but I've always wanted to."

The nurse left them alone. Ellie moved closer and ran her fingers over the babies' hands. "It happened very fast," she whispered, still in awe.

"I'm sorry I forgot to wear my pager. Roberta said you tried to get hold of me. I—I feel terrible. What happened?"

Ellie kissed his arm. "You're here now, that's all that matters. About a half hour after I started cleaning, I felt this sharp pain. It doubled me over. I went out on the deck and another one hit me and my water broke. Two landscape guys saw me and ran over. One of them said, 'You're having a baby.' He said something in Spanish to the other guy, then, 'We take you. He will drive. I have kids and know how this works. Redding is fastest hospital to get to.'"

Duane shifted the two sleeping babies in his arms as Ellie continued. "They put me in their work van. The man held my hand and patted my shoulder and talked in Spanish. When we got to the E.R., he told the staff, 'This lady having two babies, take good care of her.' Once I was on a cart, each shook my hand and they left. Then, one said he'd tell the manager he and his friend would make sure the house was cleaned before they left. Can you imagine that?"

The next day, when they arrived home from the hospital, Granny was at the house, waiting for them. She kept exclaiming, "Twins, great grandbabies. You named one after me and the other after Ellie's grandpa, James, same as Duane's grandpa."

The first forty-eight hours were a blur, with each adult trying to do everything. One baby would cry and three adults would jump to care for it. No one was getting any sleep, other than the babies who slept fine between feedings. With Granny's coaching, Ellie quickly caught on to nursing twins. On their third day home, Granny announced she was returning to her own home. "I'll come back to help in three weeks when Duane goes back to work. Ain't no sense in three of us trippin' all over ourselves. You two will do fine, and you need to get your own routines down pat."

"Thank you, Granny. We'll bring them over Sunday." Ellie looked at Duane who nodded.

Sunday afternoons at Granny's was a routine for the two of them, now it would be even better with the babies. He loved going to Granny's.

Lying in bed the next day, nursing the babies, Ellie turned her head toward the dresser. "The birth certificates and footprint certificates are in that envelope. Look how cute their tiny feet are."

Duane pulled the certificates out. The prints of their feet were cute. He also noticed the babies' last name was Bryant, nor was he listed as the father on the birth certificate. No one was. She listed their address as at Granny's, too. The same as on her driver's license. His eyes widened as he turned toward her, not sure what to say. He assumed they would be named Gleason, and he would be listed as father.

She adjusted the babies and said, "We can always add Gleason, but only when we're legal." She didn't seem angry or snotty, just calm. "You have an issue with being seen with me in public. I don't understand it, but until you can walk down the streets of Split Creek with me and our children, I'm keeping their last name Bryant."

She motioned for him to sit on the bed. "No one around here, other than the mailman, knows I live out here. I love the seclusion, as you know. It's just when we're around other White people, you seem to have a problem. You have no problems in Fair Haven." She placed Jimmy into his arms. "Now, burp him, please."

She started burping Beula. "I'm not making a big deal out of this. I love you. I'm independent. I could take these babies and leave. You'd never see them again, nor would you have any claim to them."

Duane startled, waking Jimmy. He quickly patted the little guy back to sleep as Ellie's words banged around in his head. How did he respond to that? Was she going to leave him? She was so calm.

Ellie waved her free hand at him. "Relax. That's not a threat or something to coerce you. I have no plans to leave. I love living out here without neighbors. The reality is, we can exist this way forever, but until you want your name listed as their father, and can proudly be seen in public with me, this is the way it's going to be. Now, please change our son."

Duane was glad for the diversion. He needed time to think through her comments. On the one hand, Ellie's words cleared the air, opened up his issue with being seen in public with Ellie where people would recognize them as a mixed-race couple. And now with children. On the other hand, it added to his guilt, his inability to deal with the matter. Still, how did one deal with such a situation? Who would understand? What advice could anyone give?

He carried Jimmy to the changing table Ellie also picked up at a yard sale, and changed him, marveling at how the tiny guy stretched, how strong he was becoming, how he seemed to know when he was naked and wriggle around. And pee. Too late. Jimmy sprayed him. Again. Another t-shirt to change. Duane thought he was a fast learner, but obviously he wasn't with baby boy pee-showers. He finished changing the baby and put him in his bassinette.

Ellie laughed when he came back in the bedroom and changed his shirt.

"No comments," he muttered.

In the dining room/nursery, he picked up the bucket of soaking diapers and carried them to the basement where he poured them into a tub for further soaking. A new washer and dryer sat next to the tub. Ellie insisted on using cloth diapers, usually drying them on the lines outside.

A week later, Duane showed Ellie the newspaper clipping about Ralph. She cried. "I don't understand it. What does he have against Black women? Is it just because we're Black?"

Duane cuddled her. "I don't get it either. I think it has more to do with me than you, but I can't put my finger on why." He crumpled up the article and threw it away. He had an idea why Ralph was so jealous, but did he want to go there?

Chapter Twenty-one

Friday, January 11, 2019, the farmhouse

Duane awoke and stared at the shoebox in front of him. What could be in it? Why would Retha have brought it? The box certainly wasn't from the house. He never stored anything in a shoebox. Maybe Ellie had and Retha found it while poking around. That didn't make sense.

Retha adjusted herself on the bed, leaned forward, and said, "We both got lots to talk about. I debated whether we should talk first and then I show you this box. I'm not trying to be mean, but figured what's in this box will get us both talking. And probably some crying, too."

"What's in it?" How much more could he learn?

She didn't answer. Tears were in her eyes. She motioned for him to open it.

He did. Inside, on top, were three woodcarvings. Duane sucked in a breath. One was of a little boy, one a little girl and one a woman. He cleared his throat. "Where did you find these? When?"

"That's part of my story." She motioned for him to take out the next things.

He burst into tears, sobbed, gasped, could barely get his breath as he removed five framed photos, each five by seven. One was of a little girl, one a boy, one a woman, one with the three of them and one of him and the two children. He looked around the room, saw the faded spaces on the walls where they once hung.

Retha cried out, "Granny never told them who I was."

He wanted to hold her, but didn't know how to make that connection across the table. Each could barely breathe. He wondered what she meant, 'Granny never told them who she was.' Who was she? She knew Granny, but so did lots of people. He never heard Retha's name, never heard Ellie mention her. *Oh Lord,* he thought. *I just thought her name again. Ellie.* He cried as he picked up each frame and carving. He couldn't stand looking at them anymore. Too much guilt and shame. He tried to put them back in the box.

Retha got up and placed the photos and the carvings on the buffet next to the bed. "This way, you can look at them when you want." She reached in the box and pulled out a pistol. A small one, twenty-two caliber. She put it back in the box and set the box on the buffet.

He recognized the gun. How did she have it? Why was it in the box? Who put it there?

She waved her hand for him not to ask about it.

It took a while before each caught their breaths, quit hiccupping and blew their noses.

"Part of my story," she said.

Duane looked at the frosted window. He would love to see Memory Tree. Wished he was sitting in front of her, talking, telling her his problems and issues. Memory Tree. He remembered touching her needles, breathing in the scents, listening to the soft swish of the breeze through her boughs. How much did the tree remember?

Retha patted his hand, leaned over and looked him close in the eyes, warm, but serious. "You ready to tell me about your first family?" Her words were soft. Her eyes were wet, or did she look scared?

"Yeah, it's time. Seeing the graveyard yesterday made me sad, but also, I'm glad they were buried and Granny is buried next to them. I always wondered what happened with them. Part of my guilt."

She looked like she wanted to say something, but shook her head. She slid the table out of the way and inched closer to him. "Why don't you start with how you met Ellie."

Duane told her about seeing Ellie when she was little, at the Fair Haven concerts, how her car broke down, about the pink footies, her cap, Ralph threatening her, having the babies. The birth certificates. It took a while. Sometimes she wiped her eyes, or blew her nose. Sometimes she wiped his tears. Finally, he said, "I need a break. Are there any oatmeal cookies left?"

She brought him two and a mug of green tea. He never drank green tea before meeting her, but sort of liked it. Maybe it's because she put a dab of honey in it.

When he finished the cookies, she asked him, "Did you ever go anywhere as a family, besides Granny's?"

"We did, but can I take a nap first? Somehow I'm feeling weaker."

"Of course, dear." She patted his arm and tucked him in. "This is hard work, all these memories." She teared up, climbed off the bed and hurried away.

~ * ~

Holy cow. Those are the pictures missing from the wall. And those are the carvings Dad made of us when we were six. The pictures were from when we were eight. Behind them, in the same frames, are prints from when we were six and four. They were taken with Dad's camera, a Minolta SR something. He said it was a good one with a sharp lens. Mom sent the negatives away for the prints. She bought the frames at Woolworths and surprised Dad when he got back from one of his trips. He just cried so hard when he saw them. The pistol is the one Mom kept hidden in the cuckoo clock. He had a deer rifle at home. Why does Retha have this stuff? How did she get it? I hope she talks, too. I'm so confused.

Go anywhere? I know this part. Yes. We all went to Chicago once. Granny went, too.

After Christmas, when we were eight, Mom told Dad she wanted to plan a trip to Chicago when their kids were on spring break. She wanted to take us to the big museums and see the Sears Tower. "I already got it figured out," she said. "We can stay in a cheap motel on the south side. We'll take coolers for food and buy groceries in stores when we need more. We won't need to eat out, unless it's McDonalds." Jimmy and me started yelling. We loved to go to McDonalds. She told us to quiet down, it was a long time off.

Dad looked kind of perplexed. That's a big word I learned that means not too sure what to think. Maybe he was scared. Anyway,

Mommy said, "The reason I want to go at Chicago's spring break is because there will be all kinds of kids and families. Our family will not look out of place." She told him about the science museums, riding the big busses, the art museum. "We can afford it. I've been saving money. Granny's going and will help pay for gas and the motel room. How about it? You coming with?" She kissed him and held his hand while he thought.

Me and Jimmy held our breaths. We wanted Dad to go, too. Finally, he said, "What are the dates?" He kissed her back as we yelled and ran around the house in our new Christmas PJ's.

It was so cool. We left super early in the morning. Jimmy and I were still sleeping. We went in Mom's minivan. First, we stopped at the motel and swam in their pool. Granny didn't think the room was very clean, so she cleaned it with stuff she brought just in case. Next, we ate at McDonalds. We took a train, it went above ground and underground, and we went up the Sears Tower at night and saw all the lights. In the elevator, I had to keep swallowing, so did Jimmy. We'd never been in an elevator before and this one went so fast. At first, we were scared to go near the windows, so was Granny. She kept saying, "Well, I'll be. Well, I'll be. Can you imagine bein' someplace you've read about, seen the pictures of, and now you're here in real life?"

Dad told us people lived in some of the other tall buildings. He even showed us the swimming pools on the roofs. Can you imagine that? A swimming pool way up in the air on a roof.

In the morning we went to the science museum. It was huge. We stayed all day. We went in a coal mine, saw tiny babies before they were babies in jars all lined up. Mom explained what conception meant, how a dad's sperm hits a mom's egg and starts a new life, though she said it wasn't really a human till three months before it was born. Dad showed us the old cars, they were cool, and the model railroad. We saw so many neat things, we stayed till it closed. We went back on the train to our motel, had pizza in our room, and swam some more. It's easy to swim in a pool, no yucky bottom or weeds or fish kissing your toes.

The next day, we went to the Field Museum with dinosaurs and big animals and rocks. It was cool, too. Then we rode buses to Lincoln

Park Zoo and saw all the animals. The next day, we packed up and drove to see the fish place. Jimmy and me could have stayed there longer, but we had to go to the star place. After that, we were so tired, we slept the whole way home. We didn't even know we dropped Granny off. We just woke up in our own beds and wondered how we got there. That happened not too long before the bad day.

You know, it's kinda weird Dad never added his name so we all can have the same last name. Other peoples' grandkids we played with in Fair Haven asked us once. I asked Mommy why our last names were different. Mom looked away a minute and blew her nose, like she had a cold or something. "Love is all that counts. You got a mother and father who love each other and love both of you. That's what's important. Not some church wedding or piece of paper. Who knows? Maybe someday, we'll change it." She looked at Granny who nodded. They both started talking about something else. Again.

I'm so glad Dad talked about us. I hope he tells more. I still need to hear why he never showed up to save us.

Dad's napping. I wonder how long. Oh, Retha just put her head back and closed her eyes. Gol-darn-it. I want to hear the rest of their stories.

Chapter Twenty-two

Retha McBride, age18, October, 1955

Naomi Bryant, seventeen, leaned her head onto Retha's shoulder. "How much longer till we change busses in Riverside?" They sat in the far back seat. Naomi led them back there when they boarded in Detroit. No one else sat near them. The Whites sat forward.

"About two more hours. You all right? You've been quiet, especially for you." Retha arched her back, trying to get comfortable. The back seats didn't recline and seemed firmer than the regular seats. "Hey, why did you push us way back here?"

"I know, I'm usually a chatterbox. I wanted to be alone so no one could hear us."

"You got secrets? Worried the Communists might have microphones on the bus? Girl, what's up with you?"

Naomi didn't respond. She shrugged, straightened up to flex her back. Twenty minutes later, she patted Retha's arm. "I don't want to go back to Detroit to see those guys again."

Retha was glad for that. It wasn't being in Detroit. Both girls were in love with the city after living their entire lives in Split Creek County. Both dreamed of moving there as soon as possible. They were tired of Fair Haven, tired of the huge surge in summer guests, tired of cleaning up after them, of feeding them, of many of them showing off their affluence, though that was changing as more blue-collar workers from the factories were starting to visit, tired of the continuous flirtations and sexual propositions by the musicians. Well, Retha never enjoyed that and it didn't happen much to her. Even boy-crazy Naomi must be getting tired of their interest if she didn't want to visit the guys again.

The guys played all summer in the house band at one of the night clubs in Fair Haven. There were four of them. None of them flirted with Retha. They all looked at Naomi and drooled, while she only looked at the drummer, Jesse.

"He's a dreamboat." Naomi strung him along all summer before she finally slept with him the last night the band was in Fair Haven.

"Why are you so quiet? I thought you had a fun weekend. I enjoyed the jazz and blues and meeting Jesse's folks. Didn't you?"

Naomi was quiet for several more miles. "I did it with him again, back seat bingo, in his car. I didn't like it."

"Didn't like what?" Retha was secretly glad Naomi didn't like Jesse, but if she didn't like sex, well, that was another matter.

"Doing it, you know, sex."

"Really? You been turning yourself on for all these years, thinking about sex with guys and now you don't like it? Was he rough on you? Did he hurt you?"

"No, he was real gentle, smooth, didn't rush me like the first time we did it. We even did it twice this time…I just think men…"

Retha waited for her to continue.

"Can I ask you something? Don't go getting mad. It's something I've never asked you before."

What could this be about? We have no secrets, that I know of. "Ask away. What's wrong? Did I say something that bothered you?"

Naomi inched forward in the seat, turned so she could look at Retha. "Are you queer? I've never heard you say that, but it's obvious you don't like boys. Kids at school say things behind your back…"

Retha took in a deep breath, closed her eyes and slowly let it out. "I know what they say. People in Fair Haven have been whispering the same thing for years. The answer is yes. I'm queer. I have no interest in boys. Someday, I hope to meet another girl like me. If I do, I do. If not, I won't settle for a man." She opened her eyes to find Naomi staring at her. "Does that bother you? Why are you asking now?"

Naomi leaned back and put her head on Retha's shoulder again. "I'm not upset. Can you tell me how you knew? When did you know?"

Retha leaned her head against Naomi's. "Now I know why you

wanted to sit back here."

Both giggled. "I think I knew since I was ten or eleven. You know, that age when kids started teasing each other about boyfriends and girlfriends. Just the idea of a boyfriend almost made me sick."

"Well, you were a tomboy. Look at the way you dressed."

"I know, I never liked wearing girly things, but it went deeper than that. Somehow, I realized I could never love a man or be a wife. I don't know how to explain it. I just knew I would never fall in love with a man and that left only girls. It just made sense, though I couldn't have put it in words." Retha swallowed, took a deep breath, then continued. "I don't know much about other queer women, but I heard some want to become men. I don't want to be a man. I just want to be me. I know I want love with a woman someday. Screwing with a man sounds terrible. Being naked with a woman somehow makes sense, if it ever happens." She lifted her head and pushed Naomi's off of her shoulder so she could look her in the eyes. "Now, what the hell brought that on?"

"I need time to think. Hey, can I sleep over at your house when we get home? I'm trying to figure out some things and you're the only one in the whole world I can talk with."

Retha glanced at the window. What was going on with this girl? Why was she wondering about Retha being queer? Wasn't it obvious? After all these years? She and Naomi were so different in so many ways. Naomi outgoing, feminine, just flirty enough to draw boys to her, but not enough to be called a slut. Again, why was she wondering how Retha knew herself to be queer? Retha couldn't put her finger on when, she just always knew. Wasn't it like that for every queer? Even the men? She patted Naomi's arm. "Of course, kiddo, you can stay over."

Retha called Naomi kiddo for years. They were best friends since before kindergarten. Both lived year-around in Fair Haven. Naomi's grandfather had been the postmaster. Her father took over, but he was also the head deacon at the AME church in town. The small church couldn't afford a full-time pastor, so he was the mainstay for the church. Everyone called Naomi's father Reverend. He was always busy, checking on people, wearing himself out serving others, preaching, plus sorting and delivering mail. Retha knew Naomi was worried about her dad's, Reverend's, health. So was her mother, Beula, but no one ever called Beula by that name. She'd been called Granny since shortly after she married. Her husband kept referring to her as the grand lady and she hated it. So, he started calling her Grandy. Several small church kids could only say Granny, so it stuck.

Naomi nudged Retha, stood and guided them to the regular seats. Naomi reclined her aisle seat and said, "I'm going to rest and think." She smiled one of her award-winning smiles, before closing her eyes.

Retha looked out the window, wondering what was going through Naomi's mind. Why was she wondering about homosexuality?

Naomi had always been attractive. By twelve, she looked like she was fourteen. By fourteen, eighteen, by sixteen, twenty. She was a knock-out, tall, lighter skin, eyes more hazel than dark. Her light black hair was looser, easier to fuss with and had a slight reddish tint.

Naomi's father, Reverend, tried to be strict with her, but it became harder to do as his health waned. Lately, he mostly grouched at her dress and behaviors around the busy resort in the summer time.

Retha knew she was different since she was old enough to pick her own clothes out. She hated twirling dresses, fancy shoes, white socks, ribbons, bows, hats, the color pink, baby dolls, especially the white ones, which was almost all that was available back in the early-forties.

Daniel, her father, a retired Latin teacher and principal from a colored high school in Detroit, was much older than her mother. He always laughed and abetted Retha's wishes. Ida, her mother, tried not to, but after three years, the two against one prevailed and there was peace in the family.

Retha knew she had no desire to be a boy. Hitting puberty hadn't phased her much. Her mother prepared her and insisted she wear a bra when her breasts started developing. A bra under a shirt was no big deal, even less of a deal if it was under a western-cut shirt. Something she discovered when she was fourteen, along with cowboy boots. By then, she also knew she was attracted to girls, definitely not boys, but what could she do about it? Not much. Another reason she wanted to get the hell out of Dodge.

She liked westerns, too. Read all she could and watched the ones just coming out on their wooden TV with rabbit ears. Sometimes, they went back to Detroit to visit friends and take in movies. She always begged that at least one be a western.

Both girls were now seniors in high school, with enough credits to receive their diplomas in January, if they desired. Both did well. Both wanted to get out of Fair Haven the minute they graduated.

Retha roused Naomi. Time to get off the bus in Riverside. They had an hour wait before their next bus took them north to Split Creek, making frequent stops along the way. Again, Naomi barely talked. She mostly dozed against Retha the three hours till they pulled into the small Greyhound station that was part of a gas station in downtown Split Creek. If it was summer, the bus would have swung east to Fair Haven, but not in the offseason.

During the ride to Split Creek, Naomi shifted against her, still dozing. They'd been close friends forever. Retha knew her feelings went beyond friendship, but she never shared them. Why ruin a beautiful friendship? She was surprised at Naomi's questions. Was it even possible that Naomi could be queer? Now that she thought about it, Retha was never sure if Naomi's attraction to boys was genuine, or if it was because she thought it was expected of her. After all, girls like her couldn't be queer, not that queers were talked about much in their community.

Everyone knew a few of the male entertainers who came in were a little feminine or extra masculine. Some seemed overly interested in single men. Yet there was an unspoken sense to ignore them, or at least not gossip much about what several of them might have been doing in their rooms. But queer females? Retha never heard of any, she just knew she was one and would have to figure out things as she went. She sure as heck couldn't tell anyone. Today, it was easy to say it to Naomi. Why the change? Why was Naomi asking?

Daniel, Retha's father, died the year before when she was a high school junior. He was sixty-six. A few weeks before he passed on, she was sitting on the bed with him. He had lung cancer and they knew he would die soon. He patted her hand. "You are one of the smartest, kindest people I've known." He coughed and tried to take in a deep breath, which made him cough even more. When he recovered, he added, "I know you're different. You know you're different. Don't stay around here after high school. Once I'm gone, folk will talk more boldly, be less accepting. Go to Detroit or Chicago, even New York. That's where you'll find your life." Retha recalled he dozed off and never spoke more than a few words to anyone else before he died.

With her father gone, Retha found her mother, Ida, checking on her more frequently, almost suffocating her. Retha figured her mom didn't have enough to do now that she didn't have to care for her husband. Plus, Retha thought she might have finally grasped that her only child might be queer. "People talk. You never date anyone. There's several nice young men at church."

"Let people talk, I could care less. Boys around here aren't interested in me and I'm not interested in them," Retha replied. "Besides, I've got my whole life to find someone. Why tie myself down now? Don't you want me to be happy? I won't be happy, trying to please some man and raising babies before I'm twenty." Her mother would stop nagging, till the next time she needed something to worry about or overheard another rumor.

Retha roused Naomi as the bus pulled into Split Creek. Granny picked them up from the bus stop and drove them to her home. She kept glancing at Naomi. Retha knew Naomi and her mother were very close. "What's the matter? That boy's mother said you had a nice time." Granny poked at Naomi who was staring out the window.

"Oh, Mother. Did you really talk with her? Plus, he's not a boy, he's twenty and a full-time musician."

"I told you she and me would speak. We talked before you went down and this morning after she put you on the bus. You may look mature, but you're still only seventeen. She said you seemed to have a good time, especially at the music clubs you went to. Know what else she said?"

Naomi groaned. "What? This is embarrassing."

"I'm not embarrassed." Granny turned and looked at Retha in the back seat. "You embarrassed?" Retha couldn't help smiling. Granny always made her smile. "That boy's mama said she kept a tight eye on you and never left the two of you alone in the house." She poked Naomi again. "Us moms gotta stick together. Someday, you'll learn that."

"Mom, I'm going to go in to say hi to Daddy and get grilled. After, I'm going to spend the night with Retha. Okay?"

"Yup, I'm sure Ida can use the company. She sure looked lonely at church this morning."

Retha followed Naomi into the house to say hello to the Reverend. Though he never went to a seminary or Bible college, he was ordained and given the title by a group of other ministers who grilled him on his knowledge of the Bible. Most of them were ordained in the same manner.

"Hi, Daddy, how you feeling?"

"Hi, girls, I trust you had a good weekend down there in sin city. I'm all right. The good Lord is giving me some more testing with my digestive system, but I'm going to the doctor tomorrow." He reached out and took Naomi's hand. "I sure hope you're staying pure. Makes me nervous that you're so growed up and independent-acting now. I'd hate to see something happen to you that brought lasting consequences."

"Dad, I'm fine. Just quit worrying. I'm not ready to settle down. I'm thinking of being a telephone operator, but not in this county. I already know everybody's business around here." Naomi laughed as she leaned over and gave her dad a kiss.

That night, Naomi and Retha were in Retha's bed. Earlier, they checked their homework and chatted with Mrs. McBride.

"You going to finish what you started to tell me?" Retha turned to face Naomi who looked at the ceiling.

"I don't know where to start. Something's weird. It doesn't feel right being with a man. Not because Daddy's always preaching against F-O-R-N-I-C-A-T-I-O-N or Mom's telling me to wait for someone self-sufficient. When she sees guys looking at me or me looking at them, she's always saying, 'Don't give yourself to a loser. Make sure he's got a job and can support you and babies.'" She sat up, still not looking at Retha.

"All the way home, I was thinking. It's like I'm being poured into a Jell-O mold. Be pretty. Be smart. Love God. Get a man. Get married. Have babies. Put canned fruit in with little maraschino cherries on the top. Let it set-up in the fridge. Everyone will love it at the church potluck."

"You can't help that you're pretty and smart—"

"Don't interrupt me." Naomi smacked her fist into her hand. "Just listen. I'll tell you when to talk. Even if I take a breath, you wait till I say talk. Got it?"

"Mmm, mmm." Retha didn't know whether to laugh or cry.

"I love my daddy, but I think all his beliefs in the Bible are crazy. That's God's word. Really? He only picks through it and preaches or prays on parts of it. I tried to read the whole thing through. It's nuts." She smacked her fist again. "I realized today I don't want to be in that mold. It just ain't me." She was quiet, still not looking at Retha. She got out of bed and began pacing the small room. "I had sex because I thought I was supposed to. Oh, I know it's fornicating. Still, I felt nothing. I play with myself and it feels great. With Jesse, nothing. Nothing! I tried to feel something, to force it. Nothing. Nothing. It wasn't just Jesse. They don't come much cuter or nicer than him."

Naomi turned toward Retha. "I think I've been in the wrong mold. Going to Detroit was good. Getting naked was not. I'm beginning to wonder if I'm meant to be with men." She fell back on the bed and stretched out, her hands over the pillow, staring at the ceiling. "Are there other girls like you? Girls who don't like men, but like women?" She pointed at Retha. "Okay, you can talk now."

"I hope so. There's men who like men, why wouldn't there be women who like women?" Her heart beating, she didn't look at Naomi. Didn't dare.

She heard Naomi take in a breath and slowly blow it out. "Yeah. Why wouldn't there be?" A few minutes later, she nudged Retha till they were looking at each other. "You don't feel guilty?"

"No. Of course, I wasn't raised like you, always in the church and listening to your daddy preach. My folks just went for social reasons. My dad said he thought most of the Bible was nothing more than myths that were passed on through word of mouth till someone wrote them down. Why, are you feeling guilty?"

Naomi gave her a sharp look. "No." She turned on her side, away from Retha. "I'm glad you know who you are. Thanks for talking. You're my best friend. I couldn't live without you."

Retha carefully replied, hoping the questions in her mind and desires in her body didn't come through, "No problem, kiddo. I couldn't live without you either." She turned the other way and stared at the wall. What was all that? Naomi talked about being forced into a mold and now she dropped it. Was she sleeping? Was her mind running like Retha's was? Could best friends be lovers? She adjusted her pillow. *Time will tell. I can't rush anything.*

Chapter Twenty-three

Two months later, in study hall, Retha watched Naomi jump up, grab the bathroom pass and rush out. "My best friend is sick. I'm going with her," Retha told the teacher, who replied that she was a senior and old enough to make those decisions.

In the bathroom, she heard Naomi retching into the toilet and told her to let her in the stall. She wiped Naomi's mouth with toilet paper. "What's wrong? Lately, you've seemed more distant, even when we're together."

They never resumed their conversation about Naomi feeling forced into a mold. Now what was wrong with her? Was she still bothered about who she was?

Naomi opened the door and peered out to make sure they were the only ones in the restroom. "I started gagging last week, now it's throwing up." She wailed. "I missed my second monthly. I'm starving. I can't keep anything down. What am I going to do? I can't tell Mom or Daddy. Daddy will throw me out. Mom will want me to get married to Jesse right away. She'll call his mother the moment I tell her. Retha, what should I do?"

Two White girls walked in. Retha pulled Naomi out of the stall and led her to the sinks. As they washed their hands, one of the girls snarled, "Retha, what are you doing in a stall with her? Hey, did you ever think of using the men's' room? You're dressed like some buckaroo cowboy. At least we wouldn't be afraid you're going to hit on us."

Retha snapped, "I don't hit on people. I only think about using the men's room when the women's room is filled with little princesses and the men's room is empty." She led Naomi out. "We've only got English Lit left and we're both ahead. Let's ditch and go wait in Wally's till the bus comes."

They got their coats and books and slipped out. Seniors ditching a class or two wasn't that big of deal. The Black kids went to Wally's, the White ones to the year-around A and W.

"We need a plan," Retha said, sliding a can of Vernors ginger ale and some saltine crackers across the table to Naomi. "I ordered some chicken noodle soup, maybe you can keep the broth down."

"I don't want my folks to be all embarrassed over a daughter pregnant by some summer musician, or as Mom will say, by that boy that's gotta be at least eighty percent red-headed Irish and maybe twenty percent colored." Naomi unpeeled the wrapper of her cracker. "She liked him, but every time she saw him with his folks, she always talked about how light his daddy was and colored folk having a kid that light and with that much red hair." She popped the cracker in her mouth and mumbled while chewing, "I want to get out of here. I want to leave, soon, get through this."

"So, you want to get rid of the baby? That's pretty scary. I wouldn't even know where to start."

Naomi thought. She sipped her broth, munched another cracker and belched from the ginger ale. "No. I'd rather have a light-skinned baby with reddish hair. Mine has a tint to it also. Daddy says it's from his side, but he never explained where." Her eyes grew large, tears formed. "Oh, Retha, what will happen to us if I have a baby? Should I adopt it out? I don't want to be by myself somewhere."

Retha took her hand. "Oh, girl. You know colored folk don't adopt our babies out. White girls go away someplace, have the baby, adopt it out. Not us. We keep them and love them. Our families step up and do, too. I'll help you raise the baby. The two of us. We'll make up a story, maybe we're cousins and your husband was killed in a car accident. We'll figure out something. What do you think?"

"I think if we try that story around here, we'll be laughed at." Naomi looked at Retha carefully. Seeing Retha's serious nod, she continued, "Okay, it's a deal. You're sticking with me, but how do we get out of here without everyone and their mother's uncle knowing?"

Over the next few days, they put a plan together, which included asking their parents not to buy them gifts for Christmas, but to give them the money instead. When Granny and Ida asked why they wanted cash instead of presents, the girls explained they felt too old for presents. "Besides," Naomi said, "we're trying to save up money so we can move away after we graduate." They didn't remind their folks they would have enough credits receive their diplomas in January.

In January, the evening after they finished their final exams for the first semester, they sat down with their parents. Fighting to maintain self-control, Naomi started the conversation. "Retha's eighteen. I'll be eighteen in three weeks. We have enough credits to graduate high school. Neither of us want to stay around here. Despite the fact that we love you immensely, we're moving to Detroit tomorrow. We already have our Greyhound tickets and a friend to take us to the station."

Ida, Retha's mother, wailed. Naomi's dad gasped, then started rattling something about the Bible and respectful children. "Oh, hush," Granny said, "the Bible got nothing to do with this." She looked at Naomi. "This got something to do with that redheaded drummer in Detroit? If it does, I'm going to call his mama right now."

"Momma, it has nothing to do with him. He's a loser, still living at home, can't support himself. No, it's time I got out on my own. I will never be happy cleaning rooms and houses the rest of my life for colored folk, half of them trying to Lord it over me because they're richer than me."

Naomi's dad snorted. "What the hell you got against colored people with money?"

Retha thought the Reverend might pass out, his eyes were bulging.

"Oh, hush again," Granny told him. "She's eighteen. What were we doing at her age? Huh? Remember? We was planning a wedding. Then we lost two babies. Of course, one was her twin brother right after I born him." She stood and looked at Ida. "I say let them go with our blessing. We all been there and survived. They will as well. I'd rather they go with our blessing than our curses." She turned to Naomi. "I still got this feelin' there's more to this than you're telling me, but go." She gave a questioning look to Retha, too.

Ida sat, head in her hands, sniffling. She stood, put her arms around Retha. "I always knew you couldn't stay in Fair Haven. Your father told me, shortly before he died, that you couldn't stay and don't force you to stay. Still, I thought you could go off to a town around here, maybe Riverside, and get a job, take some training, but still be closer. Detroit is a long way." She shuddered. "Who knows what kind of people live there? I've heard there's a lot of prejudice."

Retha wiped the tears off her mother's face. "Mama, we're going to live by the kind of people that come here in the summers, black folk. Couldn't live by the Whites anyway. Okay?"

Her mother hugged her back. "Well, sometimes, I guess life works in reverse. My mother didn't want me following your daddy up here from Detroit, tried to lay a guilt trip on me even though I was much older than you are right now." She stepped back from their embrace. "I'm not going to lay a guilt trip on you. You're strong, you're independent. God knows you're independent. Just write us and call when you can afford it."

Each of their parents gave them one hundred dollars to add to their combined two hundred dollars they emptied from their savings accounts, piggy banks and found buried in underwear drawers. Four hundred dollars seemed like a considerable sum of money to start a new life. Even if one of them was pregnant.

Chapter Twenty-four

The next day, the pudgy White Greyhound driver in Riverside gave them a half-smile as they climbed on. "Sit where you like. Times are a changing. If anyone puts up a stink, I'll tell them they're free to move or get off. I ain't no kiddy bus driver assigning no seats to nobody. Not anymore. I was getting tired of that crap. Bet your kind was also."

The girls noticed two colored women sitting next to each other halfway back. The seats immediately behind them were open. They stored their small bags above and slipped into the seats, ignoring the scowls of several White passengers across the aisle and the fearful looks of several colored riders seated at the rear. The bus driver closed the door and stood in the aisle, facing the passengers. He bent over and raised a Billy club he stored behind his seat. "There ain't gonna be any troubles on this bus. Yah hear? If yah don't like who you're sitting near, get off and walk. It makes no never mind to me. I'm here to drive the bus, not deal with race shit."

There was dead silence in the bus as he smacked the club against his palm, returned it, sat down and jerked the clutch, lurching them forward.

One of the ladies in front of the girls turned and whispered, "I'm glad we got this driver. On the way up last Sunday, we got a nasty one." She shook her head. "Change sure is hard and long. Now where are you young women from and where are you going?"

"We're from Fair Haven, going to Detroit," replied Retha. "We're moving to find jobs."

"Oh my, Fair Haven. I've heard such nice things about that place, but never could talk my husband into visiting. Why would you want to leave a beautiful place like that?"

The other woman laughed. "Probably because they're young and want to get away from home and nosy folks like us." She turned her head to see them better. "Speaking of being nosy, have you got a place to stay? Jobs lined up?"

Both girls shook their heads. "Nope, we're open to suggestions from nice nosy ladies." Naomi laughed. Retha knew Naomi felt relieved to be on their way to a new life. Uncertain, but new. Since Naomi said she was pregnant, Retha let her thoughts of anything other than a close relationship slip to the back of her mind. They were best friends and one of them was having a baby.

Naomi's morning sickness was almost over, and she was always starving. Retha watched her pull an apple out of her coat pocket, bite into it and mumble, "I don't mean to be rude, but I'm really hungry."

Both women smiled. The woman in front of Retha said, "We brought food to eat, too. So, you need suggestions to get started in Detroit." She pronounced it Dee-troit. She nudged her seatmate. "I've heard the plants are hiring. They don't always like women on the lines, but they're starting to change. Even if you can get in cleaning toilets or emptying waste cans, it's a start. There's a lot of colored-owned stores and businesses, too. Can you two type, answer phones, even take shorthand?"

"We both type very well, and Naomi took some office classes in high school so she does some shorthand. She wants to be a phone operator or office worker. I'd like to get on the lines. I'm stronger than a lot of men."

Retha watched the woman glance at her western attire and suppress a smile. *Dammit, it's true. I'll show them.*

The other woman said, "I'll give you a note with the area where these businesses are. There's a Negro newspaper they usually advertise in. You can read a copy at the library. Also, the YWCA is close to the city buses. It might be a place to spend several nights till you acquaint yourself with the city and find jobs. I will say, housing is tight. You may have to take a room with a shared bath in someone's home or a rooming house."

In Detroit, the four waited in line to collect their luggage from the bus driver. The women handed the promised note to Naomi. "There's more colored moving in every day, but I'm sure you'll find something.

Good luck. The Y is that way." She patted their backs and walked away.

The traffic was horrendous, loud and startling. They started walking in the direction the woman pointed them. "Look, there's a sign that says Y. Let's go in, I'm tired and starving." Naomi let the way up the steps into a large lobby. Men sat around, reading newspapers or listening to the radio. The man behind the counter looked at them, his eyebrows raised as he asked them if he could help them.

"We need a room, the cheapest. We can share the bathroom." Naomi flashed her wide smile.

"I'm sorry, we can't provide rooms for you." He must have noticed Retha straighten her back as if to say something. "Oh, oh, not because you're colored, but you're women." He laughed at their expressions of shock. "You've never been to this big of a city, have you?" They shook their heads. "See, there's a $YMCA$ and a $YWCA$. The YW is two blocks further. Got it?"

Both girls laughed. Retha heard Naomi's stomach growling. Barely three months along and that kid's an eater. Glad she's got some loose clothes to wear. Retha turned to the clerk. "Guess we are country folk, but I smell food. Can two starving girls eat in the $YMCA$ or do we have to wait to get to the $YWCA$?"

The man laughed so loud, others in the room looked up at them. "Anyone, men and women, can eat in our cafeteria. We even have some colored cooks now, so everything isn't just what White folks eat. It's cheap, too." He pointed them down the stairs, toward the cafeteria.

It took the girls five days to find jobs and a place to live. At Retha's suggestion, Naomi bought a cheap used wedding ring from a street vendor. She was now married, but her husband was in the Navy, Great Lakes, but he was going to Virginia or Florida. She figured that out from seeing some Naval recruiting information in the library, which they were learning was a great resource. His name was George Bryant, he was nineteen and they grew up near each other in Split Creek County. In public, Retha was her cousin, not best friend.

Their first jobs were with a small manufacturing plant, making carburetors for Ford Motor. Naomi was in the office, Retha kept the shop floors clean of metal shavings, dirt, grease and water. She was teased for her short hair and the men's' jeans she wore, yet she kept bugging the boss to show her how to work some of the basic machinery and teach her the assembly process. Gradually, he complied.

They found a dark third-floor efficiency room in the converted attic of a home deep in the colored section. It was near bus transportation and walking distance from their jobs. The room had one double bed, a hotplate, two wooden chairs, tiny table, a cold-water sink and a communal ice chest at the bottom of their narrow stairs. They shared a bathroom with four other roomers on the second floor. The owners lived on the first floor.

The girls soon learned their way around Detroit on the public transportations system, where to buy groceries, how to cook with limited pots and utensils on a hot plate, how to set money aside for rent and expenses.

One evening, lying in bed, Naomi pulled Retha's hand to her stomach. "This kid's kicking again. Can you feel it?"

Retha felt the baby kicking. It was exciting to feel the new life, but something else was changing. Lately, Naomi kept hugging Retha more, holding her hand after they climbed in bed together. It was driving Retha nuts. Not that she didn't like it, but because she didn't know if it was because Naomi was pregnant and wanted more physical support or...Or what? The pressure on her emotions had been building. Every night, after Naomi fell asleep, Retha's mind raced. Who was Naomi? Their conversation back home after visiting the guys never left her. Did Naomi know who she was? Could she truly be queer? She had to know where Naomi was at. Either way could be fine. It was the not knowing that kept her mind and emotions whirling.

Retha sat up. "We never finished our conversation."

Naomi glanced up at her. "Which one? We're always talking." She must have noticed the expression on Retha's face and sat up. "Sorry, I was trying to be cute, funny. Are you talking about the one in your bed back home? After seeing the guys?"

Retha nodded, afraid to say more.

"I've never forgotten thinking about who I am on that bus ride home. Even after I realized I was pregnant; it has been at the back of my mind. Now that I'm done puking all the time, I think it's moved to the front of my brain." She took Retha's hand and shook it like someone you just met. "Hi, I'm Naomi Bryant. I'm over five months pregnant. I'm from Fair Haven. I live in Detroit with my cousin, Retha. Now, I don't want her to be my cousin in our apartment." Tears came to her eyes. "I want to be her lover. I'm not staying in the Jell-O mold. I'm queer. I love you."

Retha didn't look at Naomi as she said, "Secretly, I have been in love with you for a long time. Like forever. Are you sure?"

Naomi gently pulled Retha's face till they were gazing into each other's eyes. "I don't think this is hormones. Before I missed my first monthly, I wanted to tell you, but I was so worried about being pregnant...Well..."

"I get it. I just want you to be sure."

"I'm positive. What do we do now?"

"This." Retha wrapped her arms around her and gently kissed her, first on the cheek, next, the lips.

When they broke apart, Naomi gasped. "I never felt anything like that kissing Jesse or the other boys I made out with. I never even felt horny when Jesse and I got naked in his car. My god, now I'm so horny, I don't know what to do."

"Let's figure it out. Together."

"Are there instructions for pregnant queers making love?"

"Shut up and kiss me again."

~ * ~

Naomi was well into her seventh month. One day, Naomi told Retha about her supervisor calling her into the office. "She said, 'I've been watching you for some time, but didn't say anything. You're with child, aren't you?'"

Naomi said she nodded, surprised. She thought her loose clothes hid the baby quite well. How long she could work while pregnant hadn't entered her mind. She and Retha were so in love, having fun planning for a baby, that the idea she could lose her job hadn't occurred to her.

The supervisor said, "I've waited till others, including the big bosses, said something. Honey, you can't hide babies. How far are you?"

"Seven and a half months. I'm due July first. You can tell? Really?"

Naomi told Retha the lady said, "Oh, young lady, you're so mature and sharp in many ways, but anyone who's had a child can tell when someone else is trying to hide it. Your second one, you won't even try to hide." She laughed. "What's your husband say? Is he excited? Can you go join him on base to have the baby? That would be ideal."

Naomi said she pasted a smile on. "Right now, he's in basic, then he's going to either Florida or Virginia. Once he's settled, the baby and I will join him. Are you firing me?"

"The supervisor gave me an odd look. Almost like she didn't believe me. Then she said, 'I hate to use the word firing. You're an excellent employee, but our policy is pregnant women are only supposed to work till they begin showing. I will write you a good letter of recommendation.'"

Naomi told Retha how desperate she felt. "Is there nothing else I can do here? Can't I sit in the back room, answer phones, file papers, even make calls? I learn fast. I even took a bookkeeping class. I could help with that."

"I'm sorry, there isn't," the woman replied. "However, I will call an answering service, they might have a need, but they may not want to train someone who's going to leave them to raise a child."

Naomi said, "Please call them. I can work nights. I won't need much time off. Retha and I planned to work separate shifts when the baby came. Retha's my cousin. She came with me and will stay with me till I move to my hus—"

"Oh, Naomi," the supervisor said. "That means you still will be moving away. How can I ask someone to employ you when you won't be staying around?"

Naomi told Retha she stared into the woman's eyes. "Tell them the truth. I'm not married. My boyfriend left me. I won't be moving away and I will need a job. Retha, my cousin, plans to stay and help me for as long as necessary. Besides, you don't have to worry about her getting pregnant. She doesn't like men."

Naomi laughed when she told Retha how the woman gasped. "I suspected as much. Your story about your boyfriend has never quite added up." She snickered. "So, I've heard. That Retha is a tough one, but the boss loves her work." The woman thought several moments. "No guarantees. I'll call my contact. She has a soft heart for girls who get themselves into trouble. Still, I don't think you should say anything about Retha to anyone else."

Naomi got the job, working from ten at night to six in the morning. The answering service office was on the first floor of a wooden building that held small apartments above it. One of the apartments opened up for rent and the girls moved in. One-bedroom, combined living and kitchen. The full bathroom was shared with one other tenant. There were four apartments on the third floor. The walls were thin. Only one fire escape existed for their whole floor, which originally was one large apartment. Still, it was luxury to them.

Naomi's new boss was so excited to have them living above the office, she ran a line and phone up to their apartment so that on weekends, Naomi could take a message, or put the caller on hold, run down the stairs and transfer the call. The boss even told her people could call her personally during slow times, but she couldn't make long distance calls out.

In late June, shortly after they moved into the new apartment and just before the due date, the girls received letters from their mothers. They came in the same envelope to save postage. Granny and Mrs. McBride wrote they wanted to come visit the girls and see their new digs. Retha and Naomi were unsure where their mothers picked up their slang.

Retha also thought their moms sounded suspicious. "How long before we tell them? When the baby's old enough to drive?"

"It's time. I've felt guilty over waiting this long. I wished Mother could be here, but Daddy's getting worse and we might have to explain how in love we are."

Naomi leaned on Retha's arm down the rickety steps into the office. It was Saturday evening, no one else was present and Naomi was on call. Naomi placed a collect call to her mother, who refused it and called the number back. Naomi and Retha sat close, the phone receiver tucked between their ears so they could both hear and speak.

Granny sounded thrilled. "Five months and we finally can talk. We like your letters, but this is much better, even if it costs me some." She paused. "Now, what's wrong?"

"Mother, why do you think that?"

Granny's voice tone changed to strict mother. "Because I knows you like no one else. I knowed something was up when you left. Then I went to get a Kotex and realized there should have been a whole lot more missing. You got pregnant by that light-skinned redhead, didn't you? I've just been playing along, waiting till you got the gumption to tell me. Now, when you due?"

Retha hugged Naomi as she started crying. "Around the first of July. I'm sorry, Mommy. I'm sorry. Even if I wasn't pregnant, I would have moved out."

Granny was quiet. Retha could hear her tapping the phone table. That woman always had to poke or tap something. "I understand you wanted to move out. Jist not in the middle of the school year. That didn't help my 'spicions. Listen, your daddy's right here. He's about choking right now, realizing he's going to be a grandpa."

Retha heard Granny turn from the phone and speak to her husband. "We're gonna be grandparents. That's the way it is. That's all we need to know right now. We gonna be grandpa and grandma and love that baby to death. Understand?" Retha heard the Reverend start to say something, but Granny cut him off. "Now listen. None of your preachin' or hollerin' will change them facts. Calm yourself down. Take one of those nitro pills, take two. I don't want you kickin' off the day I find out I'm going to be a grandma."

Granny spoke back into the phone. "Now, child, I jist said me and Ida wanted to come down to force you to tell us what's up. There ain't no way I can leave your father. I always dreamed of being present when my baby had a baby, but it's not going to happen. Finally, my name means what I am called, Granny, and I can't be there to granny that baby when it comes outta your tummy. Do you want Ida to try to come visit?" Granny's voice seemed tentative about the idea of Ida visiting by herself.

Retha said, "No, Granny. We'll be fine. I'll call her next so she can know we're fine and living in a safe place."

"Makes sense. Jist don't tell her anything 'bout the baby. Retha, I didn't know how to tell ya, but your momma ain't doing too well. I doubt if she could help with the baby anyway. She's mostly covering up for things she's been doin'. I think her mind is slipping. You two need to bring the baby up for a visit as soon as you can, and Retha can see what's up with her mother."

"We will, Mom. We will. Mom, thank you—"

"You're welcome, young lady. Jist so you know, I ain't gonna call that boy's mama. Goes against my grain. He should be supportin' your baby. I think it would complicate things. Retha will be better help with a baby than a worthless man. Goodbye." The phone clicked off.

Naomi hung up the receiver. Both wiped the tears from their eyes.

"Glad that's over. I shouldn't have waited," said Naomi. "I'm worried about your mother."

"Me, too. Right now, let's get you back up the stairs. How much bigger can you get?"

~ * ~

Early on July 4th 1956, Retha woke to find Naomi sitting on the kitchen chair, bent over in pain. Retha quickly dressed, grabbed the bag they prepared and helped her down the steps. They caught the bus to the county hospital.

"Who's your doctor?" asked the admitting clerk.

"I don't have one." Naomi groaned as Retha rubbed her back.

"Good grief, you're ready to deliver and never saw a doctor?"

Retha snapped, "Look, she's healthy, her water broke on the bus, her contractions are three minutes apart, we're not ignorant, now please get that paperwork done before you and I deliver this baby."

"Okay, okay. I'm hurrying. Where is the father?"

"He deserted me. He's in the Navy, doesn't know I'm even pregnant." Naomi gasped as another pain rolled through her.

Three hours later, Ellie Marie was born, nineteen inches, six pounds fourteen ounces, with a head full of reddish black hair. No shots for pain, no stitches, no complications for Naomi. Two days later, after Retha got off work, the three of them took the bus back to their apartment. The next night, Naomi carried the baby downstairs and, when not answering the few night calls, she marveled over Ellie.

Over Labor Day weekend, the three took the Greyhound to Split Creek. The two grandmas and one grandpa couldn't get enough of Ellie. That night in her old bedroom, Retha said, "Mom's not good. She's not eating, she forgets things, she asked me four times what the baby's name is, even whose it was and where have I been. I'm worried. I don't think she should be on her own."

Naomi finished nursing Ellie. "I agree, but we don't have room for her. Does that mean you want to move back here?"

Retha thought a moment. "No, our life is before us and we can't live here, not as a queer couple with a baby. I'll talk with Granny tomorrow. Maybe there's someone who can care for her."

Granny teared up when Retha asked her about her mother. "I needed you to come back and see for yourself. I kept thinkin' you'd come back sooner. I should have insisted. Several of us been runnin over there every day to check on her, but I was afraid to tell you right out what we were seeing." Granny thought a while. "Mrs. Johnson out on Oak Road is licensed with the state to provide nursing care in her home. She's White, but I know she's taken in colored before, if someone can pay for them. Even if she can take her, this ain't something you can get squared away right now. You gotta figure out her money situation, maybe get a lawyer to help you take over her affairs. It could take you several weeks, if Mrs. Johnson even has the room."

Naomi and Ellie returned to Detroit on the bus. Retha stayed home three weeks, getting her mother's affairs settled and Ida moved into Mrs.

Johnson's. When Retha returned, her job was gone, even though she kept them updated.

"What will you do, try the Ford or Chrysler?" Naomi asked her when Retha said she was unemployed. "I'm not worried. We got some savings thanks to our folks teaching us how to handle money."

Retha was rocking Ellie. "I want to try something else. I like the machine work, but I'm tired of the grime and dirt, plus the men are always bothering me. Several wanting to know if I need a good lay so I would learn to dress like a woman or not be so grouchy to them." Retha switched Ellie to her other arm and kept rocking. "When you were in the hospital, I talked with some of the colored aides and nurses. Most were aides, but they said even though they got the scut work, it was better than putting up with the menfolk in the shops and all the dirt."

Retha stood, kissed Ellie, and put her on the bed. "One of them told me the hospital runs a nursing program to train the nurses and aides. She asked me how I did in school. I told her fine, that I liked science and got A's in biology. Besides, I'm thinking I might want to help deliver babies someday."

"Wow. From a noisy factory to a noisy delivery room." Naomi handed Retha a cup of tea. "I think you'd be a wonderful nurse. Could you wear cowboy shirts over your starched white uniforms?" Naomi ducked Retha's mock swing at her.

The next week, Retha applied to work at the hospital and signed up to take nurse's aide classes.

Chapter Twenty-five

Saturday, January 12, 2019, the farm house

Retha turned her mind back to the present as her iPad buzzed. She looked at Duane to make sure he was awake. "More emails from your daughters. Anything you want to say directly? I try to update them each day. They're very worried about this storm we're in."

He looked toward the window, as if thinking how to respond. "Just...Just tell them I'm getting worse, that I love them. The storm is bad, but I've been through worse. And," his face brightened, "not to believe everything you're telling them about me."

"Pshaw, I don't need to make up things about you." She settled back in her chair and typed a few minutes, then closed the cover and laid the iPad next to her knitting bag on the floor. "They said they're doing fine. I think they understand where you're at. They sure do love you."

Duane looked away.

Retha placed couch cushions against the foot of Duane's bed and climbed onto the bed, facing him, their legs next to each other. She tucked a blanket around their legs. Mugs of sweet green tea rested on the bed table.

Branches tore at the roof. Sumac scraped the siding and windows. Even with the woodstove blasting and the heater turned up, it was hard to keep the temperature at sixty-five degrees. She kept water dripping in the bathroom and kitchen sinks so the pipes wouldn't freeze. The radio said the storm might continue for three more days.

She was worried about the wood supply. They were burning more than she thought they would, and there was no way she could get to the shed for more, not in this storm. Food was an issue, too. The grocery store called that morning and said there was no way they could deliver that day.

Probably not for another four or five days. They told her Grassy Lakes Road was blocked with snow at the curves and the county was busy trying to keep the main roads open. Eating flour, sugar and yeast raw didn't sound too good.

Duane looked at her, then glanced at the frosted window. "How did Naomi die?" Keeping his hands under the blankets, he raised them to wipe his cheeks and nose on the tea towel Retha placed for that purpose. She had to, in order to keep him warm, bringing his hands out from under the blankets could chill him. She already kept him in adult diapers. He quit eating solids, though he was drinking Ensure because it was easier to swallow, plus he said he didn't feel hungry after drinking it.

She leaned toward him. "We need to make an agreement. I'll talk about Naomi having Ellie. You need to talk more about Ralph." She waited till his leg nudged her, as if agreeing. "We both will talk about May twenty-nineth. I'm not sure how, it won't be easy, but we both need to."

She thought, but didn't say, that both needed to hear each other's story before Duane died, which was approaching faster than she originally thought.

She began, telling him of her and Naomi's love, the baby being born, their lives in Detroit. How happy she was when she got a job at the county hospital and was able to get some training in patient care. How her mother died suddenly six months after going to Mrs. Johnson's, and she used the remaining funds from her parents' tiny estate to buy a used car and some used furniture for the apartment and baby.

~ * ~

My Grandma Naomi was a lesbian? A homosexual? With Retha? They loved each other like mommies and daddies, that much is for sure.

Mommy and Granny told us about homosexuals, they said people called them gay now.

On our trip to Chicago, in the fish museum, two men—one was a Mexican, I think—two men were holding hands. Holding hands like people in love or mommies and daddies do. Sometimes, they put their arms around each other as they looked at the fish. Me and Jimmy were right next to them at the big tank, the huge one in the middle with the whales and sharks. They hugged and I heard one of them say, 'I love you.' This man and woman behind them said they were disgusting fags. That they shouldn't be seen in front of children and families. That God said they were going to die.

The men tried to ignore them. Granny wiggled through and patted the men. 'Pay them no never mind. You boys love who you want to love.' That couple gave her mean looks and walked away.

That night in the motel room, Mommy explained fags was a bad word for homosexuals or gays or lesbians, like the 'n' word was for Black people. She told us gays and lesbians was about when a man loved a man or a woman loved a woman, like she and Dad loved each other. I think we kinda got it. Granny never said anything about my Grandma Naomi being a lesbian.

Mom never said anything either. I wonder if she even knew.

Retha leaned forward and lifted a mug of tea to Duane's lips. After his sips, she set his mug down and picked up hers. After taking a swallow, she continued, "It was Sunday, October 7, 1956, warm, colors turning. My car was parked several blocks away. Parking was tight and I didn't want to give up my spot. About nine-thirty that morning, I put Ellie in her stroller, she was fifteen months old, jabbering, saying mama and trying to say momo, which was me. We took the busses to the zoo. Naomi was tired and was going to sleep in."

Retha adjusted a pillow behind her. "Ellie loved the zoo. All toddlers do. I let her run and walk as much as possible. That girl needed room to run and our apartment was small. I swear that's why Naomi was so tired out, the kid loved going up and down the stairs, up and down. I packed sandwiches and bought an orange push-up we shared. Well, shared when I could get it away from her for a sloppy lick. You remember those?"

Duane smiled.

"Anyway, about two-thirty, she was worn out and fell asleep as we left the zoo. I got us off the bus about three blocks from our building and immediately smelled smoke. I soon realized our street was blocked off. Firetrucks were still there and our entire building was charred, almost to the ground. It was horrible."

Retha grabbed her tea and took a big sip. Tears eased down her cheeks. "It was so horrible. I'll never forget it. I pushed my way up to an officer and told him my cousin, my roommate, was asleep when we left at nine-thirty. Where did the people go that lived there? He called a fireman over. 'Which one was your apartment?'"

"Third floor, back end, the stairs were next to the answering service." Retha set her mug on the table.

Duane rubbed his eyes and motioned for her to continue.

"The fireman wiped his nose. 'No one on the back of the third floor survived. The fire started in a third-floor front apartment and blocked the stairs. I hope we convict the owner. The place was a tinderbox—a fire trap. It went up in seconds.' He turned and motioned for me to move closer. 'I'm so sorry. Your roommate is at the county morgue. You need to go identify her and make funeral arrangements. God be with you.'"

Retha bent over, crying. Duane pulled his hand out and stroked her head. "I'm so sorry. I'm so sorry. All you've been through—"

"All we've been through." Retha straightened herself.

Duane looked away. "Yes, but none of this was your fault. Ellie was my fault."

"We'll talk about that, but let me finish while I can."

He put his hand back under the blankets. He didn't look convinced it wasn't his fault. "What did you do next?"

"The only way I could identify the body was by the ring she still wore and a scar she had above her left wrist. For some reason, her left hand must have been under her body when the fire swept through. Her death was quick, the man at the morgue said. She never had a chance to run or even get to a window."

Duane shook his head, waiting to hear what happened next.

"The man told me the body couldn't be shown. 'We can cremate her,' he said. 'I know that's not popular, but it's the fastest, cheapest way and you don't have to buy a casket or have her driven back home.' I told him to cremate her."

Retha silently rocked back and forth, then sipped more tea. Calming herself, she continued. "I had nothing for Ellie. We knew several friends, gay guys who owned a house and loved the baby. I drove over there and we stayed with them till the body was cremated. The hardest time was for Ellie. She was eating solid foods, but still nursing when she wanted. She did not take to a bottle easily. She was so stubborn, even then."

"She was. She always was."

"I hadn't called Granny, I needed to tell her in person. Her husband died two months before—we drove up for the funeral and spent several days—anyway, my mother was dead. I didn't want Granny rushing down here in her old car. To do what? My friends helped me get some clothes and diapers. I went to our bank and got our money out, it was in both our names, picked up Naomi's ashes and headed to Granny's."

"What did she do? How terrible for her. She never talked much about Naomi, just that she died in a fire in Detroit and she took Ellie and raised her. She never mentioned you. I don't get it. What did she say?"

"Granny took one look at my face and burst out crying. 'What did you do to Naomi? Where is she?' Of course, I was sobbing so hard, I could hardly talk. When I finally got it explained and we both settled down, she set the urn, it was a cheap box, on the bookshelf, picked up Ellie and told me, 'You need to leave and never return. This is not your child. She's mine now. You ain't gonna stay around here. There's nothing for your type here. Go start a new life.' She pushed me toward the door and stood, watching till I drove off. It was almost as horrible as the day Naomi died."

Retha doubled over and shook as Duane patted her head. "My

whole life ended that day. My dreams of living with and loving Naomi the rest of our lives were gone. The baby I intended to help raise was gone. I had no legal rights to her, not in fifty-six. Granny, the woman I considered my second mother, told me to leave and never come back." Retha rocked back and forth, wiggling the bed. Eventually, she calmed herself and sipped her now cold tea.

She pushed Duane's hand back under the blankets, slid herself forward and felt around his legs to see if his diaper was wet.

He tried to smile. "It's okay. I'm good for a while. Let me have a sip of that Ensure, maybe the chocolate will give me some energy."

He sipped his Ensure as she leaned back, her thoughts and the pain from that day as fresh as if it were yesterday.

How could Granny, a woman who was never part of the community gossip chain about me, push me out the door? The woman always found a way to make things work out for everyone involved. She was the fixer. How could she use those words? Not say anything encouraging? It was so unlike Granny. Or was it? Now, decades later, she realized Granny had no choice. But it sure didn't seem like it at the time.

Chapter Twenty-six

Sunday, January 13, 2019

Man. Why did Granny act that way? Telling Retha to leave right after Granny's daughter burned to death in a fire. How horrible.

Just think, Retha coulda been like another grandma to me and Jimmy. We never knew or even heard about her. Mommy never mentioned her. I know she would have if she knew about her.

That means, if Grandma Naomi didn't die in the fire, my mom would have grown up with two mommies.

Wait. I remember Granny said something else in the motel room. Jimmy asked how homosexuals had babies. Granny said, 'It takes a man and a woman to start a baby, but two men or two women can raise them.'

I remember Mommy looking at her funny. Granny changed the subject, like she didn't want to answer any more questions.

I have to quit thinking. Today, Dad's going to talk more about Ralph. I don't get what he has to do with Mommy, Jimmy and me.

Man, this storm must really be bad! It just keeps blowing and snowing and the wind howling, almost like coyotes do. I know we're snowed in. I heard Retha talking to the grocery store. What happens if she runs out of wood, or food? At least she's got the heater and the electricity.

Retha is putting extra clothes on Dad. She said this blizzard is lasting a long time. She keeps looking at Dad like she's worried about him. I think he's getting weaker.

What's it look like when someone dies? Can you see their stardust leave their body? Will I know when it does?

I don't want to miss it.

~ * ~

Duane stretched as much as his frail body allowed. He could tell his organs were beginning to shut down. Though he felt groggy and spoke slowly, he figured he could hold off on taking morphine till he said everything he needed to say or Retha seemed satisfied. Somehow, he knew both of them would be satisfied when he finished.

"As I said, I was eleven or twelve when Ralph showed up. He acted like he knew us all his life. He called my dad Pops right from the start and Dad didn't seem to mind. I could tell he liked the kid." Duane bent over and swiped his nose across the tea towel. "Mom seemed more reserved around him. Mostly, I think, because he could be so rambunctious, loud, cursing all the time. Dad could control him, but Mom couldn't. She finally insisted he only come around when Dad was present."

"Did you ever meet his mother? Did she become friends with your mom?"

"I met her several times. She didn't seem interested in me or Mom. Sometimes, when Dad and I would run into town for parts or to get an ice cream cone, Ralph would be out playing by the road and Dad would ask him if he wanted to come along. He hollered toward the house that he was going with Pops and jumped in, chattering away, excited to see us. I thought he was lonely and needed a father figure in his life."

Duane nodded toward his tea, and Retha held his mug up to his lips for several sips. He nudged her hand away. "You know, I lied to you."

Retha set the mug down. "When? About what?"

"I said Dad never spanked me or physically punished me. He did once, with his belt."

"Lord, what did you do?"

"It was summer, I was fourteen, skinny, just starting to grow taller. The camp group pulled in. Dad was gone and the leader told Mom they forgot one of their food bags back at the camp. They needed to run back into town to buy more food. She said they didn't want to take seven kids into the store."

"Well, I can understand that. I bet your mother volunteered to take her into town." Retha motioned for him to continue.

"You're right. Mom told her to jump in her car. The other staff member said he would take the boys on down to the launch area, unload the canoes and pack them so they could take off as soon she was back. Well, Shrimp heard all this and asked if he could stay with me. Mom said it was all right with her, that he could help me finish baking the cookies she and I started."

"Got it, but what does this have to do with getting a beating?"

"Shrimp and I finished the cookies and were playing around in the barn. Horsing around, checking out the old equipment, jumping off the hay that was stored there. We started arm wrestling. He kept beating me. So, my legs being longer, I suggested leg wrestling." Duane caught the look on Retha's face. "No, it wasn't anything sexual. I know boys that age might get turned on with the physical contact, but we weren't. Just two young teens goofing around. Anyway, Dad walked in on us. He came home early and hadn't notified us, which wasn't unusual, except this time, he was three days early."

"Oh, God. What did he do?"

"Ralph was with him and watched the whole thing. Dad yelled something about getting that Black bastard out of the barn. Shrimp took off running like a bat out of hell. He told me later, he ran the two miles to the launch site, but never told anyone why he came back. Never told a soul. I think he was afraid if he did, the camp could get in trouble for letting him stay unsupervised at someone's home."

"Go on."

"Dad was a big man and, for his age, still strong. He grabbed me, twisted my hand behind my back and with his other hand somehow took his belt off. A thick leather one. He doubled it. I was wearing old cut-off sweat pants and a t-shirt. Still holding me, he must have struck me ten or twelve times. Mostly on my upper legs, but some on my lower. It left marks. I was yelling for him to stop and trying to get away. That only made him madder." Duane paused and looked at the curtains trembling from the drafty windows. "He yanked me to a stand, slapped me across the face and said, 'Next time I find you even close to another nigger, I'll take a ball bat to you.' He punched me in the gut and pushed me to the ground. He looked at Ralph and said, 'Boy, the same goes for you.'"

"That's horrible. What did you do? What did your mother say?"

"I went into the house. Dad and Ralph started doing something with the truck outside. I went up to my room, took off my cut-offs and crawled in bed. When Mom came back from dropping the food off at the launch site, she called for me. I told her I was sick. She must have noticed Shrimp was back with the kids. Mom was suspicious. She brought me some broth and toast, tried to question me, but I was afraid to tell her what really happened. Especially with Dad around."

Duane rested a moment before continuing. "That evening, I came down to use the bathroom. It hurt too much to try and put long pants on. Mom and Dad were in the living room, watching TV. I snuck down, used the john, and was on my way back up the stairs when I realized Mom was watching me from the doorway."

"She say anything?"

"Never. Later that night, I heard her yelling at Dad. Something about her leaving when I was better. He somehow found another job the next day and left for several weeks. We never left or talked about it, though that next morning, she brought some ointment along with my breakfast. I stayed in bed for two days."

"Why were you afraid to tell her? Oh, yeah. I bet you were afraid she'd take you and the two of you would leave with her travel money."

"That's right. Where would we go? How would we support ourselves? Dad inherited the farm."

"How were things between you and your father after he came back?"

"Cool. I don't know if they ever got back to normal for us. I started high school that fall and was involved in sports and activities. Mom and I were still good. I never told her about him beating me. Two years later, he started feeling poorly, wouldn't go to a doctor. He still went off to work, but I don't think he was doing much. Mom said he wasn't making as much money, but at least he could still work. She knew how to manage money. I started cutting firewood on weekends for a neighbor. We sold the wood to summer people. I got a third. Mom worked part time at the fabric shop. We were okay."

"Didn't both your parents die close together?"

"Yes, Dad died in early April before my high school graduation, and Mom died two weeks after my graduation. Dad went downhill my senior year. He was almost seventy when he died. Mom was diagnosed with pancreatic cancer two weeks before Dad died. She died two months after he did. It was a rough time. I was eighteen, on my own. Thankfully, we could lease out the eighty acres of tillable land which paid the taxes."

"Still, what did you do?"

"I already knew I wanted to go into forestry. I managed to get a job that summer with the state parks. I cleaned toilets, patrolled, checked people in and built some retaining walls. The next summer, I got on with the state forest division which eventually led me to the national forestry as an intern." Duane leaned his head back and rested a few minutes. "It took me six years to get my four-year degree. I couldn't always carry a full load of classes. By the time I graduated, I saw the need for forestry consultants, so I had some cards printed and talked with everyone I knew. I gradually built up a business that supported me and two families quite comfortably."

"What happened with Ralph after your father died? You mentioned he was distraught at the funeral."

Duane looked past her to the window, trying to decide what to say. "Ralph seemed to adopt me. Anytime I was at home, he wanted to be with me. Sometimes, he'd sleep here for several days. He seemed surprised when I told him this wasn't his home and he needed to return to his mother. By then, they moved into an apartment in town over a bar she managed. He got into a lot of trouble, fighting, being rude. It's crazy, but when he was with me, he was fine."

"Did you feel responsible for him? Bail him out when he got in trouble?"

"No, I tried hard to ignore his problems. I had enough going on in my life without adding his crap. The funny thing is, when we were together, we got along well. Especially when we were in the woods."

Duane rested again. "We both loved the woods. Once he was eighteen, I usually got him jobs with me or near me. When I started my own business, I was able to hire him frequently for work surveying the trees, marking them, and sometimes, cutting them. Coming back home, he seemed disappointed when I dropped him off at his mother's or eventually his own place."

"You've lived quite a life. Before I catch you up on the rest of my life, I notice the wind has dropped and it's not as drafty. Let me get some hot water and I'll give you a bath, one-quarter at a time."

Retha threw an old sleeping bag she found over the heater to warm it up as she prepared hot water, soap, washcloths, and towels. Duane half-dozed as she slipped each extremity out from the covers, but kept the warm sleeping bag loose over the part of him being washed. She hummed old hymns as she washed his scrawny body. When she finished, she covered him with another blanket, warmed from the heater. She patted his head. "You keep resting. I'm going to heat up some soup."

He roused up. "There's more. Go in my suitcase. There's an old envelope in the top half. It's a letter from Ralph, just before he got out of prison."

Chapter Twenty-seven

Dad got beat with a belt by his very own father? That's terrible. Because he was playing with a Black boy?

I'm glad I never knew that mean old man. Oh wait. Is that why Dad never took us places in public around here? If his father was dead, why would it matter after he died?

I still don't get why Dad keeps talking about Ralph. He sounds weird. Why was he in prison? Is Dad or Retha going to read the letter?

This is getting so confusing and Dad is getting so weak. I just want to hear him talk about us and why he didn't come to rescue Mommy and us twins. I mean, what happens if his stardust doesn't connect with mine?

Maybe it goes to his mommy and father. Yuck. I hope it doesn't connect with his father.

What happens to mean people's stardust? Do they have any?

Do only kids' stardust go to their parents right after they die? If so, that would mean mine and Dad's aren't going to connect.

Oh, God, he has to talk.

I have to know.

Please, Dad, please.

~ * ~

"I'll get the letter, dear."

Retha finished covering him up. She pulled the suitcase from the dining chair it rested on and felt around. It was a standard size envelope with Ralph Sims and a return address in care of the corrections department, the envelope addressed to Duane at his home. The envelope was open and appeared crinkled from years of handling. Several pages were crammed inside. Scrawled across the envelope and underlined were the words, 'You better read this.' The faded date stamp read, May 24, 1985, from Split Creek. She started to pull the letter out to lay it on the lap table, but seeing the fear in Duane's eyes, she moved the letter to the buffet. He's not ready yet, she thought.

In the kitchen, she put tomato soup on to heat. She mixed it with water because no fresh milk was left. No eggs, either. There was one can left of tomato, one of chicken noodle, and a jar of bouillon cubes. A can of hash, a half box of cold cereal, and a box of macaroni and cheese was all that remained on the shelf. The coffee can next to the maker was empty. A small packet of cheese crinkled up in aluminum foil was the only leftover remaining in the fridge.

Why hadn't she given Art a longer list? She knew why. Because she was counting on having a large order of food delivered from the grocery and didn't want to burden Art with her shopping. How stupid. Art wouldn't have cared how much shopping he needed to do for them. Now, with this blizzard raging, she realized how short-sighted she'd been.

She stepped to the corner of the kitchen and counted the pieces of wood. Fourteen left, maybe enough to get them through two more days. Maybe. Another short-sighted move on her part.

She eased the kitchen door open a crack and scanned the area. The snow drifted across the porch, tightly blocking the storm door. Snow was at least three feet high on the lee side of the shed, but drifts ran four to eight feet high. She thought it would take a large county or state snowplow to make it down Access Road and up their driveway. Her minivan was a slight bump next to the light pole.

Thank God, the wind has stopped. Maybe the end is over and I can get out of here in a day or so for supplies or someone can bring them on a snowmobile. Duane's not going to make it more than forty-eight hours, if that. How long after that can I last?

Retha pulled out her phone and tapped an email to Marci at End of Life Care. She checked the soup on the stove and turned the burner off as Marci called her.

"Retha, I just spoke with the sheriff's department up there. Reading between the lines, I'd say you might be in trouble, old friend.

The wind is coming back. A deputy told me nothing is moving in or out of the county and won't be. He's got your information and knows you've been in contact with them. 'Hold tight' is what he said. By the way, Riverside is totally shut down. Grocery stores are trying to stay open—if you can get to them. They're running out of essentials. It sounds even worse up there in the boonies."

Retha replied, "I'm not worried yet. It looks like we might be getting a break in the storm. I just wanted you to know my situation. I feel like a fool for not stocking up when I had the chance." She waited, sighed. "Actually, I feel like a bigger fool for not checking the weather app and planning ahead better."

"Oh, Retha. Don't be hard on yourself. You're dealing with a dying man in the middle of a once in a century blizzard. I'm sure God will provide. I'll be praying for you. That's all anyone can do right now."

"Guess so. Thank you. I'll keep you updated." She punched the end button. *Thoughts and prayers are always so dammed effective. What will be will be.*

She yanked open the woodstove door and threw two pieces of wood in, then checked that the sinks were dripping.

Taking a deep breath, she carried the two mugs of soup, plus hot tea, into the dining room. She roused Duane and slowly fed him.

He twisted and groaned. "Gonna have to increase the pain meds, but wait awhile. You got more talking to do and so do I." He finished his last spoon of soup and took several sips of tea. "You better get started. Sounds like the wind is raring up again, might be another long night. Is it snowing again?"

"No, the snowing stopped and I don't think it started up again, just the wind." She carried the dishes back to the kitchen, returned, and climbed back into her end of the bed. Where should she start?

"After leaving Granny's," Retha began, "I have no recollection of driving to Riverside. I had a second cousin there, and she took me in for several weeks. I was able to sign up for the hospital nursing program that started in the winter. I got a job at the hospital, which I was able to keep part time once classes started. Two and a half years later, I was a registered nurse and started in labor and delivery—midnights. I got my own apartment and slowly developed some friends, some queer, the others accepting of me being different. Not all realized I was queer. By then, we were starting to be called lesbians and gays."

Chapter Twenty-eight

Retha noticed Duane was falling asleep. She tucked the blankets around both of them, put her head back and decided to rest with him. She let her mind float.

Back then, she was afraid to contact Granny. Couldn't face the possibility of more rejection. Over time, she began to replay Granny's final words to her. The ones where she used the words, your kind. 'There was no life in Fair Haven for your kind.' Obviously, she knew about the rumors that began circulating about Retha since she discovered Western shirts and cowboy boots, and never dated. Retha always ignored the rumors, plain didn't give a damn.

As the years passed, she grew to understand that the sentiment about queer women in Fair Haven went deeper than she realized. How Granny had no choice but to push her away. It was to protect Ellie.

A queer woman trying to be involved in raising a child would not have gone well in their little tight-knit community. From Granny's words and attitude when she forced her to leave, Retha grew to think that Granny also recognized Naomi and Retha had a relationship, that both were queers. No way would Granny have allowed her granddaughter to be raised with inuendo and gossip from other children and their parents. Granny didn't care much what people thought of her and her friends, but Retha figured there was no way Granny wanted Ellie to start out life knowing her mother died in a fire and had been in a queer relationship with Retha.

Retha graduated nursing school in June 1960. Other than fellow students, work acquaintances, and several cousins, she had no one close to share the joy with.

That summer, Retha gathered her nerve and sent Granny a note. *Granny, I'm in Riverside. I just graduated from nursing school. I work nights in labor and delivery. Enclosed is five dollars. Please use it to buy something from you for Ellie, who can't be much of a baby now. Sincerely, Retha.* She included her address and phone number.

Retha considered it a tiny step in the right direction when the letter was not returned. In December, she sent another note. *Granny, Merry Christmas and Happy New Year to you and Ellie. Enclosed is ten dollars for gifts, clothes or whatever is needed. I am well, have my own apartment, work lots of hours in labor and delivery and am friends with a family who foster children. Best Wishes, Retha.*

She continued similar notes each year for Ellie's birthday, plus Christmas and New Year's, always including her address and phone number. By 1965, she was a licensed foster parent and taking in emergency placements of foster children. She started including brief information about the children in her notes.

In late September 1967, approaching the tenth anniversary of Naomi's death, she sent a note. *Granny, I know you will never forget this time of year, I know I never will. We both loved Ellie. I loved Naomi. She loved me. Would you use the enclosed money to buy flowers in her remembrance? Retha.*

Four weeks later, she received an envelope with a black and White photo of flowers sitting next to the urn on Granny's bookshelf. No note. Nothing on the back of the picture.

At Christmas time, Retha received a store-bought Christmas card. Inside was signed by Granny and Ellie, signed the way you do a stack of holiday cards. No note, but a wallet-sized school picture of Ellie fell out of the card. She picked up the picture and, after gazing at Ellie, she turned the picture over. There on the back, in a young person's neat handwriting, were the words *Ellie 6th grade.*

Retha wept. Ellie resembled her mother, but shared the obvious looks of how Retha remembered the child's father.

That's how the communication with Granny went for many years. Christmas cards exchanged both ways, a school photo in the fall, following Retha's sympathy note. Eventually, birthday cards began arriving in time for her birthday. No note, signed, Granny. It became obvious to Retha that Granny didn't want Ellie to know of her, but was willing to keep a distant connection going between the two of them.

In 1970, Retha was surprised to receive a photo of Ellie in her eighth-grade cap and gown, plus a copy of her straight A report card and perfect attendance record. Again, no card or note. Four years later, a similar photo of Ellie graduating from high school.

In June of 1976, Retha was shocked to receive a handwritten note from Granny.

Retha, thought you'd like to know, Ellie had twins a few weeks ago. Beula and Jimmy. She carried them full term and birthed 'em fast. She's livin with their daddy out in the woods. She always wanted to live out in the woods in the middle of nowhere. Crazy girl.

Anyway, he's a White guy, but a good one, 'cept he's still got some hang-ups about bein' seen in public with Black folk. Ellie's too independent to get married to anyone, even a black guy. But she loves him. I started to say somethin' to Ellie about making things legal. That girl is jist like her mama. She told me to never mind. So, I don't. They got things worked out and their babies are the cutest that's ever been borned. I don't think a license will ever make much difference.

I got that part about you and Naomi figured out. Long time ago. Someday, I want to tell Ellie about you and her mother. Not yet.

Bye,
Granny

Ellie got pregnant young, too. Just like her mother. Maybe two years makes more of a difference. At least her man is with her. A White man who doesn't want to be seen in public with her. That's concerning, Retha thought. Ellie's father could have passed for White. Now, she's with an all-White man. Is that a coincidence or what?

Not many White men catch on with Black women, move them into their house. Yet, Granny seems good with him. If she wasn't, she'd say so. She never minces her words or thoughts. If Granny's okay with him, I'm not going to worry about it. Not that it would change anything if I did get all stressed about it.

I wonder why Ellie didn't go on to college. Her grades were high.

Retha recalled thinking about Naomi. If Ellie was anything like her mother, Retha shouldn't be surprised that Ellie was walking her own path. Granny said Ellie got things worked out with her man. Sounds just like Naomi, and Granny, getting things worked out. Those two were alike in that manner. Maybe two years did make a big difference after all.

Naomi wasn't trying to get pregnant. She was simply trying to figure herself out and got caught. It didn't sound like Ellie was trying to figure herself out. It sounded like she already knew.

Retha waited several weeks before replying, partly, mostly, to make sure her emotions were under control. She was a grandmother to twins. What mixed feelings tore through her? She wanted to jump in the car and drive up to see them.

Grandkids.

Yet, Granny's words still echoed, 'Ellie's not your child, she's mine now.' For all these years, Retha was patient. Showing up now could blow the whole thing.

She replied, *Granny, what wonderful news. I am so happy for you, Ellie, her man, and the babies. I can only imagine what having grandchildren would be like. Foster parenting has been a great experience for me. I've had two brothers since they were six and seven. Last year, they graduated high school and are working in the G.M. plant in Riverside, dating and living on their own. So, maybe in a few years, I'll be a grandma. They have no communication with their biological parents, so I'm their mom. I keep telling them similar words you told Naomi, 'Don't go making no babies till you love the girl and it isn't just lust, AND you can support her and kids.' Other children—I've fostered nearly twenty—have spent a few nights to several years with me. Several keep in close touch. But no grandbabies yet. You are blessed!*

Love,

Retha

Several months later, Granny replied, *Retha, sorry to be so long in getting back to you. Twin grandbabies is busy with a capital B. They're*

*smiling and cooin' and wiggling all over. Jimmy's bout to turn hisself
over. Beula switchen her little self around in the crib, ya never know
which end she be at when you get her up. I'm so glad you raised kids.
Someday, I hope you get grands. I sure do hope that.*

    Love, Granny

Both began writing longer letters, Granny's usually about Ellie,
Duane and the twins. Sometimes about Fair Haven people who passed on
or were Naomi's and her age and their accomplishments.
Accomplishments usually taking place in other locales. Fair Haven was
mostly comprised of the elderly now.

Retha chatted more about her foster kids, the mature men they
were becoming.

As the years passed, both began mentioning the idea of getting
together. Granny once asked, 'Did ya ever meet someone of your kind
and fall in love again?' Retha explained she hadn't, though she did date a
few women for short periods of time.

On Mother's Day in May 1985, early evening, Retha answered
her phone.

"This is Granny. I jist figured it's time we start talkin' stead of
writin'. Whew. I'm bout wore out. Ellie and the twins just left. Duane left
a bit earlier. I tell ya, that Eula and Jimmy bout talked my arms off.
They're turning nine in a few days and telling me how they want me to
bake a birthday cake. I finally told 'em I'd bake two, they each wanted
too much different kinds of stuff on the tops."

Retha managed to choke out, "Oh, Granny, thanks for talking.
You sound wonderful. Are you in good health?"

"You sound good yerself. I'm doin' well. Ellie and me are gearing
up to start cleaning them White folks' summer cabins. More and more
folk been comin' up earlier every year. Used to be they all started
Memorial Day weekend. Now, some start comin' around Easter if there's
no snow. Why, we had to clean seven cabins this past week for folk
coming up for Mother's Day." Granny grew silent.

"Well, that's wonderful, I'm glad you're keeping busy."

"I think it's time we tell 'em about you. You and Naomi lovin'" each other so much. Maybe you should come up in a few weeks and meet them and we tell 'em."

Retha swallowed hard and wiped her eyes. "Granny, that sounds wonderful. I'd love to come up, but what brought this on so suddenly?"

"I've been thinking of this for years. I sent you away without Ellie because our community knowed you was a lezzie. Some even figured out Naomi was too. I can't remember who, but someone stayed in Detroit and saw you two with that baby." Granny paused. Retha heard the sounds of a pencil tapping wood. "News travels around here. You know that. Ain't no way you coulda helped raise a baby around here. Plus, wasn't no way I'd give my own grandchild up. Wasn't no way you'd of been accepted. In those years, things like that jist weren't done."

"I think I understand that better now…"

"And, girl, the reason I think it's time to get open about this is because times are changin'. A few weeks ago, all of us went to Chicago, and in the middle of the Aquarium—the twins called it the fish museum—there's this gay couple walking around, holding hands. They was by the big tank right in the middle, and one of them cuddles the other and says I love you, real soft. They weren't bein' loud or show offy. This Black older couple said something nasty to them." Granny paused. Retha thought she was sipping some coffee or tea. "Anyway, it hit me like a cement truck. They was in love just like my man and I was, just like Ellie and Duane are, and just like you and Naomi were. So, I shoved my way up to them, gave that couple one of my dirty-Granny looks and told the boys to pay them old folk no never mind. I also told them they were a damn cute couple."

Retha couldn't help laughing. "Granny, I can just see you doing that. I'm so glad you did. Queers, now they're calling us lesbians and gays. We were starting to be a little more accepted, now there's the AIDS situation and straight people are scared to death. Thank you for doing that. I wished I could have been there."

"Well, that night back in the motel room—it even had a pool inside—those kids were so excited. Anyhow, that night, we had us a conversation about girls loving girls and boys loving boys. Jimmy wanted to know how they could make babies. I told him it still took a man and a woman to start a baby, but anybody could raise them just like their own." Granny paused again. "So, that's what started this, and I figured, at my age, I wanted everything right between all of us. Ellie would love to have another grandmother for those twins."

"How…? When…?" Retha paused to swallow. "When did you want to get together?" Her voice was a whisper.

"Well, Memorial Day weekend is comin' up. You can stay at my place. What do ya think? This too soon?"

"No, no, it's not too soon. I just have to work that weekend, but I could come up the Wednesday after Memorial Day. I have four days off, would have to go back Sunday afternoon."

"Bet ya won't want to go to church with me either, will ya? Ellie's just like her mom, won't have nothing to do with church, says she finds more of God in them woods and in her kids. Can't say as I disagree with her. Don't know how much longer our little A.M.E. church can keep goin' anyway. Ain't nothing but old folk and some rent-a-minister who comes in to preach and bury us. Anyway, it will be good to see you on that Wednesday. I'm marking it down on my calendar right now. Let's see, that's Wednesday, May twenty-nineth. Bye."

Granny hung up the phone as Retha sat down, nearly in shock. Some things never change, and, at times, everything changes.

~ * ~

Retha felt Duane stirring and woke up to find him looking at her.

"I think we both fell asleep," he said. "It's still your time to talk."

"I know. Let me get us some tea." She edged off the bed. "Dang, it's cold. The wind picked up again."

She threw the sleeping bag on the heater, heated water in the kitchen and came back with the tea and cookies.

She placed the bag over the bed, pulled the table close and climbed in under the covers next to Duane. "You said we could be in bed together. Hope that means we can share body heat better this way." She pulled up the warm bag, then held the mug to his lips.

"Thank you. I don't want a cookie. Start talking, I'm getting weaker."

Retha set her mug down and slid both arms under the covers. It felt good to share body heat with someone when the wind was howling again, branches scratching at the windows and roof, and you both were about to share the most terrible day of your lives.

She told him of her life after she left Ellie with Granny, nursing school, delivering babies, taking in foster children. When she started talking about the note's she sent Granny and the years of gradual reconnection between them, she realized Duane was holding her left hand in both of his, giving her gentle squeezes. He squeezed her tighter when she told of her plans to come visit Granny on May 29th, 1985.

Chapter Twenty-nine

Monday, January 14, 2019

May twenty-nineth? The bad day? Retha was supposed to come visit Granny on that day?

Did she come?

Did Dad and Mommy know she was coming? They never said anything. Wait, they didn't know nothing about Retha. Granny must have been going to surprise them. We saw Granny several times over Memorial Day weekend, even took her hunting morels in the woods, and she didn't say a word about Retha coming up. Then what happened?

Dad looks very weak. He needs to start talking. I need to know before he dies. I don't know how long this stardust thing lasts and what happens if he dies and our stardust doesn't connect? I really need to know.

I'm so scared. Scared to not hear Dad and scared to hear him. I don't like being scared.

Every time Dad naps, Retha pulls out her little screen thing, only I heard her tell Dad it's an Eye-Pad. I don't get the name. She types on it. She quit looking and talking over it with the girls, his big ones. Dad said he didn't want them to see him as he shrunk and looked ugly. They cried.

Now Retha sends them something called emails. That must be what she types. Sometimes they're long types. She must be telling them everything they talk about and Dad says.

~ * ~

Duane shuddered. He squeezed Retha's hand tighter, as if he let go, he would fall into an abyss. "That day has haunted me. I nearly committed suicide over it. I didn't. I ran away and tried to start over. In some ways, outwardly, I succeeded. Inside, I failed."

He felt Retha stroking his lower arm, encouraging him to go on. "I have to start with Ralph. I might have trouble keeping it all straight."

"Just start someplace, it will all come out the way it was meant to."

"After Ralph went to prison in the U.P., he started to write me—short notes, asking about the woods, how my business was going, nothing personal. I'd reply. Sometimes I slipped a five-dollar bill in for his commissary expenses. When his frequency increased, I chose to answer only one a month, even skip a month." He rested a minute. "I was torn between how he treated Ellie and my knowing him all those years. For several years, I think we each wrote only once or twice. About a year before he was to get out—I didn't know the anticipated date—he began to increase the frequency, including more information about his life in prison, his pride in the flower gardens he worked on, how he was getting along with everyone."

Duane laid his head back. He motioned for a sip of water.

Retha held the straw to his lips.

He took several sips. Straightening up, he continued, "Also, he began writing more about Dad, or Pops. I responded infrequently, not wanting to encourage him or any relationship. In April 1985, he sent two notes. The first said he was being released May twenty-fourth. I responded with my surprise, wished him well, but stated I didn't think he should come around Split Creek because a lot of people remembered him. I said he should get a new start in another part of the state or stay in the U.P."

Duane waited till Retha could disentangle herself enough to get his tea mug off the table. He shook his head at the offer of the tea and a cookie. He waited as she nibbled at one. The smell made him hungry, but not for a cookie. "Do we have any chicken noodle soup? That sounds good right now."

"Let me warm some up on the stove. While that's heating, I'll dive my hands under the covers and change you."

He managed a smile, put his head back and rested as she went to the kitchen. While the soup heated, he heard her mutter as she fed the wood stove, but couldn't tell what she said.

The soup she spooned into him warmed his insides and refreshed his memory. Retha snuggled into the bed beside him and took his hands in hers.

"He ignored my response and sent another letter," Duane began again. "Ralph said he wanted me to pick him up, bring him back to the house, hire him and everything could be like the good old times."

"Oh, my. What did you do? Did he know you had Ellie and the twins?"

"I never spoke of the family. I knew it was too upsetting for him, though Ellie thought he knew she was pregnant. I think he couldn't imagine I would have an African American living with me, that I could truly love her and have kids." Duane swallowed hard. "I replied I had a family. One he probably wouldn't approve of. I said I could not pick him up, and he needed to find a new life elsewhere, to leave me in peace. I didn't want any further contact with him. I even told him I never wanted to see him again." Duane paused. "God, I was so naïve and ignorant."

Retha tightened her fingers around his, encouraging him to keep going.

Duane coughed, almost a sob. "He—he sent another letter, but I didn't open it till after…"

He cried. Couldn't stop, until after Retha put her arms around him and pulled him into a hug, his head against her shoulder, like a mother would a child.

"Take your time. Take your time," she murmured, rocking him.

At last, he quit sobbing. "That day, May twenty-nineth, I was planning to leave in the afternoon for a three-week stint in the Upper Peninsula. I wouldn't come home, but we talked of Ellie meeting me near the bridge for a weekend getaway. I was getting braver in venturing out to places as a family, just not around here." Duane twisted, trying to block out the pain, both the physical and emotional. "That morning, the kids were chattering about going morel mushroom hunting. Ellie was certain there were still some to be found because of the late rains. She planned to do some fishing while the kids played in the woods near the dock. About eleven, they packed themselves a lunch and hugged me goodbye. I told them I planned to leave about one."

"What did Ellie say or do?"

"She was the same. Gave me a sexy, hip-wiggling hug, kissed me. Told me I was going to miss out on sautéed morels and fresh fish for supper. She would leave any messages with Roberta and don't forget to call Granny before I left."

"Why call Granny?"

"It became the custom, I guess. Granny loved me calling her and telling her I would be gone and for how long. It was like checking in with your mother, you know? They always want to know what's going on. Plus, indirectly, it was a way of telling her to call and check on Ellie while I was away. Ellie never felt she needed to check in with Granny every day. She was so independent."

"So, did you call Granny?"

"I finished packing the trailer, checked for messages with Roberta, ate a sandwich and called Granny. She seemed extra excited, said a friend was coming back in her life and Ellie will have to tell me all about her. 'I know you'd love her, too. She could be another grandmother for the twins,' she said."

Retha moaned and loosened one hand to wipe her eyes.

Duane paused. "I never thought about who it could be. Now I know." He tried to turn his head to look at her.

"Just go on, keep talking, I'll be fine." Retha shifted till she could face him better.

"I jumped in the shower, and, and…" He sucked in a breath, then rushed to continue. "All at once, the twins were screaming through the bathroom window screen, 'Dad, come now. Mommy said to come get you. We think a man is being mean to her. Down at the dock.' Godammit, I wanted to yell, but didn't want the kids to hear me. I knew it could be only one person. Ralph. I wanted to kill the bastard."

"My God. What did you do?"

"I shouted for the kids to wait on the porch for me. I climbed out of the shower and managed to pull on a pair of sweatpants. It took forever, being wet and all. I put some slides on my feet, you know, the ones you wear at campground showers. I was going to grab the rifle, but didn't want to take the time to load it, so I ran to the cuckoo clock and grabbed Ellie's pistol. It was always kept loaded." Duane's body shook. "I put it in the pocket of my sweats, but had to pause to tighten the string so they would stay up. I didn't want to run with a loaded gun in my hand." His speech grew slower. "When I hit the porch, I realized the kids hadn't waited. I took off. I couldn't hear them, but they probably had three to four minutes of a head start on me. Plus, I kept tripping over the roots. It's a rough trail down to the lake. I fell several times, then kicked off the slides and went barefoot, which wasn't much faster."

Retha pulled him tighter and murmured, "There, there. Keep talking."

"I heard the kids scream. They were good little runners, had good shoes on and probably had at least five minutes on me. I tried to run faster. Still, it must have took me another ten minutes to get to the clearing." He shook his head, trying to stay focused. "Just before where the planks go across the muddy area is a big tree. I saw a rope hanging from a big limb. It was a noose. Did he hang Elly? She wasn't in sight. The kids had been quiet for some time. Just as I started to move toward the dock, something struck me across the back of my head. Hard. I dropped. Must have been out for four or five minutes. When I came to, Ralph stood over me with our worm-digging spade."

Duane nodded toward the soup and waited for Retha to spoon more into him, then a sip of tea.

"Go on," she whispered.

"Ralph was always a big man, only now he was bulked up. He must have lifted weights all those years in prison. He looked like a monster muscle-man you see in a circus. He put the spade against my throat. 'You didn't read my last letter, did you?' I shook my head as much as I could. I hadn't. It arrived the day before, Tuesday. I already told him I didn't want any more communication or to see him. When the letter came, I tossed it in with my clothes that I put in the camper." Duane broke into sobs again. "Why didn't I warn Ellie that Ralph was getting out of prison? They could have gone to Granny's."

Retha waited till he calmed down. "Why didn't you?"

"I—I didn't think he'd come back here. I'd told him not to. I didn't want to upset Ellie. Oh God, why was I so stupid? Why didn't I recall his hate for Ellie? Why did I think my telling him I didn't want to see him again would have any effect on him? She could have taken her switchblade." Duane broke down again.

Retha patted and hugged him. "That's all part of the guilt, isn't it? Now take a sip of tea and go on when you're ready."

Duane shuddered, sipped the tea, then continued. "Ralph lifted the spade, but kept it ready to use. 'Maybe if you'd read my letter, we would be having a different conversation. Now it's too late. You're going to end up like that Black wife and half-breed kids of yours. Dead. Only you're the one that's gonna hang. Your brats been under water for close to fifteen minutes. Your wife for thirty-five. No way they're alive. Get up. I want you to see them first.'" Duane put his head back to rest. "I got up, but kept my hands at my sides so he didn't notice the bulge from the gun."

Retha asked him if he wanted more to eat or drink, but he whispered no.

"Ralph walked behind me, one hand on my shoulder, and pushed me across the plank walk and onto the dock. 'Keep walking to the end,' he said. I saw a big pistol with a silencer lying on the boat seat. He stopped. I could tell he must have bent over to get his gun, so I pulled my pistol out of my pocket, but kept it in front of me. 'Take a good look,' he said, 'before I take you to where you're gonna die.' I glanced down long enough to make them out in the water. There was no way Ellie could be alive. Maybe the kids. I heard him take a step toward me. I turned and fired. The shot hit him in his left knee. He collapsed into the boat, but managed to get a shot off. It went high. His gun fell on the floor of the boat. I moved closer, aimed carefully, and fired a second shot into his heart."

Retha moaned and both began rocking together. Finally, she stopped them. "What happened next? Did you go back and look more?"

Duane waited a few minutes. "I kept thinking maybe the water was cold enough that the kids could still be alive. You know, those studies about cold water slowing down death."

"I know, but was the lake deep enough or the water cold enough?"

"I dropped the pistol on the dock and dove down to them. It was terrible. Weeds wrapping around them. Eight feet wasn't that deep. The water not very cold. The twins were tied together. I pulled on Jimmy, but couldn't get any leverage. The lake bottom was nothing but muck." Duane waited to catch his breath. "I swam to the top, took another breath, and dove down again. I could tell they were both dead. There was nothing I could do to save them."

Both were silent.

"I wanted to stay with them. Drown myself. But I had to get another breath. For some reason, I couldn't take in water and just die with them. I climbed back on the dock, picked up the pistol and ran." Duane slunk deeper into the bed, before continuing, "I panicked. I knew they were down there. I killed who killed them. Would I be blamed for all the deaths? My kids and their mother were dead. They were Black. I was White. My father's words kept echoing around my mind. I slipped and slid back up the trail, sometimes dropping to my knees to sob. Somewhere I lost Ellie's gun, but didn't return to look for it. I kept asking myself why I didn't let Ralph kill me, or drown myself. How was I going to tell Granny? What would I tell her? The guilt became too much. I decided to kill myself. I made it to the truck, backed the camper next to the barn, unhitched it and parked the truck in the barn and shut the big door."

"Oh my God, two times you dove down. No wonder you carry so much guilt. Now keep talking. Get it all out."

"I got a hose and ran it from the exhaust of the truck into the cab, jumped in and started the engine, but I forgot the rear sliding window was open and the barn was so drafty. By that time, I was thinking more rationally, or so I thought. Just like not drowning myself, I couldn't kill myself. I was a chickenshit. Escape became the only thing I could think of. Run. Hide. Start over." He paused to take several breaths. "No one other than Granny knew that Ellie lived with me. No neighbors. The closest one was five miles away and never came this way. If anyone knew or suspected, they never said a word to me." His voice grew softer, his words slower. "Ellie's driver's license still listed her address in Fair Haven, so did the kid's birth certificates'. Roberta knew, but she also knew I was going to be out of reach until I checked in late Thursday." Duane wriggled as he peed his diaper.

"Don't worry, we'll change it later. It's getting even colder in here. We only have two pieces of wood left. I was going to put them in later. I'll hang something over the door into the kitchen to keep the heat from the heater in this room."

"I'm not going to make it much longer. How are you going to survive?"

"I've always survived. I can communicate with my cell phone till they can plow in to get me."

"What about food? Is there enough for you to live on for several days?"

"Quit worrying about me. The sheriff thinks they can get some food out on a snowmobile when the wind drops. Now keep talking."

"I turned the engine off, got out and gathered some clothes out of the trailer and put them in Ellie's minivan in the shed. I went in the house and grabbed my bank books and cash, my business papers, the car title, and stuffed them in the van." He took a shallow breath. "Next, I poured gasoline inside and all around the barn, turned the trailer's propane tanks on, turned the trailer's range burners on, but didn't light them. I waited a few minutes, then threw a lit flare into the trailer and ran to the minivan. The trailer exploded as I drove out. That caught the barn on fire."

"Where did you go? Why? What did you think would happen about Ellie and the twins? And Ralph? What were you thinking?"

"I don't know what I was thinking. The only thing I knew was my father sitting on my shoulder, cursing me for loving a colored person. How embarrassing it would be to contact the police and tell them my Black common-law wife was dead. I wasn't thinking." Duane rested, gathering his strength. "I drove to Traverse City, paid cash for a motel, and the next morning, traded Ellie's van in. It was titled in my name. Got a good used pickup that had a camper on it, not a trailer. I kept thinking someone would come after me, or that I'd be arrested, but I wasn't. I drove over the Mackinaw Bridge and on to Houghton, which was close to my next job. There, I got an apartment, closed out my Split Creek bank accounts, opened new ones and informed my insurance agent of my new address. He also held the life insurance policies."

Duane closed his eyes and rested his head on the pillow for several minutes, before slowly continuing. "Previously, I bought a term policy of twenty thousand to cover Ellie and the twins with the beneficiary being Granny, and I held a ten thousand whole-life on Ellie for me. I figured Granny would tell the agent they died. He'd figure out to transfer the money for the whole life policy to my new bank. I canceled the answering service, canceled my business registration in my name, and registered a new similar business under the name of ABC Forestry Consultants."

"Hold on. What did Roberta say? She'd been with you a long time. It wasn't like she didn't know you or the family."

"I told her first thing to immediately cancel my number and not to take any messages for it. I told her if anyone asked or was trying to contact me that I was fine and starting over in the U.P. I also told her that if anyone asked her about my personal life to please say she was professional, never met me in person, and only dealt with me in business circumstances."

"Well, she must have. In the papers, she only referred to you as a business client who left the area to start a new business in the U.P."

"How do you know that?"

"That's part of my story, now finish yours."

"I spent the next year, trying to stay sober enough to work, waiting for someone to track me down. No one did. I think knowing I was starting over in the U.P. was enough for the authorities. I never changed my name. Used the same social security number. Filed my quarterly estimated taxes. I finally got my head on straight and spent the next years building my business. I had a lot of contacts, all wanted to do business with me under a new company name. I met Pamela. You know the rest."

He waited for Retha to respond. She didn't know the rest.

He fumbled around under the covers till she asked him what he needed. "Could you read Ralph's letter? I feel like I want to go to sleep soon. Need to get this over."

Chapter Thirty

WOW. Dad did come down to save us. He even dove in the yucky water to save us, but we were already dead. The last thing I remember is the weeds wrapping around us as we went down.

Why didn't our stardust know Dad came down and pulled on Jimmy? Does stardust take a few minutes to start working? Does it take an hour?

Maybe stardust takes longer under water to start up. I think it was the next day before I finally understood Mommy and Jimmy wanted me to go back to the house. It seemed awfully hard to get out of the water.

I wonder, if me and Jimmy waited on the porch for Dad, would we still be alive? Wait, Ralph had a gun, too. I just remembered. It was a big pistol and it was laying on a seat in the boat. He wasn't carrying it. So even if we came down with Dad, he could have shot us.

I'm so glad Dad did try to save us. Now, at least I know that much. I just wish my stardust knew Dad tried. I wouldn't have been wondering all this time. Yeah, but what if he died with us, or in the barn? Is it selfish to wish he did that? Then he would have been with us all this time. Except his two other girls wouldn't have been born and that would have been sad, too. They're nice and my half-sisters. This is all so complicated. I think I'm just glad Dad is here and I got to learn all this.

What's in Ralph's letter? I hope Dad stays awake long enough to hear it, though he's probably read it.

Dad and I need to hear Retha's story, too.

~ * ~

Retha got out of the bed, poked around, then crawled back in, holding Ralph's letter and several newspaper clippings. "After I read

Ralph's, I'll share these clippings as part of my story." She elbowed him. "Stay awake, you can't pass out on me yet. You have to know everything."

The envelope's return address was in Houghton, Michigan, the prison's, yet the postmark was Friday, May 24, 1985, from Split Creek. Scrawled across the envelope were the words, YOU MUST READ THIS!

Retha began reading.

Jerkface, You said you didn't want contact with me anymore, but you damn well better read this. I should of told you this shit sooner, but DAD was a lot like you. A big chicken shit about who he loved. Did you get the DAD? He's MY DAD, too. DAD had TWO families. You were in the legal one, I was in the illegal one. So, here's some background. I'll know if you don't read this to the end. Keep reading, it might save your life and your half-breed family's.

Duane sniffled. "I should have read this. I just, just had no idea…And if I had, none of this would have happened."

"Shh, we don't know that. I'm thinking Ralph wasn't going to be happy till he had you to himself as a brother. At his size, even Ellie's switchblade wouldn't have helped her. Now keep quiet."

DAD met my ma when she was working at a bar over near Tawas. A sawmill was there he worked at a lot. He may have acted good around your mom, but he didn't when he was gone. For some reason, my ma liked him and he began staying with her in the apartment over the bar. She was the manager. She knew all about your mom and knew she would never have him to herself, plus he worked other places around the state. When Ma got pregnant with me, she was worried she might lose her job. What owner wants a pregnant bartender and manager? DAD bought the bar so she could keep managing. It was in both their names.

About the time I turned seven, the business failed, so DAD moved us into that crapass shack near you guys. I was thrilled to be with him even more. Plus, you didn't know it, but many times, he took Ma and me with him to where he was working, so I got to be with him even more than you. I think he started taking us after your mom said I was too damn rowdy to be around her when he was gone.

Later, Mom and me moved into town and she managed a bar there. All those years, he kept saying he would tell your mom about me, confess it, beg forgiveness, so he could be honest that I was his son and quit hiding it. He never did. That's why I was so upset at the funeral home. He had TWO sons who loved him. TWO sons who loved the woods because of him. But only ONE son inherited anything. Only ONE son kept the farm and house. Only ONE son got into a good business. Even worse, I LOVED YOU. Not as a fucking queer, but as a brother. I know I was a terror, but part of that was because I couldn't be who I wanted to be, HIS SON AND YOUR BROTHER! After a job, it killed me every time you dropped me off at Ma's or my crappy apartment and you went to the farmhouse.

Did you know his will stated to split his inheritance between his TWO sons? It said that if he died before your mother, she got everything, but if she died before him, everything was to be split between you and me. But he died first and your mom wrote her will to just you. That's another reason I was so upset.

The other thing that killed me was you being a nigger lover. I know it was your mother's influence. I know she had DAD by the balls, that she'd leave him if he fought or drank or said anything against the goddamn Blacks. I wished he would have said something and she left. 'Cept you'd have gone with her and I wouldn't have a brother. I wanted BOTH DAD AND YOU. TOGETHER. I was glad when your mother died. Maybe then we could be almost like regular brothers, but I was afraid to go against DAD's words. The last thing he told me was that he loved me, but I couldn't say anything to anybody till after Ma died.

GUESS WHAT? She died last year, there was an obit and YOU never mentioned you saw it or gave me sympathies. You knew who she was all these years. She never was mean to your face. You acted like she didn't exist, that you just accepted me because DAD did. Now, out in the woods, well, that was different. Most of that time, it felt like we were brothers, talking wood stuff, and nature things, playing games, you teaching me about tree growth and forest management and logging. I loved being with you. I hated getting dropped off at my place, especially when I knew you had two more bedrooms in that old house and part of it should have belonged to me.

Anyway, you weren't there to pick me up from prison, so I hitchhiked all the way home. A fun experience when it's before a holiday weekend and nobody wants to pick up hitchhikers around a prison town, and you hope that once you get away from there, other people don't realize your blue jeans and blue shirt and white sox and black shoes are prison-issued. But I made it home. My old place was still there and I got Ma's old car running again. I went out to the graveyard and talked with DAD. I told him I was going to have a talk with you.

I made several runs by your place and could tell you had someone living with you. I was pretty sure it was that same light-skinned bitch who shot over my head and told me to never come back. I parked down the road and walked the trails toward the house and saw them two kids and her afore you got home. I went back and mailed you this letter today, Friday.

Here's the deal. I figure you're going to be home and not leaving till Wednesday. I'm going to be at Johnny's Bar on Grassy Lakes Road on the edge of town. I'll be there Sunday, Monday, that's Memorial Day, and Tuesday, that's the twenty-eighth, at the same times, from five to nine. In case you don't get this letter Saturday, you'll get it Tuesday. Still enough time to come visit me fifteen minutes away. I'm sure your sweet little BLACK babies' mama will let you sneak away, even though you rarely leave the house and I'll bet never together with her. You're such a chicken shit. If you loved that woman so much, why would you never admit it? Ma said she never saw the two of you together in town. One or the other, never together. She knew. She thought you were stupid to fall for a Black, but also a chicken shit not to admit it. Your mother really screwed you up. Mine didn't me. She and DAD were on the same wavelength when it came to race shit. Keep them separated. Even the Bible says that, asshole.

I'm not drinking anymore, so I'm writing this sober and I'll be sober when we meet. The first thing we're going to talk about is selling the farm and splitting the funds half and half. The farm came from DAD's father and had nothing to do with your mother. It's ours. Now let's split it up.

We do this and I'll leave the area and never bother you again.

You choose not to meet with me and I'll get the farm after you and your milk chocolate family's death, which will come soon. Very soon. I ain't waiting around. You see, DAD's name is on my birth certificate. HIS will said HIS sons, I'm one of his sons and can prove it even if your mom wrote her will to just you.

Don't worry, no one will ever guess I'm the one who offed you guys. Trust me, I learned a bunch of shit in the slammer. The woman and kids will be in the lake, all bound together and you'll be swinging from a tree. Murder and suicide, front page of the County Press and everyone will know what you really are.

Your move, asshole

"This is horrible," Retha said. "When did you receive this? The Saturday or Tuesday?"

"It could have been Saturday. I couldn't remember if anyone checked the box. We get so little mail and I wasn't expecting any contracts or payments. Definitely Tuesday, but I was done communicating with him. I didn't want him in my life. I was so naïve and stupid. And stubborn. Still, I had no idea he would do this. Oh God, I should have opened it. We all could have left." Duane sighed, exhausted. He went on, now mumbling, "The will? I never knew Mom's was different than the one Dad left. When she read Dad's will, she must have realized Dad had two families. She wrote her will, leaving the farm only to me. She went downhill so rapidly, we didn't have time to talk about much, and I was so busy with graduating and lining up a job… Can I sleep now? I'll just nap."

~ * ~

No, keep him awake. I'm afraid he'll die and I still won't know some things.

Oh, wait. Retha said she's going to read these little newspaper pieces she has in her hand, then Dad can nap. I think she's not sure how long Dad will live, too.

Chapter Thirty-one

Retha folded Ralph's letter and put it back in its envelope. She had a ton of questions she wanted to ask, but decided she would read the news release to Duane, then let him rest. She checked his pulse and blood pressure, listened to his heart and lungs. He was a good twenty-four to forty-eight hours from dying, but would probably go into a coma first.

Split Creek County Press
Friday, May 31, 1985 Weekend edition
Officials Confused by Fire and Drownings
On Wednesday, May 29 at 1:30 p.m., area fire departments were called to a burning barn on Access Road, just north of where Grassy Lakes Road curves west again.

The fire was fully involved, including an older recreation vehicle parked next to it. According to officials, the hay and an older pickup parked inside contributed to the intensity of the inferno.

"We were concerned when we saw the truck that someone might be in it," Split Creek Fire Chief, Jody Nelson, said, "but when we finally got the place cooled down enough, we determined no one was in it. It was definitely arson. The boys first on the scene could smell gasoline and a five-gallon can was found near the trailer. It went up fast and burned down fast. Thankfully, there wasn't much hay inside or it might still be burning."

Property records show that Duane Gleason owns the property, but he was not at home. Later inquiries led to his answering service, owned by Roberta Kincaide, who said he contacted her about twelve thirty p.m. to state that he was leaving for the Upper Peninsula.

Gleason is a forestry consultant who travels around the state and Midwest.

Ms. Kincaide had no explanation why his truck and trailer would be in the fire.

"Maybe he bought something new," she said. "He'd been complaining about his rig getting old. I can't imagine him firing his old rig. He always seemed like an upright business man to me. Of course, we never met in person, just taking and giving messages."

The fire departments from Split Creek, Lakeside Township, and Marquette Township assisted. The firemen allowed the fire to burn down, but kept it from spreading to the shed and nearby farmhouse.

Chief Nelson said they had the fire out by seven thirty p.m., but he kept one member on duty in case of a flare-up.

The Chief could not state how long the fireman remained that night, only that there were no flare-ups when emergency personnel returned to the area again at nine p.m., on another call. This one a murder by drowning.

Retha quit reading. Duane was lightly snoring. "Young man, looks like you couldn't wait for your nap. Sleep away. I need to use the facility anyway."

She slipped out of bed and trotted to the bathroom. No water dripped in the sink, none flowed when she flushed the toilet. She caught a whiff of gas and turned the water heater to off.

In the kitchen, she relit the pilot on the range. What would have caused it to go out? Why did it seem so weak?

She rummaged around till she found a hammer and several nails. She gathered the half-filled tea kettle, some tea bags, the remaining cookies, a box of saltines and carried them to the dining room. After setting the pot on the heater, she went into the bedroom and pulled the last blanket from the closet and nailed it over the archway between the dining room and kitchen.

"Duane, we're in a bit of a jam. Well, I am. The water pipes are frozen. We're out of firewood. I used the last two pieces. There's just some coals left. If I can keep the pilot lit on the range, I can heat up some soup, but need some water. Maybe I can melt some snow. Let's see how desperate we get."

She didn't mention they were nearly out of food. Why worry him? She heard on the radio that the intermittent high winds made it impossible for people to go far with snowmobiles. Not seventeen miles from town to here.

She pulled another pair of socks on, wrapped a scarf around her head and slid back into bed. She was already wearing long underwear under her jeans and cowboy shirt, plus a sweatshirt and sweat pants. Her winter parka laid across the end of the bed, it helped keep their feet warm. Duane continued to breathe regularly.

~ * ~

Dad just fell back to sleep, but Retha seems to think it's all right. She checked him all over and kissed him on the cheek. I think if he was dying, she'd be doing different things. I don't know what, but she doesn't seem surprised or sad yet.

She just got out of bed, and it looked like she was taking pictures of Ralph's letter and those newspaper pieces with her Eye-Pad. What else can you do with those things? Now she's typing and typing on it in the bed.

I can tell you what happened that day. I now know Dad did come to try to save us, but it was too late. Here's what happened.

Jimmy and me ran back down the trail as fast as we could. It's still a long way, and when we got back to the dock, no one was around.

It was quiet.

We stood at the beginning of the dock and yelled for Mommy. Jimmy started running toward the end. I waited a second, then started after him.

The boat was hooked to the second section. You couldn't see it from shore because the brush came right up to dock on both sides of the first section.

All at once, as soon as I was past the boat, this big man—now I know it was Ralph—jumped on the dock from the boat and grabbed me.

I saw a gun—a pistol, but bigger than Mom's—on the seat of the boat. He was huge and strong.

I screamed, but he wrapped a rag or something around my mouth and tied it in the back and I was gagging. He tied my arms behind my back with those plastic tie things, next my knees, then my ankles.

It happened so fast.

Jimmy ran back and started beating on him. Jimmy couldn't get past Ralph to go for help. All at once, he had Jimmy tied up just like me.

He dragged us to the end of the dock where one of our boat anchors and some rope was. We helped Dad make the anchors out of coffee cans and cement and a metal loop thing the rope went through. It was so much fun. We made a bunch of them one year.

He wrapped us up together with the rope and kicked us over the edge into the water. His kick hurt, too. The anchor pulled us down. Dad used to say it was eight feet deep there, but who knew with all the weeds.

It was horrible. We could see Mommy lying down in the weeds, her eyes were open, but we could tell she couldn't see us. She was dead.

We started gagging and choking in the water, wiggling around, staring at each other and Mommy, trying to wiggle and fight, but we were tied too tight. We blacked out and ended up next to Mom.

I don't know how much longer—maybe it was morning—but somehow, I knew we were together, and Mommy and Jimmy somehow were telling me to go to the house to wait for Dad. It took a while because it seemed so hard to move through the water. I think stardust has a hard time getting out of water.

Maybe Mommy thought Dad would be joining us at the bottom of the lake. Anyway, we were all dead, but our stardust could signal things to each other. At least for a while.

I wonder if Dad's stardust will be able to signal right away. Sure hope so.

Chapter Thirty-two

Tuesday, January 15, 2019

Duane woke to find Retha's head on his shoulder, her hands grasping his. He squeezed her hands and felt her response. He remembered the news article he fell asleep to last night.

She sat up in the bed. "Good morning. Guess I better get back to reading." She picked up a paper from the table. "This is the next part of the article."

He nodded and squeezed again. He wasn't going to last much longer. He listened as she read.

Murder by Drowning
Wednesday, May 29, 1985
At eight p.m., the Split Creek Sheriff's Department received a call of bodies in a remote bay of Big Grassy Lake, accessible only by foot off of Access Road, across from the home of Duane Gleason, whose barn burned that afternoon.

Deputy Chet Hanson stated he met the caller in the driveway of Gleason's home, Ms. Retha McBride of Riverside, but formerly from Fair Haven. She led the officer through the woods, part of the national forest, to a rudimentary dock. At the end of the dock, lying in approximately eight feet of water, were three bodies. Officer Hanson called for help to recover the bodies. They were taken to the county morgue.

The bodies were later identified as Ms. Ellie Bryant, twenty-nine, and her twin children, Beula and Jimmy, nine. The family resided in Fair Haven with Miss Bryant's grandmother, Mrs. Beula Bryant.

Ms. McBride stated that when the family didn't return from a fishing outing, Mrs. Bryant asked her to search for them.

"They loved spending time in the woods and fishing," Ms. McBride said. "Some time ago, they discovered this fishing site and apparently were given permission to fish there by the man who built the docks. I checked the canoe access area, sometimes they go there too, then I checked down this trail.

"Granny, that's Mrs. Bryant, mentioned they sometimes go there, but she wasn't sure of the location, other than it was off Access Road, close to the old farm house and big pine tree."

When questioned why they didn't involve the police sooner in the search, Ms. McBride replied, "Ellie was very independent, but usually returned to her grandmothers' by seven p.m. or so. We weren't worried till then. This is so tragic.

"I haven't seen Ellie since she was a toddler and I came up to visit the family, only to be involved in finding their bodies. Granny would have come, too, but she sprained her ankle last night and isn't very mobile. She raised Ellie after Ellie's mother died in a Detroit fire."

When asked if she knew Duane Gleason, Ms. McBride said, "I never met him. Granny knew of him because his mother and her attended school events and concerts back in the 1960's, when Fair Haven was operating. His mother died young, as I understand it. That's the only connection I know of."

This reporter asked Sheriff Haines if they considered Duane Gleason a suspect in either the fire or the murders. "The fire looks like arson, but who knows why? I might consider him a person of interest if he shows up and demands an insurance payment real quick, but we're not sure he even had insurance on the barn. We'll be checking into that.

"I tend to think he left for the U.P. to do his work, and someone had a grudge against him. We heard several rumors that an area man, recently released from prison, was doing some barroom talk against Mr. Gleason.

"In terms of these murders/drowning's, we have little to suspect a connection between Mr. Gleason and Ms. Bryant and the children. First, they're of different races.

"Even if he gave them permission to fish, it sounds odd. He had to know he built that dock on national forest property. Why would he give strangers permission to fish on it?

"Second, the same guy we're interested in has a history of attacking black women. I think if we find him, we might solve two crimes.

"Believe me, we will be looking for him."

A spokesperson for the National Forest issued a written statement. 'We do not give permission for private citizens to build docks on public land. However, given our vast amount of forests, it may happen from time to time. In no way did we give Mr. Gleason permission to build that dock or for others to fish there.'

Duane sniffled. "So that's why they never came looking for me. They knew Ralph was back in the area. I also didn't have insurance on the barn. I did on my vehicles, but not comprehensive, nothing to replace them."

He squeezed Retha's hands. "What else do you have? Anything about finding Ralph's body or our gun?"

"Apparently, they never found his body."

"I don't understand. How could they have missed it? He was right in the boat." Duane shuddered.

Retha pulled her hand out from under the blankets and cupped his chin, turning his face toward hers. "Calm down, calm down. I made sure they wouldn't find it for a long time, if ever."

"You what? I'm really feeling pain, but maybe that will keep me awake long enough to listen to your end of the story. After that, I think it's time to start the morphine. Give me a lot, if you want."

She patted his cheek. "I agree it's time to start the morphine. I'll give you just enough so you're not in pain. I won't give you enough to kill you. With me, death has to take its natural course. You will most likely slip into a coma and fade away."

"Yeah, my death isn't far away, but can you survive? There can't be much food left. I'm guessing the water's frozen, and you're out of wood." He gave her a slight nudge. "Besides, you're not old enough to die."

Retha chuckled. "Duane, I might be. I just might be. I emailed the sheriff department about us. They replied that it could take several days to get to us. Access Road is filled level where it meets Grassy Lakes Road and the curve is as well. They have to bring in those snow blower trucks."

She pulled her hand away from his face and stretched. "He asked about a helicopter. I told him not to waste their money. He said they're asking local residents with snowmobiles to help and will put out our address as an emergency, but can't guarantee anything till the winds die down."

She climbed out of the bed and pulled the blankets tighter around him. "Don't worry about me, when it's my time, it's my time. Plus, I am old enough. Now be quiet and listen, then I'll give you a shot."

Chapter Thirty-three

I think Dad's gonna die soon.

What will it look like?

Where will our stardust meet up, if his still works? If it doesn't, what will happen to me?

Where will I go next?

Yikes. The electricity just went out. Retha told Dad. She went out to the kitchen and came back with a flashlight and a camping lantern. She told Dad she would use them when she needed to give him a shot or help him, but they could still talk in the dark.

Being in the dark doesn't bother me. I've been here forever without lights. I don't want to miss Dad when he dies.

I probably couldn't see his stardust anyway.

Nobody can see mine.

~ * ~

Retha cranked the thermostat on the heater as high as it would go. Without electricity, there was no fan to circulate the warm air. They were now dependent upon just the radiant heat. *Thank god these old heaters don't have electronic thermostats. At least I can crank the flame to high.*

Climbing back into the bed, she realized her future was even more dire. She gathered herself. First things first. Duane needed to hear her story about that horrible day as much as she needed to tell it. She snuggled her head against his chest, partly so he could better hear her and partly to share body heat. Could she stay warm if or when he died? She pushed that thought away and began.

"I arrived at Granny's that Wednesday, just before noon. She was trying to hobble around, using two canes, and fix lunch. I made her sit, iced the ankle and finished preparing the food. It did feel awkward after all those years, but I think the fact she was dependent on me—her age, my age—and my maturity somehow eased the tension for both of us."

Duane's hand lightly squeezed hers. He was getting weaker.

"I was there when you called her and said you were leaving, that Ellie and the twins were looking for morels, that Ellie planned to fish. I rechecked Granny's ankle and told her she needed a new stretch-wrapping and crutches. She agreed to let me take her into town to the drugstore and get them."

Retha paused to think a moment. "We stopped at the grocery store. She got all ticked off when I insisted on paying for the food. You know how she was, always doing for others, but not wanting others to do for her." She felt Duane's weak chuckle. "While I was fixing supper, about five-thirty, she tried calling your house, but got no answer. I could tell she was worried. 'She's always back by this time, and I wanted to tell her a little about you,' she said."

Retha thought through the sequence of events. "After we ate, she tried again, but no answer. She tried to get up to wash the dishes, but forgot to use the crutches and twisted her ankle again. Not bad, just enough that I convinced her to let me put more ice on it, more wrap and to stay in her chair while I did the dishes. When I finished them, she told me your number and I tried, but no answer."

Retha stretched. She patted Duane as if to keep him awake. "About that time, Granny turned the radio on for local news and heard there was a barn fire at your place, but no one seemed to be home. That worried her even more. 'How could there be a barn fire and no one around?' she asked. 'I can understand why Duane wasn't there. I want to know where Ellie and the kids are? Doesn't make sense.' She freaked out when the announcer also said Ralph Sims was out on parole and back home, promising to lead a new life."

Duane squirmed.

Retha nudged him not to talk yet. "'Oh my God,' Granny kept saying. 'Oh my God. He threatened to kill Ellie once and now he's back in town?' She wanted to head out right then, but was in a lot of pain. I suggested we contact the police, but she was hesitant. Said something about you and Ellie keeping your relationship quiet and not wanting you to get embarrassed, though she did say she thought you were starting to grow out of that phase of your life."

Retha felt Duane tighten. She squeezed him till he relaxed. "So, I got directions and told her I would go check. That's when she told me about the trails down to the dock. Granny also said to check the canoe access area. 'It stayin' light so long now, maybe they're just hangin' down there, havin' fun and don't even know about the fire, though I don't see how.'"

Retha took several big breaths. "By now, I was worried. Nothing made sense. I had some understanding you and Ellie led separate lives when it came to being seen in public together and that, legally, Ellie still lived at Granny's, but like I said, nothing made sense. If there was a fire, why didn't Ellie and the twins come over to Granny's? The barn burning would have been quite emotional for them."

"What did you do?" Duane spoke so softly; she felt his words more than heard them.

"Driving out, I passed several fire engines and a number of cars returning from the fire. Near your house, I could see two fire engines looking like they were getting ready to pull out, and several cars. A police officer stopped me and asked what I was doing in the area. I told him I was looking for friends who might be fishing down by the access. He waved me on."

Retha wriggled a hand out from under the blankets to grab her mug of barely warm tea. She held it to Duane's lips, but he shook his head.

After taking several sips, she continued, "I drove on to the access area. I think I might have been there once or twice as a teenager, roaming around with Naomi. No one was around. I slowly drove back. Before the house, I pulled over when I spotted the trail going down toward the bay. I had this terrible foreboding something was wrong."

Retha held her hand to Duane's heart and patted him. "It was so silent after I heard the fire engines leave. Even the birds weren't chattering. That trail is not an easy one to walk, especially the first time, when the sun is so bright as it gets lower. Just before the clearing, I saw a gun, that pistol I showed you. Now I know it was Ellie's. I didn't pick it up. Thought I might need to show it to the police. Across the clearing, I noticed something and stepped over to see a spilled bag of morels. When I looked up, I saw a rope hanging from a limb on the back side of a large tree. Like a noose. Like a lynching."

Retha felt Duane's shudder.

"That was for me," he croaked. "Ralph planned to take me at gun point and hang me to make it look like a murder/suicide."

"I know, dear, I know. He was your brother. Now save your words." She pulled the bedding even tighter around them. Radiant heat wasn't very good without a blower. "I was scared. I almost wanted to run back to the car and call the sheriff's office, but I wanted to know the full story. I was partway down the dock when I saw this body in the little boat. It was a huge man—"

"Ralph," whispered Duane.

"I looked at him. Could tell he'd been shot in the leg and the heart. I spent a few shifts in the E.R. Enough to tell bullet holes. These ones were small compared to some I'd seen." She gathered herself. "I walked to the end of the dock. There was a breeze blowing from the left to right. It took me a few moments before I could see them in the weeds. I might have missed them, but I saw the white of an anchor, the cement. Next to the white was a hand. I could then follow the shadows and outlines. I saw the other anchor and could tell there were three bodies."

Retha swiped at her eyes, then Duane's. "I had to sit down before I fainted. It took me a few minutes to realize Ralph must have killed them. I wasn't sure if he shot them first or not, but could tell he intended for them to stay down in the water. Who shot Ralph, I wasn't sure, but I knew it was with the small pistol—"

"A twenty-two."

"I wasn't sure whose it was, but somehow knew you might be blamed and I was positive you wouldn't kill your own family. I decided my daughter and grandkids didn't need to be remembered with their killer. I climbed in the boat, grabbed the gun, laid it on the dock, tied two more anchors around Ralph's legs, pulled the drain plug on the boat, got back out and used an oar to push the boat past the end of the dock. I threw the oars in the lake. The breeze started pushing the boat and loose oars to the North. Slowly. When the boat was about thirty feet out, I got the pistol and emptied it, shot all the bullets at the boat. Most of them hit. It took about fifteen minutes for it to fill and sink. The oars drifted toward the other side."

Duane moaned. "Why? Why did you sink the boat?"

"Because everything I heard about you from Granny was good. In spite of your fears about being seen in a mixed-race relationship, I knew you loved your family and would never do anything to hurt them. I had no idea why Ralph would want to kill them or who killed him." She paused. "I kept Ralph's gun and I picked up the small pistol. I also took the rope down and hid it in the woods. I hid the guns in my trunk and drove my car into the driveway. Someone was sleeping in a car by the shed."

She felt Duane moving, trying to talk and shook her head at him. "No one else was around. I figured the man asleep was to guard against the fire starting up again. There were still some embers smoldering. I went inside the house and walked around. I noticed the side panel of the Cuckoo Clock was open. There was a box of twenty-two shells in there and no clock mechanism, so I knew the little pistol would fit in there as well."

She rearranged their blankets, murmuring for Duane to not talk. "A switchblade was in there, too. I used the phone, called the police about the bodies in the lake. While I was waiting, I took the three carvings, and the photos off the wall, put them in a paper shopping bag and put them in my trunk. I waited on the porch till the police came. The guard was still sleeping. He woke up fast when the police came whipping in. Later, I threw Ralph's gun in Granny's lake."

Retha paused long enough to control her memories of that horrible day. "I explained to the police that my friend, Granny, asked me to come looking for Ellie. How they liked coming over here to explore the woods and fish. How worried Granny was when they didn't come home before dinnertime. Just like the newspaper said." She patted Duane's hand. "Other than Ralph, they couldn't make a connection with you or anyone else about a black woman and her kids being murdered right after a fire. 'Coincidence, what a weird coincidence,' the officer said. I agreed. Said I knew nothing about the barn fire and never met the owner. Which was true."

Duane wriggled as if he wanted to say something.

Retha patted his leg for him to stay quiet. "See, the police didn't even look inside the house. I didn't suggest they do so. It was obvious to me a family lived there. They asked a few more questions, said they sent someone out to get Granny's story, which matched mine. They already heard Ralph was back in the area."

Duane was rocking as much as a dying man could. "I'm so sorry. Granny, I'm sorry. Forgive me, Granny. I loved them. I loved you." His words could barely escape his lips. His head leaned against Retha's. "Thank you. I want a shot. The pain is bad. What happened to Granny?"

"Granny had a fatal heart attack three days later. We buried them all at the same time. You saw where." Retha grasped him tighter. "I'm so sorry, but I'm so glad you talked, told all this out loud, cleared your mind and heart. It's okay to be sad. Even if you read Ralph's letter and the family went to Granny's, somehow, you'd all be dead. He'd have found another way."

"That would have been better."

"Really? Yes, you lived with guilt for being afraid of what others thought, based on your father's influence and for not opening Ralph's letter, but what else did you do? You raised two more beautiful children. They love you. I emailed them earlier today that I expected you to die soon, that we may not be able to contact them. I also told them nearly everything about you that we've discussed. Now they know who their father is."

She nudged him with her elbow. "Guess what? They still love you. Duane, they know the story—your story. They want you to go in peace."

She quit talking. He needed morphine, but she wanted him to be able to express anything else while he still could.

He seemed to rest, quiet, not shuddering, still warm. After ten minutes, he whispered, "Do you think they know I love them, too?"

"Absolutely."

"Good. I do." He paused long enough that Retha looked up to see if he fell asleep. "I'm ready for the shot. If I don't wake up, thank you. I love you."

Retha prepared the shot by flashlight and administered it. "Bye, sweet man."

"How old are you? You can tell me. I won't tell." He tried to smile.

"Ladies don't tell their age." Retha slipped under the covers with him and wrapped herself around him as much as possible. "I'm eighty-three, you old fool."

She dozed off as his breathing slowed. His heart kept a regular beat. When she awoke, he was still breathing, but she figured most likely he was in a coma. She checked her iPad, but realized it needed charging.

I'm in dire straits. If snowmobilers don't get to me soon, I'll be gone as well.

Somehow, that seemed all right. Eighty-three, a good age to die. Today.

Or tomorrow.

Or the next.

Whenever.

She went back to sleep, holding a dying man, not sure how long she could live without food in an almost freezing house.

Wednesday, January 16, 2019

Retha awoke shortly before eight in the morning. She shivered. Her teeth chattered.

Why does it feel as if the heat is gone? Duane is cold, too. Bet he's gone. He's more than cold. Wish I could stop this shivering. I'm chattering so bad. I can't even reach my tea on the table, inches away.

She forced herself to stretch under the covers. *It's so silent. No heater fan. No sounds of the burner. Hey, no sounds of the wind. Did it finally die down?*

Oh, good. I'm not shivering as much. Why am I so exhausted?

Duane feels like a block of ice. At least he died at peace with himself.

Am I freezing to death?

With that thought, Retha forced herself to sit up. Her movements felt clumsy, awkward; her muscles and joints stiff. She managed to throw the blankets back and sat up, then shook her head to clear the dizziness. Grasping the bed rail with her right hand, she reached her left toward the heater and touched it. The metal grill was freezing.

It would be like licking a flagpole in the winter. There was no heat.

Had the propane gas run out?

Now, what do I do?

Chapter Thirty-four

Holy cow. Dad and I are together. It just happened.

His breathing kept getting slower and slower. He gasped once in a while. Finally, he took in a big breath and it came out all funny, like letting air out of a balloon. He never took another breath in. I kept waiting and waiting.

What did stardust look like when it left someone's body? Then I remembered, I really didn't see Mom's and Jimmy's. No one ever saw mine. I just knew when he was with me.

"So, you're waiting for me? What a wonderful surprise," Dad said. Well, not out loud. That's just the way it is for stardust. We talk without sound.

He was next to me at the top of the archway, between the dining room and kitchen. His stardust started talking right away. It must have been the water that slowed me down getting up here, after I died. I didn't need to say anything else to him. We both knew we were together again.

"Let's go to Memory Tree," Dad said. "I think whatever happens next will happen there. I've always wanted to be in that tree."

"What about Retha? Will she live?"

"She's always been a survivor," Dad said. "Besides, there's nothing we can do for her."

"Won't we get blown away, flying to Memory?"

I was scared. I didn't want to end up getting blown across the fields or into the forest. Besides, I liked staying in the house, and I was worried about Retha.

"I don't think the wind will affect us. Besides, the wind died down. See, we can't hear anything moving or blowing outside. Oh, wait. I hear something now. Sounds like snowmobiles. Look."

We watched Retha walk, like a drunk person, to the kitchen door, open it, and look across the hayfield. The sounds of the snowmobiles kept getting closer.

"We can go now," Dad said.

All at once, we were high in the branches of Memory Tree. Together. It's wonderful. I feel calm all over. Ain't scared now, either. We're just tucked away in a small cluster of needles, not far from the top. Just waiting. I don't know for what. Even if we wait here forever, I know Dad and I are together.

At first, I wondered how we would find Mom's and Jimmy's stardust, how that worked. I didn't worry, though. Dad didn't seem to be worried either.

I decided to practice my patience. Something Mommy always said I should work on. "You're a lot like me," she said. After waiting all this time for Dad, I decided I could be patient some more.

We watched two snowmobiles pull up to the house. A man and a lady took off their helmets—that's how I could tell they were a man and a lady—and went into the house. When they came out, the man carried Retha, all bundled up in a snowmobile suit and wearing a helmet. "I think we got here just in time," he said. "You're going to be fine."

The lady carried Retha's suitcase. "I'll take good care of these pictures and carvings." The lady strapped the case down tight behind her as the man showed Retha how to sit behind him and hang on.

Dad and I laughed when we heard Retha say, "I told you it wasn't my time to die. Can we hurry? I need some coffee. Eggs and toast would be nice, too."

I was worried. "Dad, they're not—they're not taking you. What about your body?"

"Oh, Eula. That's only my dead body. My stardust is right here with you. Don't worry. As soon as the roads get plowed, the funeral home will pick up my body and have it cremated. It's actually good that it's cold."

I thought a moment. "Yea, you're right, Dad. That was kinda silly."

We both watched Retha. She waved at Memory Tree as the

snowmobiles took off. I wonder if she knows we're up here.

~ * ~

The next day, the highway crews cleared Grassy Lakes Road. They even opened up Access Road and the Gleason driveway. The following day, the coroner and his assistant retrieved Duane's body.

The coroner's assistant discovered the gas pipe and valve, attached to the house near the back door, had pulled loose. Over the years, vines wrapped around the pipe, pulling and twisting it till the copper tube going into the house crimped and developed a pinhole leak. The propane tank slowly emptied, beginning its gradual escape, even before Retha and Duane moved in.

Duane was cremated as planned, his ashes saved for Ashley and Jessica, Duane's daughters.

Chapter Thirty-five

July 2019 - The Farmhouse Site

Ashley and Jessica stepped out of their rental car and greeted Reggie Slater, a landscape architect. Ashley carried a bag containing a cardboard urn. The area where the house, barn and shed once stood was cleared—the buildings knocked down and hauled off—leaving nothing but the sandy soil. Some weeds and tufts of grass grew up.

The three women paused as a vehicle sped up Access Road, dust roiling behind it. The minivan tore up the driveway and came to an abrupt stop. Retha climbed out. She pulled her old suitcase from the back seat, marched up to them and handed the case to Jessica. "I didn't trust those people at the packing store. When you said you were coming back here, I figured I'd just give it to you in person." She looked around, sighed, and shook her head. "Wow. The house and shed are gone, too. I do like your ideas for a fresh start. Everything needs a fresh start at times." She reached her hand out to shake Reggie's. "If you haven't guessed, I'm Retha, and I can't wait to see what you got planned for this place. Now, let's get started."

Reggie led them to a folding table set in front of Memory Tree. She unrolled a tube of drawings and used stones and pinecones to secure the corners. "This is the overall plan for converting the property into a nature preserve and memorial. As we discussed, it will start at the south end of the property with a savannah that transitions to the national forest."

She motioned the women away from the table and gestured across the property to where the savannah would be. Returning to the table, she continued. "Accessible trails will wind through the preserve, with benches and signs designating what is growing in that area." She used her pencil to point out the trails, a small pavilion, parking lot and an area in front of Memory Tree with benches. "Initially, the challenge will be keeping the invasive plants, like sumac, out of the area. Once the natural plants, shrubs and trees are established, that should become easier."

"I love these plans." Jessica clapped her hands and twirled around. "You have done a great job interpreting our combined families' story into a memorial."

"Reggie, we couldn't have told you the story without all the information Retha provided us," Ashley said. "As we told you, she cared for our father in his final days. We had no idea of his life before he married our mother and they had us. Every day, Retha emailed us about their conversations, how she slowly got him to talk about his life, all the tragedies involved and how they overlapped with her own life. Since, we've had many long conversations. We know the whole story now." She looked around the grounds, then at her sister. "How do we share that complicated of a family story here?"

Jessica touched the plans, then squatted to open the suitcase. She pulled out several of the carvings, plus photographs that once hung on the dining room walls. "Ohmygod, Retha. I can't believe you thought to get all of his carvings from the basement, and all the family photos. This is amazing."

"Well, my rescuers thought I was crazy when I made them go down to the basement and pack them carvings up, plus take all the pictures down. Told them even if I freeze to death waiting for them, they still had to take the stuff along and get it to you two." Retha pulled the girls into a hug.

No one spoke for several minutes.

Wiping her eyes, Ashely broke the silence. "We have a family display at our home in Seattle. Now, it can combine both families." She paused and looked around. "However, outdoors here, it feels complicated to be able to condense the lives of two families into some type of a printed display next to the benches. Reggie, what do you think?"

"I agree." Reggie paused to look up at Memory Tree. "I know a sculptor. She just graduated with her Master's degree from art school. She's biracial. I have a feeling she would love a chance to bring some ideas to you. That, plus some displays, might be more impressive." Reggie tapped the plans. "You gave me a range for this project based upon your financial resources. The expenses will be below the top of your range. I think she could still do something within your overall budget."

Reggie turned and smiled at Retha. "Her wife is also a nurse."

"Wait. She's mixed. She's a lezzie. Her wife is a nurse? Good Lord, girls. Hire her. If you need more money, I'll chip in. Those sound like great qualifications to me." Retha bowed low as the other three bent over in laughter. She sorted through the suitcase and pulled up one of the statues. It was of a man and two children, a boy and a girl.

Each person grew quiet.

Retha set the carving on top of the drawings. Patting it, she said, "I think that sculpture lady should see this one. People gotta know how this man loved all his kids."

"That's a wonderful idea. We agree," Ashley said as she and Jessica walked closer to Memory Tree. Both stared up at its majestic height. Reggie followed and stood behind them. Retha hung back and watched.

Jessica reached out to touch the needles. "Reggie, Retha told us how Dad named this tree. He loved it. When we brought him here last January, he wouldn't let us get him up the steps into the house until he could stand and look at it for a few minutes. We thought he'd die of exposure before we could get him inside."

Ashley turned toward Reggie. "We decided the name of the preserve should be The Memory Tree Sanctuary. I like your idea. I think a sculpture might tell the story far better than something that takes a long time to read. I say ask her to contact us, hear the story of this place and give us an idea."

"Totally agree." Jessica picked up a pinecone. Turning it over, she looked at its brown scales, the seeds starting to loosen, and said, "A sculpture just might complete our desire to honor our father's love of the woods and nature, his complicated relationships with race, his first family, plus us, his second family." She pulled her sister into a hug. "What a hodge-podge of a life, but then, life is a hodge-podge."

Ashley stepped back to the table and picked up the urn. "Speaking of a mishmash, we definitely have to bring our guys here. Maybe we could have a double wedding here when the sanctuary is finished." She opened the urn. "You ready to do this?" She motioned for Retha to join them.

Jessica took a handful of ashes and spread them around Memory Tree as Retha, Ashley and Reggie watched.

Jessica looked at Retha, ready to move toward the path across the road.

Retha waved for the sisters to come close to her. Hugging them, she said, "You two do the rest without me. This is something you need to do by yourselves." She wiped her eyes. "I'll be gone when you get back. I've got a client in Mt. Pleasant. Damn breast cancer came back. She's a widow, no kids." She slowly pushed the girls away, before marching off.

"Thank you for coming into our lives," Ashley called after her.

Retha paused, turned partway around. "No, thank you. I now have part of my life back, too." She turned back and briskly walked to her minivan.

Taking her sister's hand, Jessica led the way across the road and down the narrow trail toward the bay. "That must be where the floating dock used to be." She pointed to a slight gap in the brush as they entered the clearing.

"I'm glad it's gone. Our half-brother and sister died there. And their mother. They all seemed so young. Ellie was only two or three years older than we are now." Ashley reached in the urn, next Jessica, as each slowly spread ashes around the clearing.

They let the last of the ashes flutter along the trail on their way back to Memory Tree.

Memory Tree

We've been in Memory Tree for a while now. It's cool. The sanctuary was finished last spring. It's fall, now.

Down below, it's nice seeing the people come visit and walk the paths around the sanctuary. Some sit on the benches in front of Memory. I like knowing other folks talk to Memory.

We see Retha come. Not often. She's getting old. Well, she always was. Now she's walking with a cane, real slow. I wonder if she's still helping people die. Who will help her die? Will her stardust come to Memory Tree? I hope so.

People also spend a lot of time around the sculpture. The sculpture goes in a circle around a not-real pine tree. There are shapes that kinda look like people, but not like Dad's carvings. Each kinda-person is a different shade, some dark, some light, some in between.

The first two look something like a mommy and a daddy holding hands, but facing away from each other. Two kids are between them. Next is another woman—maybe it's Pamela. Then two big girls, and next, maybe a Retha; 'cause it's got kind of a baseball cap on. The Retha looks at someone next to her, someone almost like a ghost, maybe it's my Grandma Naomi. The last person in the circle is a granny-like person reaching for the mommy and kids.

Below each sculpture-person is their name, a short story and a picture. I don't know how they made them, but the rain and weather doesn't hurt the pictures and stories. Dad's picture is one of his carvings. The one with him and us kids.

People look and read the stories printed below them.

Some cry.

So does Retha when she comes here.

~ * ~

Did you know eastern white pine trees have five needles in each cluster? They do. I counted them.

Did you know trees inhale the air around them and exhale clean air? Yup. That's what trees do.

Listen, we didn't stay stardust. I figured we would eventually find Mommy and Jimmy and float off to space to form another star.

Nope. That's not the way it works.

Our stardust turned into pine needles.

That's right, we're part of Memory Tree now. Not just in it. Part of it.

Don't ask me how, but ain't that cool?

Shortly after I knew we were pine needles, I asked Dad, "Do we stay pine needles forever?"

"Nope. Pine needles like ours only live two to three years and—"

"So, we gotta die again? That means Mommy and Jimmy aren't pine needles somewhere?"

I kept thinking we'd find them or at least know they were close to us. But I kept practicing my patience. With Dad beside me it was easy.

"Sweetheart," Dad said, "life is a cycle of death and renewal. Mommy and Jimmy and Granny and Naomi were once pine needles here, or somewhere." He waited a moment. "Do you remember Mommy teaching you about mulch? How organic things die, break down and become food for new things to grow?"

"Sort of." I did remember. "So, I'm going to turn into mulch?"

That sounded yucky. Yuckier than being stardust and going back to being a star. Being a pine needle was fine, except I forgot that some of the needles turn brown and fall off the tree each fall.

"What happens to mulch?" Dad's voice was gentle.

"Other stuff grows in it. It's like food for flowers and plants and trees."

I thought for a while. I remembered what Mom taught us about mulch. Things break down so they can be absorbed—another big word she taught us—into the soil and how mulch feeds the seeds and plants and trees. She used to say everything was temporary. Nothing stayed the same.

Remembering Mom's words made me finally realize our stardust turns into needles that live two or three years, then die. The dead needles turn into soil that grows new things. That means our stardust actually does last forever.

"I get it, Dad. We aren't going to return to outer space and be another star. Our stardust becomes a pine needle that dies and becomes food for the dirt. The dirt feeds other things that grow and live. Then they die. And everything starts all over."

"That's right, Eula. Our stardust is a cycle of life and death, growth, too."

"Dad, that means it never stops. It just keeps going—oh, right, that's what the word cycle means."

"Umm, that's right," Dad said.

We both laughed.

I wonder what Mommy and Jimmy became. Granny, too. I'll bet they're something cool, like all flowers and trees and grasses are.

Granny used to say we came from dirt and we return to dirt.

Now I get it.

Someday, I hope a pink thippie grows in my dirt.

I still like pink thippies—Pink Lady Slippers—the best.

Acknowledgements

I am thankful for the support I had writing this book: Kathie Giorgio, my writing coach and founder/director of AllWriters' Workplace & Workshop; the talented and incredibly helpful members of the Beloit Public Library's Stateline Night Writers—Jerry Peterson, Diane Tibbitts, Vicki Nemetz-Poff, Karl Bell, Gina Buckles, Kimberly Vogle, Laura Nilson, Nancy Clark-Mather; beta readers Joanne Lenz-Mandt and Louis Butler; sensitivity reader, Trinica Sampson.

A big thank you to Bob Wood and Tom Montag for permission to use their poems. I loved both of the poems the instant I read them and knew they were a fit for this book. A friend, artist, writer, and musician did the cover art—thank you, Arthur Durkee.

I'm especially grateful for my partner, Rick Dexter, who has yet to grow tired of my ongoing life with imaginary characters. That's amazing, because even when that life includes me talking—or yelling—with the characters in my sleep (Ralph seemed to be the most disturbing), I only get a nudge to turn onto my side. In the morning, he reminds me of what I said. He says it's so I can write it down.

Finally, a debt of gratitude and respect for Christine Young and Arlo Young of Rogue Phoenix Press; their staff; Sherry Derr-Wille, manuscript editor; and Gene of Web and Graphic Designs.

Author's Note on Fair Haven

A history many people won't know.

Years ago, as a much younger man, I directed a summer camp—YMCA Camp Pinewood—near Muskegon, Michigan. Staff took qualified campers for canoe trips down the Pere Marquette River in Lake County, Michigan.

That first summer, I was driving an old van hauling a canoe trailer on my way to pick up staff and campers at their pull-out. I drove through an area called Luther and noticed African-Americans living and gardening there near the national forest. It surprised me.

I knew of Black people living in rural areas in the southern states, but I never expected to see any living in this part of Michigan. It was hours from Detroit and Grand Rapids, even further from Chicago. To me, a Michigan farmer's grandson, the soil didn't appear to be that great, and there wasn't any major industry for jobs within comfortable commuting distance. So, what led African-Americans to settle there?

Forty years ago, we didn't have the internet when we wanted to research something. Not only that, but my responsibilities for leading a summer camp left me with little time to explore any questions I had about the Black settlement at Luther. Those images and wonderment stayed in the back of my mind.

I am White, raised in a tiny village in the midst of a large farming area. At the time, several well-established Mexican families lived in our locale. They were accepted, grudgingly by some, even less so if the boys were dating a White girl. Other than the brief coverage in school history classes, I never studied the African-American history of Michigan, nor the U.S. Back then, I assumed that in the upper Midwest, African-Americans lived in the big cities and surrounding areas. Black people living in rural Michigan never crossed my mind.

Fast forward to 2019. As a writer, I like to research a physical setting when I'm starting a new novel. I like to look at maps. I like to think how I can fictionalize the area I'm interested in. For this novel, I knew I wanted to write about a mixed-race couple, and I knew I wanted to place them in a rural or remote area. Somehow, I recalled the African-American families living in Luther, so I pulled up a map of the area.

Bingo! That's when I discovered Idlewild. It's very close to Luther. Had I made a few more turns when I was going to pick up those kids and my staff at the end of their canoe trips, I would have driven through Idlewild.

Idlewild, I found out, was often referred to as Michigan's Black Eden. It was a fascinating African-American resort community that thrived in west-central Michigan, near Baldwin, in Lake County. It was big and robust from the 1920's to the late 1960's. In my story, I call it Fair Haven. I believe the statistics I use for Fair Haven are close to those of Idlewild.

The reason Idlewild, that Black resort community, died is well-documented. When the Civil-Rights Act of 1964 signed by President Johnson went into effect, African-Americans could soon go anyplace in the nation for their vacations, not just Black resorts in the middle of nowhere. Great progress, yes, but the Act also proved to be a death knell for Idlewild.

I urge you to dig into the history of Idlewild. It is truly fascinating. Here are some links:

https://en.wikipedia.org/wiki/Idlewild,_Michigan
https://interactive.wttw.com/chicago-on-vacation/destinations/michigan/idlewild-michigan-black-eden
https://www.blackpast.org/african-american-history/idlewild-michigan-1912/
https://savingplaces.org/stories/whats-next-for-idlewild-michigans-black-eden#.XxXz7C3MxhE

Idlewild: The Black Eden of Michigan by Professor Ronald J. Stephens, University of Nebraska ISBN 0-7385-1890-5

History: Dr. Daniel Hale Williams and Idlewild by Professor Ronald J. Stephens, University of Nebraska

"Michigan's Other Motown" Lakeshore Guardian article by Randy Karr

Urban Green: Nature, Recreation, and the Working Class in Industrial Chicago by Colin Fisher, University of North Carolina Press

Prof Ronald J. Stephens (2001). "A Context for Understanding Idlewild's Past". Retrieved 2006-08-26.

About the Author

Memory Tree is Bill's fourth novel. Bill grew up in a village in a Midwest farming community where nearly everyone had large families. Hence his proclivity for writing about families, warts and all. He began writing after retiring from careers in YMCA camping and foster care, and, he admits working with children for forty years may have affected him. Bill resides in Beloit, Wisconsin, and looks forward to again traveling. He enjoys reading, writing, photography, art and volunteering.

He likes connecting with his readers. Contact him at billmathiswriter@gmail.com. Check out his website: http://www.billmathiswriteretc.com. Keep track of and follow him and

his future books on Facebook:
https://www.facebook.com/BillMathisWritersEtc/.

For a variety of short stories read the author's blog:
http://billmathiswriteretc.com/blog/

More books are in progress.

Help Spread The Word!

If you enjoyed this book, please leave a review on Goodreads, Amazon or other similar websites; ask your local library to order a copy; invite Bill to a book club meeting either in person or via Skype, Zoom or Facebook Live; tell your friends to order a copy; post your comments on your Facebook page and Bill's page:
https://www.facebook.com/BillMathisWritersEtc/.
Thank you!

Revenge is Necessary

Shaw Skogman, a taciturn, successful farmer, erupts and attempts to kill his wife and son by firing a shotgun at them. Shaw ends up with a severe leg wound but chooses to die rather than accept a lifesaving amputation. His wife and family learn more shocking things about him as they discover the separate life he led in plain sight. Elderly farmers and their spouses died. Was it of natural causes? How did he acquire so much land? What was the relationship between him and Melvin, his nervous right-hand man? Shaw's first wife committed suicide—or did she? What roles do a gay undertaker, a closeted sheriff, and two gay teens play in discovering the answers? Finally, what secrets did his second wife have?

Chapter One

Junior: Shaw Philip Skogman, Jr., age 17
Saturday, March 26, 2011
Midville, Minnesota

Junior ran faster, his bare feet churning, sinking into the dirt drive, already muddy from three days of rain and now topped with three inches of heavy, wet, late-March snow. The grainy flakes whirled around him, pelting his skin, nearly blinding him. He didn't feel the cold yet. Where was he headed? Where could he go in his Fruit-of-the-Loom white t-shirt and tighty-whiteys at seven on a Saturday morning? His dad might come after him if he headed toward his boyfriend Beany's house.

The image of his father with the double-barrel shotgun bursting in on him and Beany in Junior's bed pulsed with every heartbeat. Beany's words as Junior raced toward the door still echoed. "Run, Forrest! Run!" The same words his mother screamed at his track meets. She loved the movie Forrest Gump. He knew Beany escaped down the back stairs as Junior flew down the front ones. Beany would be well on his way home. He was a fast runner, too. At least he had a place to run to for sanctuary.

Damn Beany. Sneaking into Junior's bedroom in the early morning, or middle of the night, still dressed, crawling into Junior's bed, ignoring the twin guest bed in the room. The bed his mother moved in over ten years ago when Beany started showing up in the middle of the night, coming in the unlocked back door, slipping up the narrow back stairway and into Junior's room without making a sound.

What caused his father to lose his marbles? Completely lose them. It's not like Beany never slept over before.

"Right, Junior. Duck right."

His mother's scream, sounding from the front porch, broke his thoughts. Made his heart thump harder. How could he be thinking about his bedroom and Beany when his father, at this very second, must have the shotgun aimed at him?

He dodged right, closer to the overgrown shrubs that lined the quarter-mile driveway. He heard the shotgun bellow and felt sharp stings on his left buttock, along the back of his upper leg. He ran faster, tried to crouch lower. Birdshot. At least it was birdshot. It smarted, but he was far enough away to realize it couldn't go deep. Must have caught the edge of the pattern. He dodged into the middle of the drive and quickly back to the right. Did that several times. Why? He wasn't sure. Maybe zig-zagging would make it harder for his dad to focus on a moving target. He knew what was in the other barrel of the gun. A slug. That would more than sting if it hit him. It would kill him. His dad was a good shot.

His mother's scream again tore through the wet, thick air. No words. It was followed by the shotgun blasting again and his dad bellowing. Was he in pain? Did he still have the gun? Did he have more shells? Junior threw himself into the ditch and lay in the cold sloppy mud and snow. Hearing nothing, no sound of a thud or a slug whistling by, he stood, turned and took several cautious steps toward the house. His mother's voice floated toward him through the heavy swirling snow. It was less shrill, but still urgent, her don't mess with me voice. "You're safe for now. Keep running. Don't come home."

What the hell did that mean? You're safe, keep running, but don't come home. He turned, lengthened his stride and settled into the eight-hundred-meter pace he ran for track. He sensed the front of his soaked t-shirt invading his nighttime warmth, but still, he didn't feel the cold. He stayed to the right of the drive, on the edge, the grass slippery beneath the snow. At 127th Street, he wanted to turn left, run one quarter mile to Milliken Road and go left a half mile to Beany's house. However, he figured if his dad was still capable, he might jump into his truck and head toward Beany's house down their Milliken Road driveway. If he shot at him once, wouldn't he shoot again? Junior remembered his father's words in the bedroom as he aimed the shotgun at him, "You're not my son." What did that mean?

Junior turned right, onto 127th Street. A half mile further was the small Lutheran church and cemetery where someone might be around and let him in. Why didn't he hear his dad's diesel pickup starting up? His dad must have ignored Beany who was probably home by now. Would he or his mom call nine-one-one? Would his dad show up at Beany's looking for him?

His feet began to sense the cold and the occasional small stone. He was glad the road was mostly dirt, not all gravel. How long did it take to get frostbite? He was approaching the fence of the cemetery when he heard a vehicle slowly splashing behind him. He glanced back. It wasn't his dad's pickup. Junior slowed to a walk as the old pickup eased to a stop beside him. He glanced in and saw Jens Hanson, motioning for him to climb in. There was a tarp covering something in the backend. It was shaped like a casket. Junior opened the door and slid into the warmth. He grabbed the blanket on the seat and pulled it around him like it was the last one on earth.

The Rooming House Gallery
Connecting the Dots

Josh and Andres unexpectedly inherit an old rooming house in Chicago. Each discovers they have a long and deep history with the place. Thrilled to have a home of their own, plus a place for Andres to make and sell his art, the two are challenged to turn the place into a community art center. The challenge becomes more personal as each deals with their own backgrounds, family issues and differing personal interests. Tough decisions are made about their new/old home, relationship with their fathers, and their conflict over starting a family. The neighboring family and new friends play a key role as they bring the art center to fruition, move into a new personal home, and begin a non-DNA family.

The Rooming House Diaries
Life, Love & Secrets

Six fascinating and touching diaries are discovered in an old rooming house that detail the lives of the owners and tenants spanning over a century of change in Chicago's Back-of-the-Yards neighborhood. An unwed pregnant teen shows up; a teen from Paris, France appears, the result of a relationship during World War I; the first Mexican in the neighborhood is given a room and eventually inherits the place, his diary describes his young life running the streets in Tijuana, Mexico and how the rooming house served undocumented AIDS clients. The matriarch leaves a long-hidden diary that details her undisclosed life of brothels. Filled with love, life and family secrets, The Rooming House Diaries prove DNA does not always make a complete family.

Face Your Fears

Face Your Fears is filled with vitality as it challenges the traditional concepts of normalcy, family, disability and love. Nate is a quadriplegic with cerebral palsy raised in a family of achievers. He must be fed, dressed and toileted, yet has unique skills and abilities he gradually becomes aware of. Jude is able-bodied, one of 10 children raised on a hardscrabble Iowa farm. He can change diapers, cook, fix equipment, milk cows, and discovers his vocation as a physical therapist. Both experience tragic teen-age losses, navigate family tragedies, and come to peace with who they are individually as gay men, and eventually together.

This book shows how normal comes wrapped in different packages, yet inside each package, people are the same, whether able-bodied, disabled, black, white, brown, green or LGBTQ+.